The Salt of the Earth by Fred M White

Fred Merrick White was born in 1859 in West Bromwich in the Midlands of England to Joseph White and Helen Merrick who had married the previous year.

Joseph was a solicitor's managing clerk, who by the time the family moved to Hereford a few years later, had become a solicitor's article clerk.

Little is known of White's early years but what is known is that he followed in his father's footsteps and worked as a solicitor's clerk in Hereford. His father by now had also become a solicitor and times seemed quite prosperous for the family.

However in the late 1880's something went badly wrong for his father and he was imprisoned.

White had by now decided that writing was a more preferable career for him than the law. By 1891 Fred M. White, now 31 years old, was working full-time as a journalist and author, earning enough to support himself and his mother, Helen. By this time Fred's younger brother, Joseph A. White, had left home and working as a glass-blower.

In 1892, White married Clara Jane Smith. The wedding took place at King's Norton, Worcestershire, and the couple went on to have two children; Sydney Eric White (1893) and Ormond John White (1895).

As the century closed Fred's father had been released from prison and was living as a "retired solicitor", together with Helen, in Worthington in West Sussex.

By the time of the 1911 census, Fred M. White, now 52 years old, and his wife Clara were living at Uckfield, a town in the Wealden district of East Sussex. As the ominous shadows of the First World War gathered White had established himself as a popular and extremely prolific author. Indeed whether it was novels or short stories they flowed from his pen with a startling speed and many of them were initially serialized in the popular weekly and monthly magazines. His clever use of science to create imaginative and highly adventurous story lines was a particular talent of his.

During the First World War, both of his sons served as junior officers in The Royal Inniskilling Fusiliers.

The titanic struggle of the First World War and his sons' war-time experiences in it greatly influenced this phase of his writing. His novel The Seed of Empire (1916), describes early trench warfare in great and gritty detail. He went on to describe how the social changes after the war created many problems for returning soldiers as they attempted to fit back into a now peaceful society.

Fred and Clara spent their twilight years in Barnstaple in Devon, an area which also provided the backdrop for his novels The Mystery Of Crocksands, The Riddle Of The Rail, and The Shadow Of The Dead Hand.

Fred Merrick White died in Barnstaple in 1935.

Index of Contents

CHAPTER I

PANDORA WAITS

Outside a blackbird was piping madly in the blackthorn, and towards the West a sheaf of flaming violet arrows streamed to the zenith. The hedgerows were touched here and there with tender green. The bonny breath of the South was soft and tender as the fingers of Aphrodite. It was the first real day of Spring, and most people lingered out of doors till the bare branches of the trees melted in the gloaming, and it was possible to see and hear no more, save for the promise of the little black herald singing madly from the blackthorn.

Thus was it outside. Inside the silk blinds were closely drawn, and the heavy tapestry curtains pulled across them as if the inmates of the room were envious of the dying day, and were determined to exclude it. The score or more tiny points of electric flames were scrupulously shaded with pale blue, so that even the most dubious complexion might not suffer. At certain places the lights were grouped in lambent masses, for they lighted the trio of Louis Quatorze card-tables, where twelve people were playing bridge. Now and again the tongues of yellow flame picked out some glittering object against the walls or on the floor, hinting at art treasures, most of them with histories of their own.

On the whole the restful room was more calculated for philosophic reflection than for fierce silent gambling, with indrawn breath, and lip caught sharply between white teeth. The room was deadly still, save for the flutter of the cards as they rippled over the tables. There were cards, too, upon the floor, glistening under the light blue like bizarre patterns to the Oriental carpet. Only two men looked on—one a thin, nervous, ascetic creature, with melancholy grey eyes, and a Vandyck beard. The average man would have had no trouble in guessing than Philip Vanstone was an artist. He had the temperament stamped upon him, both as to his features and his clothes. His companion was built in a larger mould, a clean-shaven man with a hard, straight mouth, and the suggestion of a bull-dog about him. When one glanced at Douglas Denne, one instinctively thought of Rhodes and other pioneers of Empire, who had that marvellous combination of mind, which allies high courage and imagination with the practical attributes that lead to fortune. To a certain extent Denne was a pioneer. He had amassed a huge fortune in foreign lands. He had played his part in painting the map of the world a British red, and, incidentally, he had found time during his Oxford career to win the Newdigate prize and write a volume of poems which had attracted considerable attention. If he had described himself, and why his career had been so phenomenally successful, he would have spoken slightingly, and called himself a pawnbroker with an imagination. Usually he thanked Pinero for that phrase. It saved a great deal of trouble when he found himself in the clutches of the interviewers.

And yet, despite his youth, and his health, and his fortune, he was by no means a happy man. To begin with, he was cursed with a certain demon of introspective analysis. He was bound to bring everything under the microscope, including his own soul, and the soul of his fellow men. He refused to believe in the genuine disinterested action. He put it down to temperament. It gave pleasure to the wide-minded man to do good and kind things; therefore, it could not be accounted as righteousness—it was merely a selfish method of enjoyment. Everything that happened in life, every mood and impulse of his own and of other people came under Denne's mental scalping knife, so that to him the beauty of the pearl was never anything but the poetic secretion of the oyster. Denne would have given much to have been able to change places with Phil Vanstone, the penniless artist.

He wasn't playing himself; in fact, he rarely touched a card. Playing for sovereigns was poor sport to a man who had been moved to stake an Empire upon the throw of a dice. He had come to Adela Burton's cottage at Maidenhead purely to please his companion, but was more or less scornfully amused, because Adela Burton was one of the apostles of the Simple Life. Perhaps that was why she was playing cards with a more or less notorious set of men and women, who had motored down from town that same morning, seeking the pure delights of the pink, March day. Denne watched the cards flashing across the table, heedless of the play of emotions in the rich brown Rembrandt shadows. He was as near to enjoying himself now as ever he had been in his cynical life. Presently, by a curious coincidence, the three rubbers finished simultaneously, and the players sat back in their Chippendale chairs. It was characteristic of Adela Burton's cottage, and, incidentally, of herself, that all the furniture was Chippendale, unless it happened to date back to the period of Louis Quatorze.

"Are you going to play any more?" Denne asked.

The hostess rose from her seat and came round to the speaker's side. She was very simply and plainly dressed in homespun material with a suggestion of heather blue in it, which no doubt, was one of the notes in the melody of the Simple Life. But it had cost sixty guineas in Paris all the same, as any woman who studied the fashion papers would have known at a glance.

"I will play no more this evening," Adela said gaily. "In fact, I wonder at my temerity in playing at all today. For before I sleep to-night the great secret will be disclosed. Do you know that before long I shall come into my mysterious fortune?"

Denne congratulated his hostess gravely. He was studying and criticising her now in his own merciless fashion, but, outwardly, there was little with which he could find fault. To begin with, there was no other woman of his acquaintance who had gone through two rapid seasons in London without some sign that the bloom was off the peach, and the dew dry on the flower, Adela Burton's complexion was as pure and fresh now as when she first startled society with her original methods and almost archaic extravagance. In some strange way she had retained all the innocent look of youth though there was wisdom and laughter in her unfathomable eyes, which were like green lakes under budding chestnut trees in the calm of a still May evening. Such wonderful eyes they were, with all the knowledge of the ages in them, and yet clear and innocent as those of a little child. For the rest, she was rather small, though she was not without a dominating something, which it was impossible to express in words, and yet which could be left like darkness. Two years before Adela Burton had hardly been heard of. Now she went everywhere until the time had come when she led fashion instead of following it. This is the rare attribute of the gods, and is given only to great Society ladies and inventive milliners.

Probably Adela Burton had been the first to grasp the picturesqueness and poetical advertisements to be derived from the cult of the Simple Life. Her cottage at Maidenhead consisted merely of a hall, sitting-room, bedroom, and bath-room, together with a tiny kitchen, where she did for herself. The humble necessary charwoman came every morning to scrub and scour, and, besides that, when at Maidenhead Adela Burton lived entirely alone. One had to look to the graphic writers of society papers adequately to describe the personality and menage of a woman like Adela Burton, for they were beyond the scope and intellect of the ordinary novelist. Possibly no living woman had contributed so much to the income of the paragraphists who make their living by describing the toilettes and eke the pots and pans of ladies of fashion.

"I am sure I congratulate you," Denne said, in his same grave way. "Let me see, what is the amount of this fabulous fortune? One authority, I understand, puts it at five millions."

"I haven't the exclusive knowledge of these favored journalists," Adela laughed. "But I shall deem Providence open to criticism if it is less than a million. Famous Samuel Burton could not leave his adopted daughter less than that. Now have you ever read of a more delightful romance outside the pages of a halfpenny paper? Here am I, taken from a humble sphere at a comparatively early age, and educated to the purple. I am not allowed to know what relation Mr. Burton is to me. All I know is that I get certain remittances from a New York firm of lawyers, who always warn me not to ask unnecessary questions. Ever since I was seventeen I have practically had as much money as I have cared to ask for. Now the trust has expired, and by the mail which comes in to-day I am to learn all about it. Possibly I am to have the happiness of seeing my benefactor, and thanking him in person. I rather gather that he is coming here this evening, and that is why I am not to have the happiness of winning any more of my friends' money. Now, answer me a question, Mr. Denne. Why do I always win at bridge? It makes not the slightest difference to me whether I lose or not—"

"My dear young lady," Denne said in a monotonous voice, with all the expression squeezed out of it, "you have answered your own question. And after that gentle hint you gave me just now, it is time Vanstone and myself were moving. May I be permitted again to offer you my sincere congratulations in advance?"

Denne and his companion stepped out through the crystal glass porch, heavy with the scent of tropical flowers, and gay with pink and yellow orchids, into the sweetness of the air. The former drew a long, deep breath of relief. For the moment the poetic side of his nature was uppermost.

"What a night!" he murmured. "How wholesome and pleasant after the heated atmosphere we have just left! I declare that blackbird yonder is scolding us. Well, he certainly has the best of the argument. My dear fellow, 'Idalian Aphrodite Beautiful' certainly has the popular approval. She would take the pries hands down in a beauty show, though, after all, Aurora has the dainty and more spiritual beauty of the two. Vanstone, tell me candidly, why did you bring me here?"

Denne literally thrust the question at his companion. There was a sudden and searching change in his manner.

"Oh, I'll be candid," Vanstone laughed, a trifle awkwardly. "It is no use trying to deceive you, I know. I want you to do your best to save that woman from herself. She is young, beautiful, and capable of the most generous impulses, and yet, with a soul and mind and body like hers, she is frittering away life amongst those chattering magpies."

"Making souffles instead of substantial soup," Denne laughed. "Oh, my dear chap, you are quite wrong. What a travesty it all is. Here is a three-roomed cottage, furnished with the loot of a score of palaces, a sitting room almost Ouidaesque in its luxuriance, a five-hundred pound freehold, with a couple of thousands spent on the electric light, a kitchen to cook porridge and poach eggs designed by an Eschoffler, and costing the income of an ambassador. Fancy the simple life in Paris frocks, and pap served up in Charles II. porringers! The whole thing appeals irresistibly to one's sense of humor. And, don't forget, that this enchantress is going to marry Mark Callader. Any woman who would stoop to marry Callader is absolutely beyond mortal aid. Nothing but conversion to the Salvation Army would meet a case like this."

"That is why I want you to interfere," Vanstone said eagerly. "We all know what Callader is. He has the instincts of a Squire Western, and the mind of a pugilist. I am certain that man would knock a woman about, especially if she were his wife. He would be far happier tied up to a fifth-rate variety artist. You can help me if you like, and I am going to make a personal favor of it. I am not a bit in love with the girl myself. Besides, she wouldn't look at me if I were. But I honestly believe if you took Adela Burton away from her surroundings, she is capable of becoming a good woman. I know you believe in nothing, but at any rate, I'll ask you to give me the credit of good intentions."

"I'll try," Denne said sardonically. "If there is one man I know more than another who is given to self-sacrifice you are that foolish and slightly idiotic person. Still, you might have asked me to help an honest woman."

Vanstone stared at his companion in astonishment.

"I don't know what you mean," he stammered.

"I mean exactly what I say," Denne replied in matter-of-fact tones. "Your paragon amongst women plays bridge with people who can't afford to lose. The whole thing disgusts me. Stare as you please; if you will come to a dinner party I am giving, I shall be able—but there—what does it matter? And yet perhaps—"

CHAPTER II

PANDORA SHOWS HER HAND

At last all the guests were gone, the frivolous silken rustles had died away, the mass of inane femininity had departed. Nothing remained but a subtle suggestion of effete perfumes, and the acrid insinuation of tobacco smoke. The flowers were struggling now to come into their kingdom. A cluster of narcissus in an old Ming bowl began to assert itself. With an impatient sigh Adela pulled back the curtains, and flung open the long French windows leading to the lawn. She stood drinking in the fragrance of the evening. The breath of the spring night touched her cheek caressingly. The blackbird in retrospective mood was still whistling softly on his porch. It was practically dark, and a sense of desolation swept over Adela as she turned back into the room again.

"What a fool I am!" she soliloquised. "All the more so, because I am not devoid of intellect like most of the people who have just left. I wonder what they would say if they knew, if they realised that I have actually come to the end of my tether, and have not a five-pound note in the world to call my own. I wonder if this is the end of it? Perhaps the funds are exhausted, for it is scarcely likely that those American people would have written intimating that it was useless to apply to them for further money, and that, in future, Mr. Burton would communicate with me himself. Is it possible that some rich crank has been playing a joke upon me? No, that is hardly credible. I don't think that any man, however rich, would keep up a joke, which, from first to last, has cost him a hundred thousand pounds. I have not long to wait. I shall soon know my fate."

She stopped to gather up the cards which lay on the floor, like the gaudy parti-colored leaves of an autumn forest, and placed them methodically away. She emptied the ash trays, and sprinkled the sitting-room with sanitas so that the flowers in the Prinus jars began to pick up their heads, and the whole atmosphere became sweeter. It was so dark that the purple shadows beyond the French windows were almost menacing. With a shiver of apprehension, Adela closed the shutters and pulled down the blind again. It seemed to her fancy that she heard a footstep on the gravel. With a smile at her cowardice she put the fear from her. As she stood waiting vaguely for something to happen, as one does in moments of nervous tension, she imagined she could hear the bathroom window raised gently and closed again. It came upon her with overpowering force that it was half a mile to the nearest house, that she was alone, and that there was booty enough here to keep a score of burglars in afluence for the rest of their natural lives. Instinctively she walked across the room to where the telephone receiver hung. She had her hand upon it when something touched her arm. All her combative instincts were awake. She was ready for real, palpitating danger. It was only the intangible that frightened her. Her eyes gleamed with anger.

"What are you doing here?" she demanded.

The intruder made no reply for a moment. He pressed his hands to his sides. The panting of his breath filled up the silence of the room. He might have been some fugitive seeking sanctuary. But for a moment his limbs failed him, and he staggered to his fall. There was time for Adela to gaze at him from under her long purple lashes. She had it in her to study him calmly and critically.

Evidently this was no creature to be afraid of. In age he was about sixty, with a mass of white hair, and grey moustache that dropped over the corners of his lips. His face was handsome in its way, though seared and lined. He gave an apprehensive glance over his shoulder which told its own tale. For the rest, he might have been a broken down derelict cast off from some cavalry regiment. He certainly had the air of a man who had seen service—a man who would be at home amongst refined surroundings. His eyes were blue, small eyes, that told of cunning and wickedness, eyes that spoilt what otherwise might have been a benevolent face. He was dressed with some attempt at smartness, though his grey frock-coat was faded and discolored, his patent leather boots were down at heel. Adela knew the type. Doubtless this had been a man of clubs in his time, a man to whom the topography of the West End was as an open book.

Beyond question, this man had come to beg and whine, to plead some pitiful tale, more or less true, and in her indolent way Adela was already feeling in her pocket. A deal of promiscuous charity has its origin in indolence rather than generosity. The man seemed to realise what was passing through the girl's mind, for he raised his hand protestingly. It was a long, slim hand, and Adela saw that the nails were pink and filbert-shaped. She saw, too, what puzzled, and, at the same time, alarmed her. The hard, sly cunning had died from the intruder's blue eyes. His whole face had changed its expression to one of deepest interest, and almost filial affection. Adela would have found it hard to express her feelings at that moment. Disappointment and fear and horror were uppermost.

"What are you doing here?" she repeated.

"They followed me," the man gasped, as a curious dry hard cough seemed to choke him. "They nearly had me outside the station. I was an accursed fool to come back again. I might have known that I was not forgotten. There are a score of men in England to-day who would go a long way to put a spoke in the 'Colonel's' wheel. And now, my dear, how are you? Ha! There is no need to ask that question. If ever I saw anyone with the true air about her, you are she, ruffling it with the very best of them, too. Oh, bless you. I have read all about it in the papers. Laugh, well, I should think so. But, you see—"

A fit of coughing choked the speaker's utterance again. He pressed a dingy handkerchief to his lips, and Adela saw a faint smear of red upon it. She was standing opposite the speaker, breathing quickly and rapidly herself, and unable to overcome a feeling of evil.

"Once more, what do you want?" she demanded. "From what you say, you are flying from justice."

"That is so," the man replied coolly. "I thought you would enjoy the joke, and so you will when you have heard it. How like your mother you are, to be sure!"

Like her mother! The words seemed to be tangled and twisted in Adela's brain, just as a physical pain starts at the touch of a raw and bleeding nerve. Had this degraded wretch known her mother, the mother she did not remember herself, whom she naturally thought of as someone exalted and beautiful? Yet he spoke of her as though they had been on the most familiar terms.

"Did you know her, then?"

"Know her! I fancy I did. Why, there wasn't a man or boy in New York twenty years ago who was not familiar with the name of Sophie Letolle. But people are soon forgotten in these days. Ah, there was a woman for you? Handsome? Handsome's not the word. Daring and ambitious, too. What a queen she would have made! I ought to have married her myself. I should have been in a very different position now if I had. But she never cared for anybody but poor Jake, who was a feeble sort of creature at the best. Ah, my dear, it is not from your father's side that you inherit your brilliant qualities."

"Jake!" Adela repeated the word again and again. It was suggestive of some handsome, degenerate bar-loafer—the type of man who often attracts the admiration of a dashing and clever woman. Yet there was something almost amusing in the suggestion. That man could not be Adela's father. It was incredible that she had had her being in some gorgeous butterfly known to man as Sophie Letolle. Oh, no, surely she had a clean and more refined ancestry than that. Adela had assumed so much from the first. She had known no care, no spoilt darling in Society to-day occupied a better position than she. The whole thing was a mistake. This man had come to the wrong house; he had taken her for someone else. She must put him right at once.

"Stop!" she said. "There is something wrong here. Do you know who I am?"

An absurd, almost senile affection gleamed in her visitor's eyes.

"You are Adela Burton, the adopted daughter of the celebrated Sam Burton, the American millionaire. It is astonishing what the British public will swallow if you only go the right way about it. I could sit down and laugh when I see you in the lap of luxury, with your portrait in all the papers, and ever so many peers at your feet. What would they say if they knew the truth? The paragraphs about you I have read, heaps and heaps of them! The gorgeous things they have said about Sam Burton! And all the while there hasn't been any Sam Burton at all. At least, not in the sense that people suppose. My dear girl, I hope, for your sake, that you are an admirer of Dickens' works."

"I have a great liking for most of them."

"Then you will remember 'Great Expectations?' Do you recall Pip and his wonderful fortune?"

Adela nodded. It was coming to her mind with illuminating flashes. She recollected the story of Pip and his phantom fortune—that memorable scene when Pip's fairy godfather appeared in the shape of the desperate hunted broken-down convict, whom the lad had helped so many years before in the old churchyard on the marshes. And as this picture began to stand out warm and tangible, a dreadful fear gripped Adela by her white throat and held her speechless. The man was mumbling, but a horrible grin overspread his features.

"Don't you see the analogy?" he said. "Pip helped a convict, and in after years the old man helped him. There was a time when you helped me. You were only a tiny tot, and probably the incident has faded from your mind. But your pluck and courage got me out of a tight place, and I've never forgotten it. I was always a sentimentalist at heart. Besides, you were fond of me then. I fancy I can feel those kisses of yours on my lips now!"

The power of speech returned to Adela in an uncontrollable torrent. A thousand questions trembled on her lips, but she kept herself in with an effort. The atmosphere had grown suddenly cooler. She felt cold and shivered from head to foot.

"You had better tell me whom you are."

"So you haven't guessed? Do you mean to tell me that you are in the dark still? Then let me introduce myself. I am the famous millionaire; the only and original Sam Burton."

CHAPTER III

TRAGEDY OR FARCE?

Adela groped her way to a chair, as if she were blind or fumbling in the dark. It never occurred to her to doubt what the intruder said. She took it all absolutely for gospel. There was no hint of mirth about the speaker. Evidently he was in deadly earnest. He stood with his hands under his long coat tails like a statesman in the hour of his triumph. The leering look of affection was on his face. Adela shuddered as she wondered whether he would expect her to kiss him.

But one fact stood out as clearly as a beacon light on a stormy sea. The man was a criminal. He had not told her so, but Adela knew that as plainly as if the facts had been proclaimed in a court of law. The veriest tyro in crime would have stigmatised Burton as a shy man with a shady reputation. He had the tone and accent of a gentleman, it is true, and he had passed most of his time, doubtless, in cultivating refined society. But there was no getting away from the hideous suggestiveness of his mouth, and the wicked cunning in his blue eyes.

Nor could she escape the fact that this man had loaded her with benefits. If this were Sam Burton, and the girl saw no reason to question it, she was under a debt to him that she could never repay, and she could not even claim relationship. For years past he had devoted his life to her happiness and comfort. He had educated her, paid her extravagant bills unmurmuringly, surrounded her with every luxury and extravagance that the heart could desire. He had confessed to being a sentimentalist. This was the one clean, sweet romance of his otherwise spotted existence. He had been carried away by the genius and power of Charles Dickens' work. He had elected to play the role of the old convict, and Adela was Pip in another form. Was this a ghastly tragedy or a screaming farce?

For the first time the girl laughed. It was a hard laugh with a touch of hysteria behind it. She glanced from the self-satisfied figure standing before the fireplace to the evidence of wealth and refinement around her. She could see the outlay of a fortune almost within reach of her own slender ringed fingers. This picture had a history of its own, and the halo of the big cheque about it. There was a carpet, which had cost half a score of lives to make. Here was a piece of statuary beyond the purse of anyone but a millionaire. And this was only Adela's country cottage. There was a flat in St. Veronica's Mansions, Westminster, compared with which this bungalow was simplicity itself. Every penny of the money had come from the pockets of the imagined millionaire, but was probably the fruit of audacity and crime! Possibly the stranger had a suspicion of the trend of Adela's thoughts, for he stretched out one of his long, slim fingers and pointed to a Corot half hidden behind a feathery bank of palms.

"I remember that picture," he said. "It used to hang in the house of a virtuoso in Florence. You would laugh if you knew how it came into my possession. Didn't I send it you on your twentieth birthday? Yes, I am sure I did. I remember it because I forwarded those old Dresden beakers at the same time. We got lots of stuff from the chateau of that mad Hungarian Prince when his castle was burned down. As a matter of fact, there wasn't any fire at all. I think that was about the best and most simple scheme I ever invented. Over forty thousand pounds' worth of plunder, and no one so much as suspected. I sent you a certain trio of Rembrandts, too. Where are they?"

"In my London flat," said Adela feebly. She was past emotion, or anger, or tears. She lay back in her chair limp and listless, fascinated in spite of herself.

"That's right," Burton said encouragingly. "I am glad you are taking it in the right way, because, you see, the game is pretty well played out. I am not the man I was, and if the doctors tell me truly I haven't very long to live. I daresay you remember that business a year or two ago in Paris over the Countess De Trouville's diamonds. I believe the affair created a considerable sensation. I got it bullet in my left lung then, and have never quite recovered. But for that I might have kept up the glorious game to the finish. But, what does it matter to a clever girl like you? You are in the very first flight. You pass for a girl with a fabulous fortune. You are even more beautiful than I expected you to be. Ah, the salt of the earth— that's what you are—the salt of the earth."

The speaker turned the phrase around his tongue a dozen times, as it he liked the flavor of it.

"You'll get nothing more from me," he said. "I am played out. I have enemies, too, ready to give me away. The police know that I am in England. It was only by the greatest good luck that I escaped them to-night."

The speaker stopped to cough again. Once more he pressed his handkerchief to his thin lips. For the first time Adela noted how white and drawn he was. She became conscious of his labored breathing. She was recovering, now. The first crushing weight of the blow was passing away. No wild desire to cross-examine troubled her. She knew that this man was speaking the truth. She felt very much now as Pip had felt when the hunted convict turned up in the old chambers at the Thavies Inn.

At one stroke the whole fabric of her dreams had been shattered. As a matter of hard, cold fact, she was not the salt of the earth at all. She was merely the offspring of some impossible creature whose face had been her fortune and whose audacity had been her bank-book. Of all the carved and gilt frauds at present haunting London she was the worst. For the last year or two she had been courted and flattered, she had basked in the smiles of royalty, she had been the guest of more than one ducal house. Modern society without Adela Burton seemed almost impossible. Of course, there had been a good deal of anxiety of late, especially since the American remittances had ceased. But Adela had not seriously troubled about that. She had looked forward to seeing her benefactor, but she had never dreamt to meet him in a guise like this. Now she knew she was an big an impostor as himself.

Her path lay clear before her. But would she take it? In her heart of hearts she knew she would do nothing of the kind. Besides, she could always fall back upon Mark Callader. Callader was going to marry her for her money. Indeed, he had made little disguise of the fact. On the whole, Adela would have the best of the deal.

"Won't you sit down?" she asked.

Burton did not appear to be listening to her. He stood up rigidly, as a fox might do when he hears the hounds. His tense expectation, the hard, drawn lines of his mouth filled Adela with apprehension.

"There is nothing to be afraid of," she said.

"Not for you, my dear, you are all right. The police don't know everything yet. Little do they dream of the connection between myself and Miss Adela Burton. But I should like to know—what's that?"

Adela heard the sound of footsteps crunching on the gravel, the quick, impatient ripple of the front-door bell. The whole aspect of the man changed. A cruel, vengeful light lurked in his eyes. He was breathing thick and fast. A moment before he had been holding an envelope in which something sparkled. He placed the contents in his breast pocket, but the envelope slipped, unnoticed by him, to the floor. Before Adela could speak he had vanished in the direction of the bath-room. Then she heard the front door open, and a man strode into the roam.

"Are you quite alone?" he asked.

"Yes," Adela said mechanically. "But what are you, of all men, doing here?"

"I came with the police. There is a man I am looking for. I ran against him by accident at Victoria, but he managed to elude me. I suppose he hasn't been here?"

"Is it likely? Is it a new society fad to hide criminals? Doesn't it strike you that you are behaving absurdly, Mark?"

Mark Callader shook his head doggedly.

"I am sorry," he said. "Of course I had no business to come in like this. But we actually found that fellow's foot-prints in your garden. Funny thing he should have come here, wasn't it?"

"Very," Adela said indifferently.

Mark Callader frowned. He stood there big and strong, a little embarrassed, and conscious of the fact. He was clean-shaven like most of his sort. He had the face of a pugilist, the heavy square features of the man who gets his living in that way. There was a blue tinge on his skin, which was slightly indented like the rind of an orange. One could imagine him in evening dress, spending his time in a sporting den, and gloating over the sickening spectacle of two human beings pounding each other to a jelly for a purse of gold. The same type of face and form is familiar at race meetings. For the rest, he was well-dressed, and up to his neck had the semblance of being a gentleman. Mark Callader could boast of a long line of ancestors, and the possession of considerable property. But there the resemblance to the man of high caste ceased. He had the courage and dogged resolution that distinguish his class. He was always at one end of the gamut of passions. There was no limit to his love and his hate, and Adela could imagine him like another Othello with his hand on the pillow and murder in his heart, should the Desdemona of the moment play him false. To sum up, he was rich, and in the smart set to which he belonged this covered a multitude of sins. A sullen, sleepy look of admiration lit up his eyes—the small, deep-sunk eyes, which he turned upon Adela. Perhaps because she loathed the type and the manner, Mark Callader fascinated her; but it was largely the fascination the snake has upon the bird.

"I am sorry I intruded in this fashion," he stammered. "But you know I never stop to think."

"Oh, I know that; I was merely thinking it strange you should have traced this fugitive here. I am afraid you have had your journey for nothing, as far as I an concerned."

"Sure you haven't seen him?"

"My dear Mark, have I not already said so?" Adela responded. There was nothing for it but to lie. However she might despise herself, she must be loyal to her convict. "As a matter of fact, you are detaining me. I ought to have gone out before now."

A sudden suspicion seized Callader.

"Then why are you not dressed?" he retorted. "You can't go out and spend the evening in that rig."

Adela would have given anything to get Callader out of the house. She hoped he would not see the evidence of her falsehood, proof which literally was at his feet, for upon a Persian prayer rug lay Burton's stained handkerchief, and close beside it the envelope which had dropped from his pocket. If Callader saw either he would never rest till his suspicions were dispelled or confirmed, and even as Adela was racking her brain for some plan to induce him to leave, he stooped down and picked up the envelope from the floor. She could see it shaking in his hand, and noticed how the blunt thumb-nail was pressed into the thick, white paper.

"What's this?" he said hoarsely. "An envelope addressed to Douglas Denne, and something inside it, too. Hang me, if it isn't a Mazarin ring—the Mazarin ring, mind."

The tiny circlet of gold glittered in the air as Callader held it up to the light. The gold workmanship was quaint and artistic. A series of claws held three engraved diamonds in a kind of cluster. Adela recognised the ring at once; indeed, everybody with any knowledge of art had heard of the Mazarin ring. It was no time to wonder how it got there, to marvel how it had come into Burton's possession, or how it managed to slip from his pocket. It was fortunate, perhaps, for Adela that Callader was gazing at it with rapt admiration. His love and knowledge of antiques of all kinds was the man's one redeeming feature.

There was no dealer in London or Paris who could teach Callader anything on the subject of art. He had the Renaissance at his finger tips. His own collections were well nigh priceless. It was known to a few that he made large sums by dealing. If he cared to run any risk to mortgage his soul for anything, it would only be for a piece of rare furniture or a famous picture. Mephistopheles himself would have chosen such bait for him.

"How did this come here?" he demanded.

"The thing speaks for itself," Adela said. She had recovered her self-possession. "Mr. Denne has been here this afternoon with some of the others playing bridge. No doubt he dropped the ring and envelope out of his pocket. Perhaps it is a good thing I have found it. Now, if you don't mind—"

"Oh, I am going. I suppose I shall see you at Denne's dinner to-morrow night. You will have a good opportunity to give him the ring back."

The front door closed. Adela was alone at last, and threw herself into a chair. She tried to analyse her confused and painful thoughts. She was like one cast away and derelict on a dark and stormy sea.

"Is it tragedy or is it farce?" she pondered. "So I am the salt of the earth? What would they say if they knew?"

CHAPTER IV

THE KEY OF GOLCONDA

Denne's offices were a dominant note in the architectural harmony of the Thames Embankment. The building stood out light and graceful as some Venetian palace, the whole structure being of marble, most of which had been imported. There were well-kept walks and gardens and lawns trim and velvety, as if they had been laid for a century. The ground floor was principally devoted to business purposes, and above were the magnificent suite of rooms where Denne kept his art treasures, and were he entertained his friends in his own lavish fashion. To a certain extent he had followed the lead of the New York millionaires in Fifth-avenue, but there was a note of originality which inspired everything that Denne did. He had his own swimming bath and tennis court; its fact, he had enjoyed the building of his palace, and was tired of it long before the last nail had been driven into the last carpet. In his cynical way he was wont to declare that he had built the place to oblige his friends, though who his friends were he would have found it difficult to say.

Denne was seated in his private office playing with his correspondence. Despite his many interests, and the score of irons he had in the fire, he was by no means a hard-working man, for, like most of his class, he had the gift of picking out the right men to do the work for him. Without this attribute it is impossible for a man to be a multi-millionaire.

So long as Denne rode the whirlwind and directed the storm, the rest followed automatically. He pushed aside a pile of signed letters and shrugged his shoulders. What an easy game when one came to understand it! How comparatively simple to pile up money when the information is right, and one has the exclusive use of a private cable. There were times when Denne was sick of making money—and this was one of them. He pressed one of the numerous buttons by the side of his writing table, and gave an order to the clerk who appeared in reply. A moment later a little man with a shiny bald head slid noiselessly into the room.

He was a strange-looking creature, small and slightly bent. He had a face of exceptional pallor, save at the roots of his hair, which was a bright parchment yellow. The skin on the face was devoid of a single wrinkle, the restless dark eyes had all the fire and sparkle of youth. The man's moustache and whiskers were black and lustrous and unstreaked with grey. His hands were soft as if well manicured. There was a touch of the effeminate about him, and yet a close observer would have noticed that in some faint intangible way Paul Lestrine suggested ripe experience allied with the full weight of years. As a matter of fact, the man was old, so old that he could hardly recollect how many years he numbered. All cities seemed one to him; he was equally at home in Paris, or Rome, or Vienna, and spoke half-a-dozen languages fluently. There was Italian, French and Russian blood in his veins. He was Ishmaelite to his finger tips, but clever, close, and secret as the grave.

There was a strong affinity between these two men, though they repelled one another, and Paul Lestrine hated his patron with a malignity that left nothing to be desired. But Denne was a generous employer, and Lestrine loved money. He was fond of it for its own sake. The mere touch of gold in his palm was to him like a draught of wine to a weary traveller. Who he was and whence he came Denne had not the slightest idea. It was enough that he was a man who carried out strange commissions and secret orders swiftly and silently without question. Nothing that Denne could suggest caused any surprise on the part of Lestrine. It was merely a question of money, and for a handsome cheque he was prepared to do anything that Denne put in his way.

Denne nodded curtly, and Lestrine bowed.

"Did you manage to get it?" Denne asked.

"Even so, sir," Lestrine replied in perfect English. "I have done exactly as you wished. It cost me more money than I expected, but the picture is in my office. Perhaps you would like to see it."

Denne nodded again, Lestrine slipped out of the room, and returned a little later with a square brown paper parcel which he proceeded to lay upon his employer's table. He stripped the covering aside, and there stood revealed a portrait of a woman of rank in the best style of Velasquez. Denne laid his hand almost lovingly on the canvas. Here was one of the few things likely to stir some of the sap of his dead enthusiasm.

"Magnificent," he said. "Ah, you are even cleverer than I took you to be. So this is the Velasquez."

"It is, sir," Lestrine went on in the same voice. "This is the picture which was stolen some two centuries ago from the Royal Palace at Madrid. For two centuries collectors have been seeking it in vain. According to so eminent an authority as Hoppenheim, the picture was originally brought to England and came into the possession of a man of family in the North of Scotland. His successors were ignorant of the value of their treasure, and, indeed, for some thirty or forty years the Velasquez was used as a fire screen in the hall."

"Yes, we know all about that," Denne said. "But suppose we send the picture to Christie's, what will it fetch?"

"Forty-five thousand guineas," Lestrine answered promptly. "That is what the picture would bring. Am I over wrong in matters of this kind? But surely, sir, you would never sell it. You couldn't find it in your heart to part with a treasure like that. Besides, it has already cost you half that sum."

"Quite right," Denne smiled. "I haven't the faintest inclination to place it under the hammer. As a matter of fact, I am going to give it away."

Lestrine expressed no surprise or indignation. On the contrary, his back curved to a rounder angle, his features were pinched and condensed into a kind of silent mirth which had something almost Mephistophelian about it. There was a dry, hard joke somewhere, and it touched Lestrine on his humorous side.

"Ah, what it is to be able to dispose of things like a Napoleon," he chuckled. "When I go to the theatre, all the world becomes the stage, and the men and women merely players at a wave of your cheque-book. To whom do you think of giving this picture, sir?"

There was no sign of mirth on Denne's face. He permitted Lestrine to indulge in an outburst like this sometimes.

"To Mr. Mark Callader," he said. "I think you have already had the pleasure of meeting Mr. Callader. He does me the honor of coming here to eat my dinners and use my tennis court. He even brings his friends also. My good Lestrine, tell me in confidence, what you think of Mr. Callader."

"Yahoo," Lestrine said with a convulsive grin. "A choice blackguard, my patron. Oh, I know there is nothing one can put one's hands on. But that man is an out-and-out blackguard. If he had been poor he would have found himself in gaol long ago. Half the women in London are running after him, and yet I wouldn't place any dog of mine under his care."

"He is going to marry one of the handsomest women in the world," Denne said inconsequently. "I suppose you don't look upon Miss Adela Burton as a lucky girl."

Lestrine made a movement as of one who handles a whip.

"He will beat her. He will abuse her. It is in the nature of the man. And so it is to him that you are going to give this beautiful picture! Do you know what I would do with you if it were safe?"

"Knife me, perhaps," Denne laughed.

"No, my master," Lestrine said coolly. "Violence is not to my taste. I would poison you rather than you should part with this marvelous treasure. I would rob you of it now if I could. I would keep it under my humble roof where I could worship it day by day. In all the wide world there is nothing like art. It is the one thing in all the wide world that satisfies and never deceives you. But I am rambling. What do you want me to do?"

"I was coming to that," Denne said thoughtfully. "Out of all the singular commissions I have given you this is, perhaps, the strangest and most unaccountable. You know Mr. Callader's place in the North, the seat in Northumberland, which he is nursing till his nephew comes of age?"

"Do I not?" Lestrine responded. "Is there a single palace or castle in Europe whose treasures I have not inspected? I tell you all such things are wasted in Callader Castle. There are almost priceless works of art in those dark rooms on which the blessed sun never shines. I don't suppose Mr. Callader even knows what he has got. It is strange that so fine a judge should be so careless as to the disposal of family treasures."

"Well, I am not complaining," Denne said. "What you have pointed out to me is a distinct asset in the game I play. Now, what I want you to do is this—of course, nobody knows that the great Velasquez has come into our hands."

"Not a soul."

"Very good. Then you are to go north with the picture. Find some pretext for visiting Callader Castle, and take the Velasquez with you, ostensibly on the ground that you wish to compare it with other pictures there. You will contrive to leave it behind, concealed in some out-of-the-way place, and later on some virtuoso must find it, so that it will appear quite natural that all these years the finest Velasquez has been hidden away at Callader Castle. There will be no trouble over this. Much the same thing has happened to a score of famous pictures."

Lestrine expressed no surprise.

"Of course the thing can be managed," he said. "It is not for me to ask why you are putting all this money in Mr. Callader's pocket. It is only for me to do as I am told."

"I have my own ideas," he said. "No matter what end I mean to achieve. Take the painting away and do exactly as I tell you. I want to be alone."

Very carefully and tenderly Lestrine wrapped up the painting, hugging it to his heart as it it were a beloved child. He passed out presently on the side stairs, muttering to himself as he went, a puzzled frown knitting his brows.

"What's his game? That is the only man in the world who baffles me, and the world seems to understand him well enough. I would give five hundred pounds, aye, a thousand pounds, to know what this means. Timeo Danaos et dona ferentes. I would not stand in the shoes of Mr. Callader, not even to own the Velasquez."

CHAPTER V

THE LAST GUEST

It was past six o'clock when Denne closed the door of his private office, and went upstairs to his private apartments. He was giving a big dinner party in the evening, but for the moment he had forgotten all about it. He had had other things to occupy his attention, but now it came back into his mind, and he smiled as he retired to his room to dress. He came down presently, and glanced into the dining-room, a self-satisfied smile crossing his lips as he looked at the table. Everything was in red from the shades of the electric lamps to the masses of flowers. The prevailing note was accentuated by the pale, cream-colored panels on the walls. A servant or two hovered discreetly in the background, probably waiting for the approval of their master. With a word or two of praise he slipped into the salon, where he awaited his guests. One of the first was Vanstone.

"You are a wonderful man," the artist said, as he dropped into a chair. "You are the only rich man I have ever heard of who has a genuine love of art. Most millionaires buy art treasures because it's the correct thing. I suppose it is the only way they can get rid of their money. Now, your case is different. I always like to come here early so that I may feast my eyes before those chatterboxes come and spoil everything. By the way, have you thought any more as to what I said to you about Adela Burton?"

"What did you say about her?" Denne asked.

"Oh, come, you know perfectly well what I said. It is a thousand pities that she should throw herself away upon a man like Callader. If she were one of the ordinary social butterflies I would not care. But that girl has a great soul in a beautiful body. She is capable of noble things. That is why I asked you to go out of your way to save her from Callader. I hope you haven't asked her this evening?"

A peculiar smile crept over Denne's face.

"Indeed, I have," he said. "My dear fellow, I will do all I can to help you, but I cannot permit you to come between me and my amusements. You see, being a very rich man, I have so few of them. How do you propose that I should help Miss Burton? Do you wish me to marry her?"

"You might do worse," Vanstone laughed, in spite of himself. "To quote one of your own sayings, 'a man of means can do anything.'"

"I believe he can," Denne said coolly. "Anyway, make your mind easy. I don't think Callader will marry Miss Burton after all. I admit the girl fascinates me, and it would be a shame if she married a bounder like Callader. No, I am not going to tell you anything. But, touching the little matter of the bridge party the other night—"

The arrival of a couple of guests put an end to further confidences. The salon was filling up rapidly, and there was a general murmur of conversation from the secluded corners, where people were already arranging themselves. Presently the door opened and Adela Burton entered, her face serene and smiling. There was no hint of trouble or despair in her splendid eyes. She floated gracefully to her host's side, and held out her hand. If the shadow of the convict hung over her, she knew how to disguise the knowledge from Denne. Close behind her came Callader himself, heavy, stolid, and smiling as usual, yet with a certain air of possession which caused Denne a passing irritation. It was like Bottom and Titania up-to-date; the simile was trite, but it rose swiftly to Denne's mind. He smiled as he bowed over the girl's hand.

"I have not seen you," he said, "since you came into your fortune. I hope that everything came up to your expectations."

Adela smiled brilliantly. Callader nudged her awkwardly.

"Don't forget the ring," he muttered.

"Oh, yes, the ring," Adela echoed. Her dazzling smile had become fixed and mechanical. "I had quite forgotten it, but I have it in my hand. You see, Mr. Callader insisted upon my bringing it. You were careless the other night, even for a millionaire. See what you dropped in my room."

The diamonds flashed and glittered as the girl held them out in her slim fingers. Denne was taken by surprise. It was the Mazarin circlet beyond the shadow of a doubt. He had paid a fancy price for it some time before, and could have sworn that the ring was at that moment safely locked away in one of his safes. But it was no time to ask questions, with Callader standing there, sudden suspicion glowing in his dull eyes. He might find an opportunity later to cross-question Adela as to how the ring had come into her possession. For the present, her eyes mutely appealed to Denne for silence and discretion, and the man of fortune responded. He took the ring coolly and gracefully, and slipped it in his waistcoat pocket.

"That is very good of you. I don't know how I came to drop it, and, believe me, I had not missed the ring. You have not told me whether your fortune came up to expectation?"

"I cannot tell you, for the simple reason that I don't know," Adela laughed. "As yet, Mr. Burton has not put in an appearance. Probably he was detained by business. At any rate, I am still in the position of pleasurable anticipation."

"I daresay Mr. Burton has a good excuse," Denne said. "He is a most peculiar man, and has his own methods of doing things. He will appear probably at the time when you least expect him—to-night, perhaps."

Adela's eyes opened wide. A certain pleasing doubt assailed her.

"Do you mean to say that you know him?"

"Well, yes," Denne said, gravely. "I have known the man who calls himself Samuel Burton for many years. I have not always been in my present position. Time was when I had to work hard for my living like the rest of us."

Adela listened, her lips slightly parted, her eyes shining like stars. Yet she hardly dared to ask the question that trembled on her lips, and it was almost with a sense of relief that she was swept aside by other guests. She shook Callader off and crossed the room to a far corner, where she seated herself apart from the rest. Vaguely disturbed, she began to wonder if she had been the victim of some deception. Surely Denne could never have been on friendly terms with the seedy impostor who had forced himself upon her. Perhaps she would have an opportunity of asking questions presently and justify the mystery of the ring in Denne's eyes.

She sat there thinking the matter over, till the last guest had arrived, and the company drifted in pairs to the dining room. Adela noticed that one of the seats was empty. Her host was explaining that one of his guests had not yet put in an appearance. Then it seemed to Adela that the name of Samuel Burton was floating around the room.

"I hope to have the pleasure," Denne was saying. "It will be quite a dramatic surprise, and give a certain eclat to the evening. It will be a sincere happiness if the meeting between Miss Burton and her fairy godfather took place under my roof."

Adela looked up from the table from her contemplation of flashing silver and crimson, and the dazzling red of flowers.

"Is that possible?" she asked.

Before Denne could reply one of the servants threw the door open, and stood there erect and stiff.

"Mr. Samuel Burton, sir," he said.

Adela's heart gave a great leap, and her eyes fell. For the moment she sat white and trembling.

CHAPTER VI

TOUJOURS L'AUDACE

In her mind's eye Adela plainly pictured the denouement. She could almost pick out the phrases in which the paragraphists would describe the scandal. It was only a question of when the blow should fall. A score of people present would be only too pleased to pass on and retail the delicious morsel for the benefit of other frivolities who lived mainly for bridge and tale-bearing.

Well, if she had got to go through it she would know how to behave; it would be better so, than continue the horrid masquerade of being a woman of wealth and fashion when she was nothing but a penniless adventuress. With an easy smile on her face, she sat calm and collected, waiting on events. She had done nothing wrong thus far, and would be an object of pity rather than of scorn and blame; but if she allowed the opportunity of disclosure to pass, she would then deserve all that fate might have in store for her. The people round her were mostly supposed to be her friends; she saw them in a kind of mist, a dreamy tangle of gleaming arms and shoulders, of glittering jewels, of draperies light and frothy, as sea foam on an August morning. She wondered how much longer her environment would consist of shaded lights and feathery palms and ferns, priceless pictures and rare carpets from the Far East. It would be, perhaps, better to cut it short there and then, and take to an honest, if monotonous livelihood. Then the tangle straightened itself out again, and Adela was herself once more.

At any rate, it was not for her to take the first step. She would wait for the inevitable explosion, which possibly might come from Mark Callader. Would he recognise, in this man Burton, the fugitive whom he had pursued to the cottage at Maidenhead? If so, the catastrophe would be immediate and spontaneous. Much with the feeling of one who follows some moving stage tragedy, Adela glanced at Samuel Burton.

He was the same, and yet entirely different. The shabby frock suit had vanished, giving place to an evening dress which bore the unmistakable hall-mark of Bond-street. The cunning half-cringing fugitive looked every inch a man of fashion. There was not a crease in his coat, nothing in his attire from top to toe to which the most fastidious might take exception. His tie was beautifully knotted, his linen was spotless; he was well groomed, too, his white hair lay smooth and sleek, his grey moustache was perfectly tended, He might have passed for an elderly buck of the military type, and a club lounger in the most exclusive coteries. His manner was natural and easy, as he came forward and shook hands with

Denne. He turned with a smile, at once paternal and patronising towards Adela. Most of the women were watching him under their eyelids. Callader stood with a moody frown upon his coarse, red face. He was evidently trying to place this man, wondering where he had seen him before. He seemed to give up the problem presently, for he shrugged his shoulders slightly, and said nothing.

"Now this is really very good of our friend, Denne," Burton murmured. "My dear child, you scarcely expected to see me?"

Adela's smile was non-committal. She was waiting for a lead, and flashed one questioning glance into Burton's eyes. It was the first step which marked the understanding in the conspiracy between them. She ought to have said, of course, that she had not seen Burton before, and to have asked for an introduction. But with all those Society women about her, she lacked the necessary courage at the moment. Not one of her supposed friends but would have rejoiced in Adela's downfall. She had been too self-willed and overbearing; had led too long not to have made enemies on the road. Perhaps, for the first time, she was beginning to realise how cold and cruel the world was and what an artificial thing was this fetish called society.

"I thought so," Burton went on. "It was Denne's idea that we should meet here. I have done business with my friend, and I was inclined to agree with him. I hope, my dear child, I shall come up to your expectations. I hope you will find Samuel Burton, the millionaire, less formidable than some people seem to think. Denne, will you introduce me to these acquaintances of yours?"

Adela could only sit smiling and admiring. It was impossible to believe that this well-dressed, easy, cultured man of the world was the broken-down fugitive who had crept into her cottage asking for protection from the police. She could see him now as he had stood then, breathless and panting; she could see the dingy handkerchief pressed to his lips, and stained with blood. His cough seemed to have vanished, everything seemed to have changed, and Adela was certain that at their last meeting that well-trained grey moustache had had no place upon the criminal's face. She wondered whether Denne was in the conspiracy, whether he knew anything of the amazing history. But Denne was gravely piloting his friend around the room, introducing him to one and another of the curious women. They were more than civil, of course; for the most part they went out of their way to make themselves agreeable to this handsome, debonair old man, for was he not reported to be worth five millions at least? Callader alone stood aloof with a puzzled frown on his bulldog face, and a steady gleam in his deep-set eyes. On the whole, Samuel Burton was a success. Evidently he was a man to be taken up, to be made much of. Presumably he would take a house in town, and entertain largely in honor of his adopted daughter. Most of the women envied Adela, and did not hesitate to show it. They crowded round her now with fulsome compliments.

Her spirits were rising. A certain recklessness possessed her. After all, there were the elements of comedy in this strange drama, which would be in the cheap press tomorrow, and fill a column or two of the weekly papers; the dresses and the dinner would be described, and Adela would have more than a fair share of journalistic adulation. She was amused to see the easy way in which Samuel Burton appeared to dominate the conversation. Her only fear was for Mark Callader. He had taken her into dinner, and sat by her side moody and preoccupied. He was still watching Burton in that intent patient way of his. Perhaps it was some trick in the old adventurer's voice, perhaps some gesture of hand or arm which brought illumination to him, for his heavy face seemed to light up, and he turned and glared at Adela. Then he faced round upon Burton and paused for a lull in the conversation.

"Haven't we met before?" he asked.

Burton smiled in a patronising way.

"That is exceedingly likely," he said, "for I have been in many countries, and most cities. I suppose it must be forty years since I left the army, and set out to make my fortune. My name was not Samuel Burton then, but that is a mere detail. Now that I come to look at you, Mr. Callader, you do remind me of a man I met some years ago in Paris. I am afraid I am not exactly complimentary, because the man I am speaking of was a particularly choice scoundrel."

To Adela the words, softly spoken as they were, appeared to convey something in the nature of a challenge. She saw Callader pass his tongue over his lips much as a savage dog might have done, and waited breathlessly for what was to come next. She could hear the ripple of conversation, she could catch the rustle of silken draperies, the clink of glass, the soft tread of the servants as they moved about the room. This was the setting rather for a brilliant comedy than for the hideous tragedy which loomed so close at hand.

"Now, that's a strange coincidence," Callader said in his sullen way, "for the man you remind me of was a scoundrel, too. And, strange to say, I met him by accident in London recently. He was very like you."

Burton laughed as he lifted a glass of champagne.

"Ah! well he must have been a good looking man. Now, my acquaintance happened to be a man in an exceedingly good position. Only one life stood between him and one of the oldest titles in England. I understand he was the young man's trustee, too. I forget where the family seat was, but it was a magnificent old place, crammed with art treasures. Do you know what that man was doing? Why, he was actually selling the pictures and plate, and having them replaced with copies, so that he could put the money in his pocket without the slightest risk of being found out. A picture he offered to a friend of mine first aroused my suspicions. I took the matter up and soon discovered that my surmise was right. Now, what do you think of that for a new and ingenious form of swindling? Fancy the son of an English marquis playing a trick like that! You see how little chance there was of his being detected. The pictures and art treasures were heirlooms, and consequently there was no chance of their ever coming into the open market. An expert might question the genuineness of the copies, but, then, the family would have only smiled at his doubts and innuendos. I can tell you more stories of the same sort."

Callader's eyes had dropped. He was worrying at a nectarine on his plate as if the fruit had done him some harm, and he was taking his revenge upon it. He was still the watchful bulldog, but the dog had received a severe thrashing, and was safe upon his chain. Adela could see how the blood crept into his face and down the back of his thick neck. She knew he was fuming with sullen passion, and yet some instinct told her that for the present, at any rate, his rage would have no vent. What Burton was saying was so much Greek to her, but it was plain that Callader understood. It was plain, also, that he had determined to take his defeat with the best grace he could, for he turned to Adela with a forced smile on his lips.

"Your fairy godfather will be a success. Have you met him before?"

There was something behind the question, and Adela parried it discreetly. It would not do to tell Callader too much.

"I was as much astonished as anybody else to find Mr. Burton here this evening. I suppose he thought he could not do better than announce himself at one of Mr. Denne's dinners. But have you met him before? Is he like the man you were speaking about just now?"

"Marvellously," Callader grunted.

"Then I must beware of him," Adela smiled. "I shall have to beware of you, to, for that matter. What a scandal if it were proved that you were in the habit of selling the Callader pictures!"

The jest appeared to find no favor in Mark's eyes, for he muttered that Adela was going really too far.

"Pardon!" she said. "It was a thoughtless jest. Those nectarines look very tempting. Please pass me one."

CHAPTER VII

THE PICTURE FRAME

After dinner the smoke of cigarettes began to drift across the table, and Adela and her companions were in the drawing-room. She would have given much to be alone, to think this matter out. Even as she sat smiling and chatting, her words were spoken almost mechanically, and she had little idea of what she was saying. For she had taken the plunge. She had permitted this hideous fraud to pass, and, morally speaking, was part and parcel of it. She had been swept off her feet by the resistless tide of events, and felt that a cruel fate had been altogether too much for her. But, then, what could she have done? She could not have risen to her feet directly Samuel Burton appeared and denounced him as a criminal, a man who had not earned an honest penny for twenty years. Besides, the man had been kind to her, extravagantly, grotesquely kind. She was no relation of his, she had no claim upon his purse, she was merely the daughter of a notorious woman, whose name had once been a by-word in American drinking saloons. And this Samuel Burton had chosen to make her the centre of the one romance in his life. For twenty years he had lavished money upon her, and surrounded her with every luxury. He had worked and slaved for her till her position had become unassailable. Yet if these women knew, oh, it they only knew!

What would they say? What would they think? At least half a score of women around her were known to some of the greatest in the land, and were familiar with the atmosphere of Courts. But if one might read their secret hearts, perhaps they might be no better or worse than Adela herself. Still, they were the smartest of the smart. Their sole object of idolatry was Money wherewith to procure the luxury and extravagance upon which their whole souls were centred. That was why they were making all this fuss of Adela, why they were descanting on Samuel Burton's fortune, and speculating about its amount. In imagination they were already making the millions fly.

"You will know how to handle him, Adela," one of them was saying. "I don't know anyone better able to lead a guileless millionaire the way he should go. He is very fond of you."

"He has imbibed the very best of American traditions," another remarked. "A man should slave to amass money, and a woman should have nothing to do but spend it. Well, dear Adela has lived up to her part honorably. She has neglected no opportunity of spending. You will start with a house in Park-lane, of course, my dear. It is fortunate that the Bendorf smash should come just now. The Bendorf mansion in Park-lane is quite lovely. Then you will have a place in Scotland, and a country house not too far from town, and a beautiful steam yacht for your friends. No doubt many other brilliant ideas will occur to you. These hints will suffice for the present. There is a deal of enjoyment to be got out of five millions. I am told that is what Mr. Burton is worth."

Adela shrugged her shoulders carelessly. She was looking her best and most brilliant. A faint pink had over spread her cheeks, and her eyes were sparkling. There was something malicious, too, in her amusement. It pleased her to see how these women flocked around and flattered her, for this evening she would play the game. What to-morrow might bring forth she would leave till to-morrow. She knew the bubble was bound to burst, that before long the glittering sphere would vanish into nothingness, leaving naught but disaster and disgrace. For Samuel Burton had come to the end of his tether; he had told Adela so plainly. She thought of the handkerchief with its faint stains of blood. Samuel Burton was a dying man; he had no longer the energy or audacity of youth, and though he was carrying his head high just now, the collapse might ensue at any moment.

"I don't know what my plans will be," Adela explained. "As yet I have given the matter no consideration. Of course, it is impossible that things should go on as they have been doing, now that my benefactor has come to England. I have no doubt he will be good to me, and continue to spoil me, but as to the future—"

The girl paused; it was irksome to keep up the society small-talk, and she longed to be alone. For the first time for many years it was borne in upon her that somewhere or somehow there surely was a better and a higher and a purer life. The artificiality of the present mode struck her and rendered her discontented and weary. She would be identified with the audacious swindler who called himself Samuel Burton, and might have to stand in the dock, and stand her trial for colossal fraud. It tried her courage to the utmost to sit laughing and chatting with these people with such a weight and gloom hanging over her, and she gave a gasp of relief when the men came filing into the drawing-room, and Denne walked over to her side. He appeared quiet and subdued. Most of the men, indeed, were not in their usual lively spirits. Samuel Burton had not appeared, and, somewhat alarmed, Adela looked up questioningly at her host.

"Where is my—Mr. Burton?" she asked.

"I was going to talk to you about him," Denne replied. "I am afraid Mr. Burton is not at all well. He had a kind of fainting fit a little while ago, and we had to take him into the open air. At present he is in my smoking room. He declined to let us send for a doctor; in fact, he made light of the whole affair. He says it is nothing unusual, and he will join us in a few minutes. Perhaps you would like to go and speak to him. I think you know where he is to be found."

Adela was nothing loth; indeed, she regarded the incident as an intervention on the part of Fortune. What Denne had said had escaped the chattering women about her, so that she managed to leave the drawing-room without attracting any attention. She came presently to the smoke room—a large apartment close to a corridor leading into a winter garden. Here she found Burton seated in an armchair with his head in his hands. He looked up with a queer smile as he saw the girl approach, but his lips were white and he had some difficulty in breathing.

"It is all right," he whispered. "I am getting better. A few more attacks like this, and there will be an end of Samuel Burton. It is my heart, my dear, and the attacks are none the less painful because they are my own fault. Now go back to the drawing room, and talk to your aristocratic friends and leave me alone. I shall be quite myself in a few minutes."

"Don't you think we had better go? I want to speak to you. I must have this matter settled one way or another. I am bewildered and frightened, too. For the first time in my life I know what fear is. How you came here tonight and managed to deceive clever Mr. Denne I haven't the remotest idea. But Mark Callader suspects you. He knows there is something wrong."

Again Burton's face wore that queer smile.

"Don't worry about Callader," he said. "You have nothing to fear from him. Dogs do not fight dogs, at least not when they are about the same size. I should have liked to give you a word of warning before I came tonight, but there wasn't time. My child, it will be all right presently. That dear, delightful Mr. Burton, the millionaire, will take his adopted daughter home, and then we can have a talk. Now return to the drawing room, and enjoy yourself."

Such a notion brought a smile to Adela's lips, but Burton refused to say more. So she joined the women again. She could play her part for half an hour longer, but the half hour expanded to three-quarters, and still Burton made no sign. Adela flashed a glance across at Denne, and he came over to her.

"I think we had better go," she whispered. "Evidently Mr. Burton is no better. I will take him home if you will ask one of the people to call a hansom."

Denne obeyed her wish. When they reached the smoking room, Burton was standing before the fire-place with a cigarette in his long, slim hand.

"I am better now," he said. "But I think, if you don't mind, Denne, I'll get back to my hotel. I shall be all the better for a night's rest. It was good of you to leave me alone, and give orders to your servants to keep away. What a lot of beautiful things you have in this room! If there is one thing I admire more than another it is pictures, especially when matched with fine old frames. Look at that frame on the table. Did you buy it for an Old Master?"

"It's a painting," Denne explained, "and a very valuable one, too. The Florentine frame suits its perfectly."

"But there is no picture in it," Burton protested.

Denne smiled as he strode across the room. Then his face changed and an exclamation of annoyance broke from his lips.

"This is very extraordinary. At dinner-time there was a picture in that frame, and what is more, it was one of the most perfect specimens of a Velasquez I have ever seen. I have an agent called Lestrine who is a perfect marvel at picking up works of art. He bought this Velasquez for me, and took it away for a time, but must have brought it back to show me something about it. That is how I know it was in its frame. Perhaps he has removed it from the frame for greater security."

Burton seemed to be mildly interested, and walked up to the frame.

"But it hasn't been removed," he exclaimed. "Look for yourself! The canvas has been cut clean away from the stretcher. The job has been very neatly done, too. The picture has been cut."

Denne bent over the frame. It was characteristic of the man that he made no fume or outcry.

"A robbery," he said. "One of the many artistic thefts perpetrated by the same clever gang. I am much obliged to you for calling my attention to it. I will ask you to keep this matter a secret; it is important it should not be talked about, or get into the papers. But I had quite forgotten that your hansom is waiting."

Denne turned to the door as if nothing had happened. He saw his visitors down the lift, and into the street, put them into the hansom, and bade them good-night.

"I will see you to-morrow," Burton said. "Oh, by the by, I have forgotten my umbrella. I walked here to-night, and I brought it instead of a walking stick. You might ask the porter to fetch it."

CHAPTER VIII

SOLDIERS OF FORTUNE

Adela gave the necessary directions to the driver, and as they drove along the dismal position of her affairs again occupied her thoughts. It would be no longer possible to pose as a great heiress. Even the immediate future looked black and threatening, for she had no money, and was deeply in debt. A few days ago the debts seemed nothing; they would easily be wiped out by a cheque from her benefactor; but now they would overwhelm her. How could she pay them? Looking listlessly out of the cab, she passed a score of shops, at each of which her account was very large, at each of which she was welcomed with a smile and the obsequious always shown to the lavish customer. Half unconsciously she began to reckon up her indebtedness, and its amount was appalling. Five or six thousand pounds at least would be required to set her free.

But where was the money to come from? Certainly not from the man by her side. He had shot his bolt. The end to the meteoric career of Samuel Burton was at hand. The passer-by might not deem the brilliant man of the world played out. But Adela had been permitted to peep behind the scenes, and she knew.

Indeed, Samuel Burton looked anything but done for.

There was a smile upon his face, the snatch of an operatic air upon his lips. He seemed to be perfectly at ease, and interested in the bustle of the traffic, and recognised a score of people in passing vehicles. He was chattering gaily enough when Adela's flat in St. Veronica's Mansions was reached. He criticised her drawing room with the air of a connoisseur.

"Very nice, indeed. I like your tone colors immensely. Your scheme of letting pictures into the panels has my warmest approval. Perhaps your lamp shades are a trifle too effeminate, but, on the whole, it is a most charming room, a sort of restful place that brings out all one's best qualities. But it must be expensive, my dear child, very expensive. Have you ever considered what this costs you?"

Adela shrugged her shoulders and Burton smiled benignly.

"I thought not," he said. "From what I could see of the hall, I presume everything is on the same gorgeous scale. I remember, about a year ago reading in one of the New York papers an article all about your flat. My dear, you can't think how interested I was, and I was not the less amused because just at that time I was suffering from a temporary reverse of fortune. In the language of Brer Rabbit I was lying low, hard put to it to obtain the bare necessities of life. You can't tell how curious it was to me to feel that I was the founder of your great reputation. But keep it up, my dear child, keep it up. You will probably marry a Duke and become persona grata at Court."

Adela was feeling a sense of shame that tingled through every nerve, the pain was physical as well as mental. She loathed herself and would have liked to strip all her finery, to have done anything to stand before the world with a light heart and clean conscience.

She had met many frauds and shams in her time, but not one of them was so empty or pretentious as herself. She was no more than a splendid lie, a living, breathing falsehood. Ah! and she might be worse before long.

"Give me time to think," she cried. "Your society chattering unnerves me. Can't you see that you have done a bitterly cruel thing? Can't you see how much kinder it would have been to leave me alone? I have brains, courage and resolution, and could have made my way in the world. You assure me you befriended me because I once did you a kindness. What have you done to me in return? You have ruined me body and soul. You have allowed me to believe I was a great heiress, have forced me into a position I was not intended to occupy, and will compel me to sink under a burden of shame and ignomy and disgrace. You must have known that it was impossible to keep this up for ever. Nor is that all, for you have deprived me of the consolation of feeling that all these years I have been spending honestly earned money. On your own confession you are a criminal and a thief. From your own lips I have learnt that all this wealth was the result of fraud and crime. Now you are an old man, past further conspiracies, with one foot in the grave. Do you want to drag me down with you? Do you want my creditors to prosecute me for robbing them as you have robbed other people? Oh, I know it is useless to protest. I know that my indignation goes over your head. But I didn't think you were going to be as cruel as this. I did not expect you to lower me to the level of a swindler and adventuress."

Adela paused for sheer want of breath. She stood, a beautiful, glowing figure of righteous anger, her breast heaving tumultuously, the diamonds around her neck sparkling and quivering. Burton leant back in an armchair, regarding this lovely picture through narrowed eyelids. He did not seem in the least ashamed or annoyed at her outburst. He might have been a painter viewing one of his own masterpieces with critical approval, chastened by experience.

"My dear child," he protested, "my dear child, really, you are going too far. You might give me credit for a little feeling, for a certain amount of affection. Now, let me see, it must be something like eighteen years since I first met you. I was in a very, very tight place then. I daresay you have forgotten all about it."

"I haven't the smallest recollection of it."

"Ah, but I have. You were the prettiest little thing, and you learnt your lesson so easily. You had only to tell a little lie or two to put people off my track. You had only to play a little game of pretending. Naturally, I am a hard man. I have had to fight my own battles all my life, but I confess that I was touched upon that occasion, and the more I thought about you the more did my scheme expand in my mind. It was only when I heard your mother was dead that I began to put it into execution. I removed you from your relations. You were running about with bare feet and were clad in miserable rags; your features were pinched and drawn for want of food. Do you know what you would have grown up to if I hadn't taken you away as I did? You would have been a criminal, my dear child, or the wife of a criminal. At the very best, you could only have expected to marry a laborer. Fancy you, a slum mother, with half a dozen children clamoring for food you couldn't give them! You may smile, but that was the life I saved you from."

Adela shuddered and sat down.

"I suppose you meant it for the best."

"I did," Burton went on. "Every penny I could rake together I spent on you. I gave you the best of educations, and started you in life. I am responsible for the position you occupy to-day. Yet I am exactly what you stigmatise me—a cosmopolitan thief and adventurer. Things were different at one time. In my younger days I bore an honored name, and held a commission in a crack cavalry regiment. I will not excuse my exit from the Army; I disgraced my name and my family, and was cashiered. I was too clever, my dear, that's the thing against me. I tried to get an honest living for a year or two, but why go into that? I am what I am, and I shall never be anything else."

"But that doesn't help me," Adela protested. "How am I to pay my debts? How am I to get out of this mess? You have little money now, and will have still less in the future. What will people say when I leave my tradesmen unpaid? If I had enough to satisfy them, the crash would only be a nine days' wonder, and my name would be saved."

"How much do you want?"

"Ten thousand pounds, at the very east," Adela said desperately.

Burton sat nodding his head thoughtfully.

"It seems a pity to give it all up, doesn't it?" he asked. "Why do it at all? I shall be able to find the money you want, and after that it is possible you may have to provide for yourself. You are a woman of the world, and I suppose you have contemplated the possibility of making a good marriage."

"I suppose so," Adela said carelessly.

"There you are, then, what more do you need? And the very man is to your hand. I don't like him; there's too much of the brute and bulldog in his nature for my taste. But if you are wise you won't think twice about accepting Mark Callader. He is rich, and all you want is a hold over him. That sort of man is always kept best in hand with a big stick, and you shall have you big stick Adela. I will show you later how to keep Mark Callader in order, and when he comes into the title and estates in a year or two—"

"You are dreaming. His cousin is in the way; quite a boy, and a very healthy one, too."

Burton snapped his teeth together with a clink.

"I know what I am talking about," he said. "Within two years from now Mark Callader will be Marquis of Kempston. I do not go about with my eyes shut. Besides, in his way, the man is in love with you, and if you play your cards properly, you won't be unhappy. I can find the money for your present wants, but as to the rest, it is in your own hands. Of course, if you like to tell the truth, you can get out of it all without a stain on your character, as they say in the police courts. But will you do it, my child? Are you willing to wear ready-made frocks and live in a bed sitting-room with two meals a day? I doubt whether you are. Think it over. You know you can have Mark Callader for the asking, and as to this money, I'll see that it is paid into your bank by the end of the week. I am going. You'll give me one kiss, won't you?"

Adela held back. There was an expression in her eyes that brought the thin blood into Burton's cheeks. Something like a sigh escaped her lips. Then he laughed good naturedly, though he seemed disappointed.

"Very well," he said. "Perhaps it is too much to expect at present. I don't think you realise how fond I am of you. Good-night. I declare I was going off without my umbrella. I must not forget that whatever I do."

CHAPTER IX

IN UPPER BOHEMIA

It was a fine, warm night, and there were plenty of people about. They were mostly in evening dress, some coming out of restaurants, others strolling up the steps of clubs. Fleeting visions of women, cloaked and smiling, flashed by in hansom cabs. It was familiar enough to Samuel Burton though it was some years since he walked up St. James' street, and along Piccadilly. Here were the old landmarks still, the clubs he had known back in his youth. As he sauntered along as if to the manner born, he made out more than one figure which was known to him. They were slightly changed, it is true, but Burton knew most of them. He smiled as he wondered, what they would say if they knew he was so close at hand. He had belonged to some of those very clubs, and, if he shut his eyes, could conjure up the old rooms. In imagination he could hear the stereotyped chatter on sport and play and women.

He looked like one of them, too, as he strode along the broad pavement. He was well-dressed, and well set up, and might have passed for a man of position, or a retired officer with a clean life and a clear conscience, who was going to his club to pass an hour or so away.

Burton had no regret for the past. He was too cynical and hardened a scoundrel for that. As a matter of fact he rather pitied his former confreres now, grey and respected, and, some of them, high up in the councils of the nation. He would not have changed places with any of them. From his point of view, there was nothing so dull and tedious as respectability. He had gone out from among them without shame or remorse. He had thought nothing of his father's pride humbled to the dust, and of his mother's sorrow. Throughout his tortuous life there had only been one soft spot in his heart, and that was for Adela Burton. Interest in her had been started in a whim, but, as he became older it had grown upon him. He was a man, too, with the saving grace of humor, and had always admired the genius of

Charles Dickens. Gradually he had conceived the idea of playing the convict to Adela's role of Pip, but on a larger and more gorgeous scale. He had had his success in all quarters of the globe; for twenty years there had not been a more plausible villain than was known to the police in every capital in Europe, to say nothing of America. Yet, during the long campaign against law and order, he had been laid by the heels only once. Many great robberies had been ascribed to him rightly, but the proof was a different matter altogether. For twenty years he had lived freely and luxuriously, and during that period the depredations could not have amounted to less than three millions. No wonder it was easy come and easy go with him, and it had never occurred to him that the time might arrive when he would be fit for this strenuous life no longer.

The knowledge had reached him all at once, so to speak. He had awoke one day to the fact that his heart was hopelessly diseased, that the nerve and audacity which had served him so long were beginning to fail. He had heard clean-living sportsmen speak regretfully of the fact that they could not ride so straight or so hard as they could in their youth, but he had smiled at them. Now he was comprehending that the weight of years made all the difference in the world. Sooner or later he had intended to put Adela beyond the need of considering ways and means. But he recognised that the opportunity was gone.

He recognised, too, that there was something in her point of view. To give him his due, he had never intended to be hard or cruel. On the contrary, he had taken the greatest pride in Adela's career, and oft enough had pinched himself so that nothing should interfere with her triumphal progress.

The girl was right; he had placed her in a false position. She might find herself before long an object of pity or contempt, if not worse. Still, there was a way out, and Adela would have to take it. The chance would have to be seized quickly, too, for those heart-pains were getting worse and worse, and Burton trembled to think what would become of Adela when he was no longer behind her.

As Burton walked along he began to see his way. He turned into a brilliant bar, where his quick eye noticed all that was going on. He saw the people from the theatres drifting in and out of the glittering restaurant. He saw self-sufficient youth sitting with hat tilted over its left-eye. He picked out unerringly the lad who was doing wrong, and whose account was nearly full. He picked out the other type which was enjoying itself modestly and discreetly. For Burton's instinct was perfect. It was one of his great gifts that he knew how to chose his tools. Moreover, though they and not he had suffered, they had never betrayed him. He turned presently and walked on until be reached his destination in Frogmore-street, and knocked at the door of a house.

Even from the outside the place conveyed a subtle suggestion of art. The door was painted a deep green, and bore an old brass knocker. A neat-looking butler answered Burton's summons.

"Is Mr. Marner in?" he asked.

The butler replied that Mr. Felix Marner was at home. Would the gentleman be so good as to give his name? Burton produced a card, and a few moments later was following the butler across the spacious dim hall into the library beyond. A tall, slim figure in evening dress rose and extended a hand of welcome. Marner was a striking-looking man with a brown, sensitive face, obviously the face of an artist and a dreamer, thought the lips were firm and well-cut, and the nose aquiline. As to the rest, his white hair reached almost to his shoulders, and he carried his clothes with an air of distinction. It takes a deal for a man to attract attention in London, but when Marner walked down the street, people looked after him, and asked each other who he was.

In point of fact, he was once a painter, a poet and a critic. His knowledge of art was deep and profound, he was a final authority upon anything debatable or dubious. He had married the daughter of a deceased bishop, who was exceedingly prominent in charitable affairs. In upper Bohemia no couple were more respected than Marner and his wife. They did not entertain largely, but their hospitality was discreet and choice, and many people, and good people, too, preferred the entree to number sixteen Frogmore-street to a call to Park-lane or Grosvenor-square. No notable gathering was complete without these two. They took their places easily and naturally. Their own house was a veritable museum of all that is true and honest in matters literary and artistic.

Felix Marner smiled in his grave, gracious fashion, as he bent to shake Burton's hand, but directly the door was closed his face grew hard, and his eyes flashed.

"Why the devil do you come here?" he said, hoarsely. "Are you mad or drunk? Aren't you afraid of being recognised? You know it was part of our compact not to see one another. You know that absolute security lies behind the fine reputation which I have built up for myself, and that it must not be jeopardised?"

"Your position is unique," Burton said, without the slightest embarrassment. "I daresay Lord Leighton never surrounded himself with an atmosphere quite like yours. They tell me that the elect of Boston make pilgrim ages to the shrine in Frogmore-street. But, my dear sir, needs must when the devil drives. We have done a great deal of business together in our time, and I must have put a great many thousands of pounds in your pocket. I have never been here before and I don't suppose I shall ever come again. The fact is, I have got my verdict from the doctors. I may die at any moment. I may expire at your feet even as I am talking now. I have done a foolish thing, Marner. In one particular instance I have allowed my heart to rule my head."

"I think I understand; you are speaking of that extraordinary girl, Adela Burton. Well, it is no business of mine, though I must confess I have watched the experiment with some interest. But has it never struck you what is likely to happen to the girl when you are out of the way. I don't suppose you have saved a single penny. Men of your class never do."

"Precisely, my dear Felix. We conceive the brilliant designs, we have the pluck and courage to carry them out, and a timid rascal like yourself finds the money, and walks off with most of the plunder. I don't deny that you are clever in your way—on the whole, I should say your intellect is more profound than mine. I have the very deepest respect for you, my fellow rascal."

Marner waved his thin hand impatiently.

"Please come to the point."

"I am here to-night because I need money, and I need it in a hurry. In the ordinary way I know it takes about three weeks to get behind that wonderful chain of fortresses you have built up between yourself and those with whom you do business. I wonder what people would say if they know that Felix Marner was, after all, nothing better—"

"They would say nothing, for the simple reason that they would never know. Once more, will you kindly come to the point? I don't want you to be here when my wife returns. She knows nothing, as you are perfectly well aware. The question is, what have you got, and what do you want for it?"

"I am prepared to pledge my umbrella, and I price it at ten thousand pounds. I take it like this, and I open it so. What have I got inside? Nothing less than a picture. I have had to roll it rather tight, but that doesn't matter. A hot iron on the back will put that right. Now behold, my dear Felix, a veritable masterpiece by Velasquez. There is no doubt that this is the master's work, as you will see at a glance. This is the very Velasquez which biographers of the Spanish master's work say has been missing for generations. What do you think of it?"

Marner spread out the canvas on the table. He examined the painting with loving care. His face lighted up with a fine enthusiasm.

"You are right," he said. "This is the missing Velasquez beyond question. It will require careful handling, but I believe I can dispose of it at a price. What did you say you wanted? What will be your share?"

"I have already told you," Burton said. "I cannot take a penny less. You can take it or leave it, as you please. I know it is well worth the risk, and I must have the money on Saturday, you see, as I am the only one who has the least idea where you get your money."

But Marner did not appear to be listening.

"Very well," he said presently. "You shall have your price. Perhaps you will tell me how you would like the cash, and where it is to be sent."

CHAPTER X

THE SPELL BEGINS TO WORK

Douglas Denne, his day's work over, was sitting in his den, deep in conversation with Lestrine.

"You seem to have been exceedingly busy," remarked Denne, "but so far as I can make out you have discovered nothing. Now confess it, you haven't the least idea what has become of the picture."

Lestrine shrugged his shoulders.

"Ah, I thought so," Denne went on, a note of triumph in his tone. "I take it, of course, that you have strictly adhered to the letter of my instructions. You have not said anything about my loss to the police?"

"That is right, sir," Lestrine replied.

"I have my way of going about those things. A man who has been all his life amongst art treasures has two classes of thieves to guard against. One is the swindler, who takes his risks on the off-chance of disposing of his stolen treasures in America, and the other is the genuine collector who ought to know better. There are men in England to-day, sir, rich and respected, who would not stick at any fraud but for the fear of being found out. These are enthusiasts, men who love art treasures for their own sake, and are content to worship them in secret. There is a friend of yours who wanted one spoon to complete his set of Apostle spoons. You may recollect that a short time ago a full set were offered for sale at Maxby's, and that on the day of the sale one was missing. That spoon is now in your friend's collection. He stole it. It may seem strange to you—"

"Nothing appears strange to me, Lestrine. Every man has his price, only one likes the pill gilded in one way, another in another. The longer I live the surer I am of this. I have made my fortune largely on this assumption. But don't let us waste time discussing the ethics of business. You must admit that you are baffled to know where the Volasquez is; you have not the remotest idea what has become of it?"

"No more than you yourself, sir."

"Ah, if you knew as much about it as I do you would have been more successful?" Denne replied with an inscrutable smile. "I have my own ideas as to the whereabouts of that picture, and shall develop my plans when I feel absolutely sure of my ground. I want you to put the Velasquez out of your mind altogether for the present, and to procure me something equally costly, something really unique. It need not be a picture. It may be a vase, or a cup, or a fine piece of statuary. I don't care what it is, so long as it is so rare as to be unfamiliar to collectors. I am prepared to pay for it. Only there is no time to be lost. Now, do you know anything of the kind?"

Lestrine's face lighted up with enthusiasm.

"I could tell you of a dozen. There are castles in the Black Forest into which the connoisseur has never penetrated. In one of these is a Saxon cup, a veritable masterpiece of the goldsmith's art, that would create a sensation if it came into the market. This I could get for you, but you would have to pay a fancy price for it, and it would necessitate a journey to Germany."

"Go and got it. Ask Delaforce for a blank cheque and let me have the thing here in a week. Understand that you are to leave the missing Velasquez to me. Good-day!"

Lestrine left the room in his quiet way, a sort of grudging admiration in his eyes. He was doubtful whether he hated or admired Denne most. In regard to art matters the man was a lunatic, the type of collector of whose idiosyncrasies he had spoken so contemptuously. There were certain pictures and treasures for which he would not have hesitated to connive at murder. But Lestrine was puzzled and annoyed to find that his efforts to recover the lost Velasquez had proved unavailing. He knew the sort of criminal who stole for the sake of gain, the man who would stoop to theft for the sake of his collection. And up to now, in these matters, Denne had always taken him into his confidence.

After Lestrine had gone, Denne gave orders that he was not to be disturbed. He pushed his books and papers on one side, and lighted a cigarette. He sat immersed in thought for the best part of an hour, and all this time Adela Burton was uppermost in his mind. He was beginning to find the girl attractive; something in her personality fascinated him. In a way, he was sorry for her, for he knew the whole circumstances of her case. He recollected how Philip Vanstone had declared that the girl was worth rescuing from the shoals and quicksands of the smart set, and that it would pay a man to save her soul alive. Few were the people upon whom he was inclined to waste his sympathy, but there was something pathetic in Adela's isolation. Denne was a cynic, and shrewdly suspected that Adela had no friends. She was too beautiful, too ambitious, and clever, and overbearing to make real friends, especially with her own sex. She had come to the front, had made a great position for herself out of nothing, was disposed at times to be harsh and arbitrary, yet her position was precarious, and she would be a thing for contempt and laughter, and endless scorn when the truth came out, as it must do before long. In any other instance nobody would have watched the comedy with more callous amusement than Denne, but it was very hard upon the girl; she was likely to be compromised through no fault of hers. She had honestly believed herself to be a great heiress, and even now, when the crash was impending, she was holding her head up high and bravely. The mere accident of circumstance had put Denne in possession of all this information, and he was pondering the mass of evidence, as a dramatist might think out the plot of a new play. Was it worth while saving the girl? Should he be the god in the car and use the wand of his wealth to ward off the cyclone which promised to sweep Adela Burton out of existence? From the bottom of his heart he despised the women of Adela's set. He shrank from the idea of seeing her the sport of their wit, and the butt of their mean witticisms.

Perhaps Vanstone was right. Perhaps this girl did really possess those sterling qualities of heart and mind which pointed to the highest ideal. Vanstone rarely made a mistake, a poet seldom does in such matters. If the girl was to be saved, then, at any cost, her marriage with Mark Callader must be prevented. That the girl had made up her mind to marry him Denne did not doubt. Callader was rich, he might some day be the possessor of a proud title, and some of the finest estates in England. Denne paid Adela the compliment of feeling sure that she had formed an accurate estimate of Callader's character. But, then, what did it matter to society? Denne could think of a score of beautiful, refined, intellectual women who had married brutes of the Callader type for the sake of their money or position; he was still thinking the matter over when he went up to his room to dress, for he had just recollected that he had asked Vanstone to dine with him.

The poet came presently, quiet and subdued, as usual. They dined in one of the small rooms, an oak-panelled octagon, with a few choice flowers on the table. There were no pictures or elaborate furniture, for when Denne dined alone he liked to get as far away as possible from the magnificence of his surroundings. It was a plain meal, too, but washed down by good Burgundy. There was no champagne and no liqueur with the coffee beyond some old brandy.

"I think you prefer this kind of thing, Philip," Denne remarked, as he lighted a cigar. "I fancy I have heard you say so before. According to the traditions, all great poets are simple-minded people. Let us drink to the unadulterated life."

"That's right," Vanstone said absently. "We all like to get back to the beans and bacon sometimes. But don't let's waste time generalising. Are you going to Adela Burton's theatre and supper party to-night? I know you had been asked."

"I thought of going."

"Oh, you had better come. Have you thought over what I said about Miss Burton. She must not waste her life amongst that frivolous lot. You will laugh, but I should like to see you married to her."

Denne chuckled in amused fashion.

"I daresay you would," he said. "I didn't know you had any ambition to be a dramatist. Am I to be a puppet in one of your comedies? But, seriously speaking, my dear fellow, I have been thinking a good deal about Miss Burton. She will need a friend before long."

Vanstone looked up quickly.

"Is there anything wrong? You don't mean to say that the millionaire, Samuel Burton—"

"Indeed I do," Denne interrupted. "This must go no further. Burton is no millionaire at all. He is a devilishly clever old swindler, perhaps the smartest chap that ever baffled the police of two continents. I shall be able to deal with him when the time comes, because he has put himself in my hands. I laid a little trap for him a night or two ago, and he walked straight into it. We need not go into particulars, but you will understand that Miss Burton is not an heiress. There will be a mighty crash before long, which will keep scandal-mongering journalists in funds for weeks. But that need not trouble us."

"Quite so," Vanstone said softly. "The real problem is Miss Burton. What is to become of her?"

"My dear fellow, of course, she has already worked out her own destiny. Mind, I don't suggest that she knows what is going to happen, but I think you will find her prepared for emergencies. Emergency will take the form of the transformation of Miss Adela Burton into Mrs. Mark Callader. How is that for a situation in your comedy?"

CHAPTER XI

IN SOCIETY

Vanstone pulled hard at his cigar; and his thin, delicate nostrils flicked angrily.

"That is what I was afraid of," he said. "It's the very thing we have to avoid. Upon my word, the idea of that dainty woman selling herself to a brute like Callader makes me turn cold. Why, the man is a cross-grained cad whose chief amusement lies in the arranging of prize-fights. It is inexplicable that such a man should be such a fine judge of art matters. But he mustn't marry that girl, Denne; he mustn't indeed. She is a superb creature, and it is not her fault that she has drifted into a smart set where she shines so brilliantly. That woman would make an ideal queen. A statesman would find her a perfect helpmeet. Oh, you may laugh and say I am in love with her myself. I am. But not in the way you think, Denne, not in the way you think. I worship her from afar—the desire of the moth for the star. I don't suppose a materialist like you can follow me. But I want you to give me your promise, Denne; I want to hear you say that Adela Burton shall not marry Mark Callader."

The whimsical smile which at first spread over Denne's face faded presently.

"All right," he said; "anything to oblige a friend. But, seriously speaking, my dear chap, I think I can make that promise. Adela Burton shall not marry Mark Callader. She may go so far as to be engaged to him; in fact, she may be engaged to him now. But she shall never become his wife. I can't tell how I shall manage my plot—you must leave the details to me. The novelty of the situation will cause me some interest, and even amusement, and a rich man's amusements are few and far between. You see, most of them have to be bought, and that is never satisfactory."

Vanstone's features beamed with boyish pleasure as he glanced at his friend. Then he rose to his feet and moved towards the door.

"Thank you, Denne, thank you," he said. "Now we had better be moving, it is past nine o'clock—quite time we joined the party at the Minerva."

"I didn't pledge myself to go," Denne replied. "Still, on second thoughts, I think I'll come. Callader is sure to be there, and he always amuses me."

They walked to the Minerva Theatre, and found themselves presently in Adela Burton's box, which was decorated with flowers, the prevailing tint being coral red. The hostess was in red herself, and wore corals in her hair and about her dazzling throat. Most of the women were similarly attired, and they were attracting the attention of the audience, which was a consummation most devoutly to be wished for. They were there for no other purpose, for the society's journals would gush over Adela Burton's latest fad, and colored theatre parties would be the rage for some time to come. The curtain had just fallen on the first act when Denne and Vanstone joined the party. They were received noisily by the women, and Denne wondered why it was that the smart set were always given over to noise. Their behavior was only a shade less vulgar than a Bank Holiday crowd in Epping Forest, and their hilarity was far less hearty and spontaneous. Adela welcomed her guests with a smile and a few gracious words. She was never noisy herself, never silly, never flippant. She left all that to her todies and sycophants.

Adela was looking her best, though her face was unusually pale, and there was a suspicion of sadness in her splendid eyes. Behind her chair hovered Callader, hard and dull and sullen, and the suggestion of proprietorship in his manner which set Denne's teeth on edge. He had seen them together before, without being in any way affected, but now, without knowing exactly why, he was annoyed and disgusted. Callader might, for all he know, have already made his position secure. Certainly his manner hinted at something of the kind. He reminded Denne of a coarse sportsman who had come into possession of a pedigree spaniel. Very quietly and persistently Denne put Callader aside and dropped into the seat by Adela. Her attention appeared to be fixed upon the stage, and she replied to him absently and in monosyllable. Denne had never seen her in such a mood before.

"Did the girl already know?" he wondered. Or was she still ignorant of the tempest which so soon was to break over her devoted heart? There was nothing in Adela's manner to point to this conclusion. When the curtain fell on the last act, the party withdrew to the Dominion Restaurant. That fashionable resort was full as they entered the supper-room. The band was playing behind a bank of ferns and flowers. The whole apartment glittered with gay dresses, and sparkled with jewels. In the centre was an oval table with coral-red flowers and lampshades, a replica of the decorations in the box of the theatre. A hundred pairs of eyes were turned on Adela as she stepped into the room and threw back her cloak. She was gay and smiling, and appeared to be whole-hearted and happy as she marshalled her guests round the table, but her animation only concealed the care that was gnawing at her heart. Was the game worth the candle? Could she actually bring herself to abandon this mode of life, which was to most of her party the be-all and end-all of existence.

It would be a wrench, she knew; perhaps what she most feared was the laughter and contempt of those she called her friends, of the flattering women who had so long fawned upon her. After all, there was something in it. It was good to be queen even of a set like that. It was nice to be waited upon. She would miss the sleek subservience of her servants. She would miss her dresses and her jewels, and the subtle satisfaction of knowing that wherever she went she was the centre of attraction and admiration. Could she give up theatres and suppers and dinners, dispense with the wild excitement of Ascot and Goodwood, the week-ends at country houses, and the homage of the crowd of men who always followed her? There were times when she longed to get away from it all, when she would have given much to be in a cottage by the sea, or in a country garden amidst the roses. But for ever? There was the rub.

Well, it was in her own hands. It she liked to speak the truth she could come out of it cleanly and honorably, but at a sacrifice. If, on the other hand, she delayed for a month, it would be too late. There was no occasion to decide at once, for could she not marry Mark Callader? She had checked a blunt proposal on his lips more than once lately; she knew she had only to be alone with him, and that one glance from those liquid eyes would bring him headlong to her feet. She knew the sort of man he was; on that score she had no delusions. He would probably tire of her, and drift back to the society of the women he most liked and admired. He might ill-use her. But on the other hand, he had a past, and Samuel Burton had promised to give her a whip with which she could scourge Mark Callader into obedient subjection. All she needed was his name and his money, and, possessed of these, there was no occasion to be afraid of anything.

She came out of her reverie with a start, conscious that Denne was speaking to her.

"A penny for your thoughts," Denne said.

"What! Do you want to make capital out of them?" Adela smiled. "Would you like to turn them into a syndicate? Well, if you will promise to respect my confidence I will tell you. I was wondering if all this gaiety were worth the time and money it demands, or whether I should ever get tired of it and turn my back on it all."

"Aren't you tired of it now?" Denne asked boldly. "Aren't you sick of the whole thing? I know that I am. But woman seems never to have done sowing her wild oats. She is always so anxious to see what the crop will produce. I daresay later, when you have married and settled down, you will find a place in the country to your liking."

Involuntarily Adela's glance travelled across towards Callader. He was sitting on the far side of the table, dull and moody, regarding Denne with no particular favor.

"So he is the lucky man," Denne went on audaciously. "May I venture to congratulate you? Oh, that was clumsily put! I mean can I congratulate him?"

A wave of color flushed over Adela's face. She was afraid of Douglas Denne, and sometimes considered him a thought-reader.

"No," she said coldly. "You may not. I think it is exceedingly bold of you to say so much. What made you think that?"

"Only the theory of contrasts. Nowadays the most beautiful women frequently marry the most repulsive men. I can call to mind a score of cases. If you look round the room you will see several instances before you."

"I see the ladies," Adela smiled. "But the men are conspicuous by their absence. What becomes of your argument then?"

"Oh, my argument is all right, because it is founded on fact. Entre nous, I am glad there is nothing between you and Callader. But I must not say any more now. I should like a quiet chat with you, because I want you to do me a favor. May I look in to afternoon tea when you will be alone? I know it is a great deal to ask, but believe me—"

"When a man talks like that I always doubt his sincerity," Adela laughed. "But you can come round on Friday if you like. I daresay I can spare you an hour then."

Denne thanked Adela gravely, took a little memorandum book from his pocket, and made an entry therein. Callader's gloomy brows were bent upon him. He set his own teeth together, and registered a mental vow which would not have pleased Callader if he could have overheard it.

"That is very good of you," he said. "I must do my best to show you that I—"

Adela turned aside for a moment, for a waiter had handed her an envelope containing a visiting card with a few words scribbled on it. The card bore the name of Samuel Burton, and the line, "Come and see me at once. A messenger is waiting outside to bring you here. If you fail, you will be sorry for it ever afterwards. S.B."

CHAPTER XII

"EAST IS EAST AND WEST IS WEST"

Almost involuntarily Adela glanced at Mark Callader. She hoped that he noticed nothing, that her face showed no signs of the uneasiness she was feeling, but, fortunately, he was consulting his watch. He half rose from his seat and turned to his hostess.

"It is past twelve," he said. "If you don't mind I must leave. I must go to the East End to see a man about a sporting event which is coming off at one of the clubs shortly. I ought really to be there now."

Adela acquiesced in a conventional phrase. She was glad to find that it was past midnight, for they would all have to turn out soon. She beckoned to the waiter, and asked him to tell the messenger to remain a few moments. The incident passed as if nothing had happened, and Callader's powerful frame disappeared amongst the maze of guests who were leaving the restaurant.

"You are in some trouble," Denne whispered, "You have had bad news. Can I do anything for you?"

Adela looked gratefully at the speaker.

"You are very clever; you seem to understand everything. Yes, I have had bad news about an old friend who has fallen on evil days. When we reach the street I shall be very much obliged if you will take charge of the party for me, so that my absence will not be remarked. These frivolous-minded creatures need not know that I am bound for a dubious part of the town in a cab at half-past twelve in the morning. I am sure you can manage this!"

Denne was sure of it, too. It was not a difficult matter in his capable hands. A few minutes later the last motor had disappeared, leaving Adela standing in her wraps as if she were waiting for a friend. Then from out of the shadows there appeared a queer little specimen of humanity half man, half boy, who regarded her with a certain reverent admiration not altogether unmixed with impudence. He might have passed for sixteen, but this was belied by the cunning of his face and the keenness of his intensely black eyes. He had a mop of snaky curls, a tremendous nose, altogether too big for his face, and his brown skin shone as if it had been oiled. He was well enough dressed in a suit of flannels, and lifted his straw hat politely, and brought his diminutive patent leather heels together as he bowed. In spite of her anxiety and perturbation, Adela could not repress a smile. There was something boylike about this queer little creature, yet his easy assurance pointed to one who knew his world thoroughly, however dark and shady it might be.

"I beg your pardon," he said, in a husky sort of bark, "but I think you are Miss Adela Burton."

Adela bowed gravely.

"I received a message just now," she replied. "Did you bring it? Do you know anything about it?"

The messenger winked knowingly. Adela could have boxed his ears for the sheer audacity of his admiration of her. He walked round her once or twice much as a would-be purchaser inspects a horse. Adela brought him up sharply and inquired what she was to do.

"Oh, you come with me, miss. But I had better introduce myself. I am Max Cordy at your service. The old 'un sent me here to-night. He wants to see you very badly, indeed. It's a risky business, but he said you would understand and ask no questions. He's very queer to-night is the old 'un. Got into a bit o' trouble this morning, he did, and that's why he couldn't come and see you. Besides, it's not quite safe, not altogether prudent. 'Max,' he says to me, 'I don't think the West End air is likely to agree with my constitution at present, so you go round to St. Vericona's Mansions, and get a reply to this note. I was told there where I'd find you, and that's why I followed you here, lady."

"Mr. Burton is ill?"

"Well, he is and he isn't," was the non-committal reply. "But we are wasting time here."

"You had better call a cab,"

"Oh, I think not," Cordy said with a familiar wink. "I venture to think not, my lady. But I don't know; it won't do for you to walk in our parts in that get-up. I tell you what to do. You get into a cab and drive to St. Mark's Church in the Borough, and wait for me there. I shall be there almost as soon as you, because I've got a bike. If I hadn't been a fool I should have brought a dark cloak for you from your flat."

Adela listened with a sense of utter helplessness. It was strange how this funny being was taking her in hand, but this was part of the chain of deceit which she was beginning to drag in lengthening links behind her. She felt not unlike a criminal trying a fall with justice. She wondered what the cabman would think of the address she gave him, and how often he drove a brilliant fare like herself to so shy a neighborhood. But she would have to go; she was being dragged along resistlessly. It was part of the price she had to pay in the struggle to maintain a position to which she did not belong, and to which she had not been born.

Still, she was not afraid. Fear was not her prevailing emotion. After dismissing the cabman she had to wait for Cordy, who soon came up noiselessly on his bicycle. The streets were deserted, save for a few miserable-looking wayfarers, who regarded Adela with suspicion. Cordy pointed out that it would be as well to avoid curious policemen, who might be disposed to ask what a beautifully dressed stranger was doing in that locality at that hour with such an escort. They turned presently from the mean street into a street of dirty, forbidding-looking houses, which for the most part were let out in tenements. It was hard to believe that this district could ever have been respectable or that some of the slums occupied the site of open fields. Cordy searched up and down the street before he knocked at a door which was opened by a slatternly-looking woman apparently under the influence of drink. She exchanged a few words with Cordy in a tongue that Adela did not understand, though it sounded like a mixture of slang and Romany. Then the door closed, and Adela was invited to ascend the stairs. Cordy preceded her, and jerked his thumb in towards a room on the landing.

"When you want me," he said, "knock on the floor twice. I'll see you back to the church, where you can pick up another cab. Anything to oblige a lady. I don't often get the chance."

He leered horribly, his little eyes twinkling with pleasure. Adela murmured her thanks, turned the handle of the door, and walked into the room.

A feeble oil lamp stood upon the bare table, and the rest of the furniture comprised a couple of chairs and a black iron bedstead pushed into one corner. On one of the chairs Samuel Burton sat. He was dirty and untidy. There was a ragged beard of several days' growth on his chin. His moustache had vanished, and with it also the society manner which he had carried so well and naturally on the evening of Douglas Denne's dinner, He was once again the hunted criminal, the broken-down, whining, cringing creature he was when she first saw him. He smiled affectionately; there was something almost senile in the fond glances he threw at the girl. His forehead was bound up in a dirty rag, on which certain dark stains appeared. It was almost impossible to believe that this was the man who had shone so brilliantly and easily at Denne's party. He took Adela's hand and mumbled over it, but on the whole she preferred him in the role of the hard, business-like, keen, audacious criminal.

"I knew you would come, dearie. I knew you wouldn't leave the poor old man by himself?"

"What do you want?" Adela asked coldly.

A fit of coughing racked the emaciated frame, and it was some time before Burton could speak.

"I sent for you because I had to," he wheezed. "I have got into trouble. I was a fool to come back to England, but I couldn't resist the temptation to see the old place before I died, and I also wished to see how my little girl was getting on. I wanted to see her ruffling it with the best of them. Many a time, when I have had to step out of doors, because the police were after me, I have pictured you living here flattered and sought after, and the thought warmed me. Come what may, I have done the fair thing by you."

Adela repressed a shudder. For the life of her she could feel nothing but loathing and contempt for this wicked old rascal, who, to gratify his own whim, had placed her in this dreadful position. Yet she owed him everything. No high-born girl in the land, no princess, had been more pampered and surrounded with greater luxury than she had. Her heart smote her and she tried to throw something like feeling into her words.

"I am very, very sorry," she said. "Is there anything I can do for you? Do you want money?"

Burton smiled cunningly as he rose from his seat and drew a portmanteau from under his bed. He took from it a rustling packet of paper, and fluttered the crisp, clean notes in his trembling hands. They were bank notes, as Adela could see.

"Here are ten thousand pounds," he said hoarsely. "They came into my hands this afternoon, and every penny is for you. You needn't be afraid to use them, but in spite of all this wealth, I haven't a penny to go on with. I have been betrayed, and the police are after me. I have to thank your friend, Mark Callader, for this. But I shall be even with him; oh, yes, I shall be even with him before I die. I can't move a step from here, and I don't know which way to turn for this money in my possession!"

"I cannot understand it," Adela protested.

"Because I dare not handle the paper. Those are all fifty-pound notes. Not a soul in this house would dare to try to cash one of them. The thing would be madness. That's why I sent for you. Put them in your pocket, my child. Don't be afraid, there will be plenty more when the time comes. Samuel Burton may be old and worn out, but he isn't quite done for yet."

CHAPTER XIII

THE MAN AND HIS METHOD

Slowly and mechanically Adela thrust the packet of notes into the bosom of her dress. She felt that she was fettered hand and foot now. It was impossible to refuse, impossible to turn her back upon this old man to whom she was indebted for everything that had made her life pleasant and triumphant. Besides, surely there must be some good in one who, throughout a misspent life, had held loyally to a romantic idea, which was sincere and honest, and as Adela looked into his face she realised that the end was not far off. She cared not to quietly fold her hands and see Samuel Burton spend the rest of his days in gaol.

"What do you wish me to do?" she asked.

"Turn one of those notes into gold and bring it to me. Fifty pounds will be enough. With that money I can lie low till one or two schemes mature, and then you can have as much as you want. I'll write to you when it is safe to come here, and when you come down you will bring me certain things I need. I can't stay here, and if I don't get away into a purer air I shall be really and truly ill. But you needn't worry about that. I'll plan it all out before you come again."

Adela was trying to think out a way out of this impasse. Such a life of deception should not continue. She would make some excuse for moving into the country, where she could be alone and nurse this broken old man back to health. Then she could fade away out of her gay life altogether, disappear abroad, and in a few months everybody would have forgotten Adela Burton. She began to speak of this, growing keener and more enthusiastic as she proceeded. As she went on, Burton lay back in his chair convulsed with silent mirth, his cunning features wreathed in a grin that brought the blood to her face and caused her to wish she had not spoken so freely.

"I couldn't do it, my dear," Burton said. "This sort of thing is the breath of life to me. An existence like that you describe would drive me mad in a month. Now just do as you are told, dearie, and don't talk sentimental nonsense. You don't seem to know how proud I am of you. There you stand, the best-dressed and handsomest woman in London, a welcome guest in half a score of ducal houses, and all owing to poor old Sam Burton. I have worked and slaved for this, and I am proud of the result. But for me you might have been—never mind what. You go on, my child, you stick to it. Marry Mark Callader, and you'll be a marchioness one day. I was going to let him know what it cost to play the traitor to Samuel Burton, but I have thought better of that, and I wouldn't have sent for you tonight if I could have helped it. There are only two men I can trust in the world, and at present they are both in America. Max Cordy, of course, hardly counts, though he would do anything for me. But it doesn't do to trust any of them too far. I think it's time you were gone."

Anxious as she was to leave, Adela hesitated. The atmosphere was close and oppressive, the sour smell seemed to pinch her throat and cause her difficulty in breathing. The floor was dirty, the walls were wet and greasy, the ceiling was black with smoke. Every now and then from the streets below came the riotous cry of a drunken brawler, or the scream of an angry woman, or, occasionally, the whine of a child. Truly, the way of the transgressor was hard. She marvelled that Burton could bear his troubles so philosophically, that he was so ready to change the comfort and luxury of his hotel for an unspeakable existence like this. She made no allowance for the spirit of adventure, for the love of cunning and audacity which spurs every great criminal onwards. Samuel Burton would doubtless have told her that it was all part of the game, that the downs of the profession rendered the ups all the more enjoyable.

"I will go now," she said. "I will bring you the money and the things you need directly you send for them. Is there anything else I can do? It seems so dreadful—"

Adela paused and turned her head away. She heard Burton give two sharp knocks on the floor, and a moment later the snaky head of Max Cordy appeared round the doorway. He bowed with exaggerated politeness, his beady eyes still expressing audacious admiration. He chattered with easy confidence as he walked by Adela's side until the church was reached.

"Stand here in the porch," he whispered, "while I fetch a cab. I shan't be long."

The minutes dragged till they totalled thirty, and still there was no sign of Cordy's return. Adela was becoming impatient. She could not remain there all night. Probably she would meet a policeman, who would show her where to get a cab. She walked swiftly along the road, forgetting what a strange figure she must cut in her opera cloak and satin shoes, and diamonds glittering in her hair. She grew conscious presently that someone was following her, and she quickened her steps. Then, from out of a side street, a man lurched against her, and she staggered back in alarm. The man behind closed up, and Adela was terror-stricken as she looked from one repulsive face to the other. They were new types to her, they had never come within her purview, but she knew by instinct what these men were and how great her peril was.

"There's no call to be frightened, my dear," one of the men said hoarsely. "It's all right. I've lost my way, too—taken a wrong turn coming home from the opera. This is not a very nice neighborhood, and you had better let me take care of those pretty stones for you. They'll be safe with me."

Adela gave one despairing glance down the deserted street. There was no policeman in sight, and as she turned to fly a rough hand was laid upon her shoulder, and another dragged her back by the throat. As she opened her lips to scream that awful grip tightened, the world swam round her, a million sparks danced before her eyes.

"You are quite safe," said a voice that seemed to come from a long way off. "All you've got to do is to behave yourself, and you won't come to any harm."

Adela trembled in every limb, but she saw clearly that her safety lay in obedience. She had heard of outrages in which the victim had disappeared, never to be heard of again. She could feel a rough hand fumbling in the coils of her hair, and pulling at her jewels. Then the ruffian who was handling her fell back with a curse and a cry. A third man had appeared upon the scene, a welcome intruder who took in the situation at a glance. Her two assailants turned upon him threateningly, and she fancied she saw the glint of steel in the light. Then, in a dreamy kind of way, she realised that Mark Callader was standing by her side, with a peculiar grin twitching his hard mouth. His face was dark and set, and his eyes gleamed angrily.

He stepped back a pace or two, then with lightning speed he lunged forward, Adela heard the stinging impact of flesh upon flesh. She saw one man measure his length upon the pavement, the back of his head coming down upon the stones with a sickening crash. Then Callader seized the other man by the throat, and banged his head against a wall until he collapsed, a white, convulsive heap, by the side of his mate.

Adela stood with clasped hands watching it all. She was glad, almost vindictively glad, and at the same time filled with terror. She had all a woman's admiration for strength and courage in a man. It seemed to her that Callader was splendid, almost god-like. There was no mistaking his magnificent nerve, his confidence in himself, his assurance of victory. The light of battle was in his eyes, he fairly revelled in the fray. It was all over in the twinkling of an eye. The two ruffians lay moaning and groaning, and as Adela put her hand to her head, she felt that her diamonds were safe. Then the elation died and gladness died out of her heart, and fear took their place. She was grateful for Callader's championship for the kind fate which had brought him to her rescue, but he was the last man in the world whom she wished to meet in the circumstances.

For the moment he said nothing, but merely offered his arm, which Adela accepted in silence. He piloted her along the road with the air of a man who knew where he was. He did not appear in the least disturbed. Even his dress tie had not shifted in the struggle. It was not till a cab was found at length and the driver awakened on his seat that Adela spoke.

"I cannot sufficiently thank you. Can't I offer you a lift as far as—"

"Oh, I'm coming," Callader said coolly, as he stepped into the cab. "I haven't asked for an explanation; there is plenty of time for that. Rest yourself till we reach your flat. I am going to see you safely home, and perhaps you will give me a cigarette and whisky and soda."

Quiet as his tones were, yet there was something truculent about them. He paid the cabman, and followed Adela into the drawing-room. How refined and luxuriant and grateful it looked, Adela thought, after the vile-smelling den she had just left. The scent of the roses and Parma violets was grateful to her nostrils. She was thankful for the shaded lamps which somewhat hid her features from the scrutiny of those close-set eyes. She threw back her cloak, and stood in all her resplendent beauty. She passed over the cigarettes, and poured out the whisky with a trembling hand, Callader watching her as a cat watches a mouse. His dull, coarse face spoke of admiration as well as suspicion, and Adela had an unusual feeling that she was utterly in this man's power.

"Well," he said, "aren't you going to tell me anything."

Adela forced a smile to her lips.

"Have you any right to know? Of course, I am profoundly grateful to you, and you behaved splendidly. I never saw anything more magnificent. But if you want to know what I was doing in that neighborhood, I am afraid I can't tell you. I had to go and see an old friend who is in distress, and was foolish enough to try to find a cab myself. That is all."

"Oh, indeed," Callader replied. "Was it a man or a woman whom you went to visit? If I were not particularly interested in you, it would not in the least matter."

Adela laughed as she dropped into a chair, and was beginning to recover control of her nerves.

"Mark," she began, "you are intolerable. You forget that you have no right—"

Callader crossed, and laid his hand upon her shoulder.

"No," he said hoarsely, "but, by heaven, I mean to."

CHAPTER XIV

GOLDEN FETTERS

The touch of Callader's hands seemed to bear Adela down much as if she were being forced into some abyss from which there was no escape. They were such strong, capable hands. She was conscious of the springy muscles. How easy for a man like Callader to choke the life out of her. She had all the sensation of one who is drowning. A feeling of suffocation filled her throat, and she trembled lest she might lack the courage to keep this man at a distance.

She could not but admire his pluck; indeed, this was Callader's greatest asset. All women are attracted by that; it is perhaps the quality they admire most in men—a survival of the pre-historic instinct which was obtained when the cave-dwellers took their wives by force, and brute strength was their first and final argument.

Yet, there was nothing brutal about Callader just now, nothing but a suggestion of certainty which filled Adela with more fear than any outburst of anger or vituperation. She knew perfectly well that Callader could compel her to do anything at that moment. She had no illusions, either, no affection for him; nothing, indeed, except a shrinking fear and detestation.

As he looked down into her face she hardly dared try to read his eyes. She would have given much to be alone, to have this trying ordeal ended. But there was no mercy in Callader's eyes. Adela knew that he would not be denied a hearing.

"You are hurting me."

"Don't talk like that," Callader retorted. "I am not hurting you in the least. Why do you behave like this? What's the use of you pretending you don't know how much I love you?"

He had taken the plunge, and with it Adela's courage was returning. After he took his hands from her shoulders she seemed to rise to the surface again.

"Do you?" she asked thoughtfully. "Now, I wonder if you really care for anybody? I wonder if you ever consider anybody in your life but yourself?"

"I don't know that I do," Callader said candidly. "But that does not affect my question."

"Oh, doesn't it? I should have thought it made all the difference in the world. What you take for love is a merely passion—the animal instincts of a strong man. My dear Mark, believe me, you don't know anything about love at all. How could you? Your have always had your own way. You have always been headstrong and reckless. You have never counted the cost of anything. Love is self-sacrificing, disinterested, unselfish."

Callader laughed openly.

"What's the good of talking all that sentimental nonsense?" he said. "Honestly, I don't know what you mean. But there's one thing I'm certain of, and that is, you shall marry me. Everybody is looking forward to it as a matter of course. Perhaps I am a fool because I know so very little about you."

"You are candid," Adela smiled. "I suppose that is proof of your disinterestedness. The fact is that you know nothing about me is in my favor, and the fact that I know a good deal about you is, perhaps, greatly in your disfavor."

Adela spoke quickly and nervously, possibly on the off chance of putting Callader off the track. But he nodded with a grudging admiration. The strange light in his eyes, however, gave Adela concern and discomfort.

"But it's true I don't know anything about you," he urged. "Nobody does. You are a brilliant mystery with the command of plenty of money. Your social position is not in question; there are hundreds of better men than myself who would be proud and willing to call you their wife. Still, you are a riddle. Tell me something about yourself, about this mysterious Samuel Burton. Who is he and where does he come from?"

"You know as well as I do," Adela said discreetly. "I have only met him once, but if I am not mistaken you have met him frequently. Do you take me for a fool, Mark? Do you think I didn't notice that passage at arms between you and Burton at Douglas Denne's the other night? It is for you to tell me who Samuel Burton is. I know nothing. I am his protege. For aught I knew he may have picked me out of the gutter. Rich men have these sort of whims sometimes, but they can afford it. Come, enlighten me on the subject of my benefactor. Where did you meet him first? Why do you hate him so heartily?"

Callader knitted his brows in a frown, and his coarse, red face grew darker and more angry.

"You are a devilishly clever girl, far cleverer than I am. But your imagination is bolting with you. I haven't the slightest idea who Samuel Burton is."

"Why lie?" Adela asked coldly. "You are afraid of that man, and he is afraid of you. You want him out of the way. But I don't ask your confidence!"

Callader was disturbed and uneasy. He could have given Adela much information had he pleased, but the time was not come for confidences of that sort. Samuel Burton's reputation or his past was no immediate concern of his. There would be time enough later to speak freely of these things.

"Very good," he said bluntly. "You have your secrets, and I will respect them. I have mine, too. What does it matter who you are, and where you come from, or how Samuel Burton made his money. I came to-night to ask you to become my wife, and mean to have an answer. I shan't interfere with you—you will be allowed to go your own way much as you do now. It will be more of an alliance than a marriage. Don't forget—"

Callader paused, conscious, perhaps, that he was about to say too much. The blood had flamed into Adela's face, her lips were parted and she was breathing rapidly. She knew the time had come when she must make up her mind, for here was the parting of the ways. If she said 'No' to Callader, then she would fade out of the set in which she had queened it so long, she would drop out of the race, and her place would know her no more. What did that involve? It meant a hard life in the future, possibly a sordid struggle, the relinquishing of her ambitions, and the luxuries and pleasures which had become a second nature to her.

Could she do it? Could she face this dismal future? As she glanced round she noted the artistic objects that gave an air to the room and the pretty things that gladdened her aesthetic sense; even the flowers in the vases appealed to her. In a mirror opposite she remarked the glint and glisten of her diamonds as they rose and fell upon her bosom, the dainty robe in which she looked like a picture by some consummate artist. She also observed Callader, standing rough and sinister, waiting for an answer. She could get out of her present difficulties, for she had the money to clear herself; she could feel the notes crackling as she breathed. But she must decide here and now.

"It shall be as you wish. No, don't come near me, don't come near me at this moment, or I swear that I shall change my mind. You are free to tell everybody, if you like, you may go to your club, late as it is, and break the news, but go at once. Do you hear me?"

The words fell thick and fast from her lips. She had risen to her feet, and stretched her hand towards the door. It even seemed that she was on the point of a physical encounter with Callader, for he came towards her with gleaming eyes, and there was something in his face that caused Adela to shrink and tremble. Then he stopped abruptly and laughed.

"Have you own way. You are in one of your moods to-night. I suppose you don't mind me coming to see you to-morrow? Good-night."

The room was the fresher and sweeter for his absence. Adela gave one glance round, then switched off the lights passionately and went to bed. She was tired and weary. She slept, as she told herself, like a condemned criminal the night before his execution, but did not analyse her feelings further.

In the morning she thought it impossible she could fulfil her promise of the previous night. She would send for Callader and tell him so. She would break with her friends, sell everything, and pay her debts. Burton should have his ill-gotten gains back again. Adela had quite made up her mind before she had finished breakfast, and was in the same mood as she entered her sitting-room. Here someone was waiting for her, a well-dressed man, polite and obsequious; but anxious and ill at ease. Adela knew who he was. He was a jeweller from Regent-street with whom she had had dealings more than once. He had a house not far from her cottage at Maidenhead, a pretty wife, and two charming little children; indeed, Adela had seen the children by the river frequently. She was well aware why he was here. Doubtless he had bribed one of the servants to procure him this interview.

"What do you want?"

The jeweller was profoundly apologetic. He was exceedingly sorry to worry Miss Burton, but he was in great straits for ready money, and there was an account of over twelve hundred pounds which had been out-standing for a long time. His position was serious, and he must have the money. He pointed out that at least two years—

"Really?" Adela said. She had lost something of her cold manner, and her conscience was pricking her. "I am very sorry, Mr. Braxton. It is very careless of me. Must you have the money to-day. You can't wait a week, I suppose?"

The jeweller appeared to be swallowing something hard.

"It is a matter of bankruptcy. If you discharge this account I shall be able to see my way clear. Believe me, madam, I would not have troubled you, but I have a wife and family, and it comes very hard—"

There was no need to say more. The man was plainly telling the truth. Besides, he was only asking for his own. With something like a sense of shame upon her Adela unlocked her desk.

"Please don't make a favor of it," she said. "I won't give you a cheque, but I have notes which come to the same thing, eh?"

The receipt was signed, and Adela was alone again. She smiled bitterly as she turned the key in the desk.

"Fate is too strong for me. I never meant to do this. I never—but, oh, why try to deceive myself? I have burnt my boats, and there is no re-crossing the stream."

CHAPTER XV

THE CUP OF TANTALUS

Douglas Denne had dined, but his dinner had afforded him no consolation. He was vexed and disappointed, and these, usually, were emotions which he did not allow himself to indulge in. The Curacoa he was sipping had no flavor. He must really change his cigar merchant. He was annoyed, too, because he had permitted outside influences to trouble him. Really, why should he worry? Why should he feel upset because Adela Burton had fulfilled expectations, and become engaged to Mark Callader? It had been the one theme of conversation during the past fortnight. The marriage was discussed in the clubs and Callader was deemed to be an exceedingly lucky man. There were armchair philosophers who wondered what Adela could see in him. They pondered thoughtfully the decrees of Fate which allowed men of the coarse, animal type to marry the most beautiful women. The girl was an heiress, too, which made the thing all the more inexplicable.

Denne was not only irritated, but he was, perhaps, also inclined to be jealous. He had always admired Adela. She possessed to the full the qualities that peculiarly attracted him. Her nameless style of beauty came very near to realising his high ideal. He had thought a good deal, too, of what Vanstone had said, and had not forgotten his promise that Adela should not marry Callader. He refused to admit that he was in love with her himself, but there were moments when the conviction was forced upon him.

"I am a fool, a sentimental fool. Despite her beauty and talent, Adela Burton is little more than an adventurer. I wonder if she knows all about Burton. I wonder if she knows that he is the son of an Earl, who was kicked out of his regiment for one of the dirtiest frauds that ever disgraced a British officer. I wonder if she knows he has been in gaol. I wonder if he is really a rich man. At any rate, he has command of plenty of money, and the way in which he stole my Velasquez was clever. I can't think how he managed to smuggle it out of the house. I don't relish this business at all, nor am I sure that I am wise in trusting Lestrine so far. It looks uncommonly like conspiracy. There are one or two judges on the Bench who would take that view. Fancy my being mixed up in a thing like this! Well, we must wait and see. But Adela Burton shall not marry Mark Callader, even if I have to marry her myself. I am jealous, that is what is wrong with me—a nice thing at any time of life. The question is—is she worth it?"

But that was a point that Denne could not decide off-hand. He threw his cigar into the fire-place and pushed his glass aside. He had half a mind to remain indoors for the rest of the evening and read, but he was too restless for that. He glanced casually through his diary with a view to selecting the engagement which was likely to afford him the greatest relaxation. He smiled grimly to himself as he saw the name of Felix Marner. That would do very well, he thought. Felix Marner and his wife were holding a reception at which everybody would be present, and it was pretty certain that Adela Burton would be there. Denne would go to Frogmore-street.

About eleven o'clock he ascended the Florentine staircase which a great American had tried, but had failed to purchase. The rooms were crowded. Here was an ambassador, there a financial magnate, behind him a Cabinet Minister, talking to a great singer; in fact, the whole place was a heterogeneous collection of celebrities gathered from two continents. Priceless tapestries draped the walls, and every picture had a history. Every object of art was the finest and best that the world produced. Felix Marner looked grave and picturesque in his evening dress, the subdued light glistening upon his grey hair. Of the many notable figures he was not the least conspicuous.

Denne exchanged a few words with his host and wandered aimlessly through the rooms. He came presently to the object of his search. Adela was sitting in the corner of a room with half a dozen men around her. Marvellously dressed in some dreamy confection of green, she suggested sea foam in the sunlight. The jewels which sparkled in her hair were as so many sunbeams. Her face was wreathed in smiles, and there was no shadow of trouble or anxiety in her eyes as Denne went forward and shook hands. By and by he managed, in his own fashion, to draw Adela away, and got her entirely to himself.

"I have not seen you for some days," he said. "I suppose this thing I hear is true?"

"I presume people tell the truth about me sometimes," Adela laughed gaily. "But what are you alluding to?"

"Oh, you know perfectly well—your engagement to Mark Callader. Am I to congratulate—no, not you—but him?"

Adela's face flushed ever so slightly.

"The paragraphists are right for once," she said. "This is the only veracious thing they have written about me for years. But why don't you congratulate me?"

"There's nothing to congratulate you about," Denne said coolly. "You must not be annoyed; I am generally allowed to say what I like. But I am sorry to hear this. Between ourselves, I don't like Callader. The man is bad tempered, and you won't be happy. Now, if I didn't take an interest in you, I shouldn't talk like this. I am sure you could have done much better."

Adela laughed again.

"You are frank," she said. "But one must settle down some time. Now, why don't you marry? It is your duty to do so, and there are so many nice girls."

"I think not," Denne said in his gravest manner. "You see, it is difficult to persuade a man to be content with a substitute. Besides, it is not flattering to one's vanity to be cut out by a man like Mark Callader."

"You are jesting," Adela said coolly, "and your joke is not in good taste. If you meant it—"

"My dear girl, I do mean it, which is my only justification. If you had not promised to marry him, I should have asked you to be my wife. You know enough of human nature to believe that I didn't make this discovery until I found it was too late. You would have done so much better with me. My position is assured, but you can't say that about Callader. A strange conversation this, isn't it? But I never do anything like other men. Now you know why I can't congratulate you. But I don't intend to give up yet. There's many a slip 'twixt the cup and the lip. Of one thing I must assure you—whatever happens, you will always have a friend in me. Never hesitate to come to Douglas Denne. Try to think as well of me as possible, and whatever trouble you are in, and however badly you behave, it will make no difference to me. Because I love you, my child, and that accounts for everything. I am sorry I did not find this out sooner, because I believe I should have had a better chance than Mark Callader. That sounds egotistical, but some day you may remember it. Now let us change the subject."

Adela looked up curiously into the speaker's grave face. At first she had thought he was jesting, but she could see plainly now that he was very much in earnest. All the anger died out of her heart, and she was filled with a sense of gratitude which brought the unaccustomed tears into her eyes.

"You are very good," she said. "Really; you are a most extraordinary man, Mr. Denne. If you knew everything you would be inclined—but we need not go into that."

Denne strolled off presently. He appeared to be concerned about nothing, though he was watching carefully, and awaiting the advent of Mark Callader. The latter arrived in his sullen, moody way, and the air which he had in society of being absolutely out of place. Denne saw him make a sign to Marner, and the two drifted off together towards the library. Denne waited a moment or two, and then followed them. The door of the library was closed, but he opened it without ceremony, and strode into the room. He had a cigar in one hand and his matchbox in the other.

"I beg your pardon," he said, "I strolled in here to have a smoke. I know Marner doesn't mind."

For once in his life the great critic betrayed confusion. On the table before him stood a small, plain-looking gold cup, fashioned in the shape of a Gothic font, such as is still to be seen in some of the older churches. He was regarding it with his head on one side, his eyes filled with a certain fatherly affection. He appeared to have been speaking, but stopped abruptly as Denne came in.

"Does that belong to you?" Denne asked.

"Eh, what?" Callader said. "Oh, no. Marner was just showing it to me. Wonderful work, isn't it?"

"Please understand, it isn't mine," Marner explained. "It has been given to me to dispose of. I should like to keep it, but it is beyond my poor means. I suppose that cup would fetch at least twenty-five thousand pounds. It is the veritable Cup of Tantalus, which Geisler alludes to in his illuminated manuscript in the Bodleian Library at Oxford. For the last eight or nine centuries the cup has vanished, and I understand it recently turned up in some castle in the Black Forest. The finding of the cup has quite a romance. Perhaps you would like to have it, Denne? Only a millionaire like yourself could afford to purchase such a thing."

But Denne did not appear to be interested. He said he had no sympathy with sentimental values and sauntered out of the library, leaving Marner and Callader together by the side of the table.

"You got well out of that," he heard Callader remark.

"I think so," Marner replied. "Besides, Denne was not interested. All the same, it is as well to take no risks, and I was foolish to leave the door unlocked."

Meanwhile Denne was walking thoughtfully homewards. When he reached his quarters, he rang up Lestrine.

"I am here, sir," Lestrine said. "Can I do anything for you? I am quite ready."

"That's right," Denne responded. "The mouse is in the trap, Lestrine. It is time to kill it."

CHAPTER XVI

THE WEARY ROUND

At times Adela thought she could not stand the strain of her mode of life any longer. Of course that was unreasonable; her life had the defects of its qualities, and she could not have it both ways. She had accepted existence as it was. It had seemed natural to turn night into day, to be always on the stretch, and she was beginning to feel the wear and tear. Many friends and acquaintances had fallen out of the race. It was nothing now to hear that this or that one had been ordered south, or was in the hands of a fashionable doctor. But Adela had regarded them as poor creatures, not physically fit to enter the arena.

Nevertheless, she could not herself keep up the pace much longer. There was no rest or relaxation anywhere. Whether the scene were London from March till July, or Cowes, Goodwood, Scotland, Homburg, or Monte Carlo, there was the same false excitement, the same constant worry and rush, the weary monotony of familiar faces. Adela was beginning to wonder whether this was enjoyment at all, and was getting to loathe it from the bottom of her heart. She longed to be by herself in the country. If she could only sleep, perchance she might be able to think, for the power of concentrated thought was leaving her. She had strange lapses of memory, could not rest indoors or out, started at a shadow. There was always present the fear that something was going to happen.

Yet she could not tear herself away from it. It was absolutely impossible to do so. Her stock of money was beginning to dwindle again. Her daily correspondence grew more insistent and oppressive. There were plenty of establishments still where she was received with bated breath and whispering humbleness, but even these were shrinking, and it was not nice to dash up to a palatial shop in a thousand guinea motor, and be called aside by a polite, but no less determined partner, who, in a few well-chosen sentences, intimated that no further credit could be given until a cheque had been received. These instances were growing more and more frequent, and Adela fancied her very servants were lacking in the respect and obedience to which she had been accustomed.

Freedom was unobtainable. She was too fast in the golden fetters for that; still in the world of fashion and excitement. Her engagement book was crammed with pressing promises. There were theatricals here and house parties there, to say nothing of stalls at charity bazaars, and all the odds and ends of the frothy flippery in which the woman of fashion revels.

What Adela wanted most was time—time to rest, time to think, time to form a plan of campaign. If she drew back now her large army of creditors would take alarm, swoop down upon her in a body, and only disgraceful bankruptcy ensue. She was beginning to realise her own hopeless weakness, to see more and more clearly that there was no escape from her promise to Mark Callader. If she were only well, she might take the plunge. Hitherto she had laughed at women's fads and fancies. It had amused her to see the pathetic way in which some women clung to their doctors, but now she was feeling the need of advice herself. Not without a sense of self-contempt, she drove to Harley-street. The great man consented to see her at once, though a score of patients were waiting in his dining-room. He extended a slim, white hand to Adela. His manner was confidential, almost caressing. He placed her in a seat and began to ask questions in his blandest and most soothing style. Sir Charles Haviland knew his world thoroughly. He saw at a glance exactly what was the matter, though it would not be discreet to blurt it out.

"You are run down, my dear lady. Let us ask ourselves a question or two. How long is it since you took a holiday?"

"Isn't my life all a holiday?"

Sir Charles shook his head gravely.

"A delusion," he said. "I don't know any woman who works any harder than you do. Why, you work as strenuously as a poor woman who is compelled to earn a living by making cheap clothing. From the time you get up in the morning till the time you go to bed you never rest. Nor do you have sufficient sleep. You are never in bed before two or three, and probably breakfast at nine, and this has been going on day by day for the last four years."

It was true enough, as Adela was bound to admit. She had never seen things in this light before. Sir Charles took her hand in his, and gravely consulted his stop-watch. He was looking a little more serious, and murmured quietly that he must use the stethoscope. Adela waited for his verdict with more or less indifference.

"You must go away at once," he said. "You must put your present life behind you for at least three months. There is nothing radically wrong, but you are completely run down. Now, don't come to me again, because prescriptions are of no use, and you are merely wasting my time. What you want is to drop this racket for two or three months, and then you will be all right again. Otherwise, I must decline to answer for the consequences."

There was no mistaking what the famous physician meant, and Adela looked more thoughtful than usual as she drove away in her car. She was conscious, however, that she was attracting attention, and was being pointed out and spoken of. Doubtless there were hundreds of people who envied her, and would have given much to stand in her place. What would they have said if they only knew? As she drove along, she could hear the boys with early copies of the newspapers calling out the latest details of the Courtfield case. This was a sensational action which must mean either the triumph of a brilliant adventuress, or imprisonment and irretrievable ruin. Adela knew Nita Courtfield. Lots of people who had taken her up were sorry for it now. Yet it seemed to Adela, criticising her own self freely, that she was not a whit better. The only difference was that she had not yet been found out, and the other woman had. On the whole, what was there to choose between them?

Adela rolled along in her car, a car that had been specially built for her, and had been the thing of a hundred paragraphs. She was beautifully dressed; there were judges who said she was the best-dressed woman in London. She was exceedingly beautiful, too, as many an admiring glance testified. But Adela was feeling very keenly how false and hollow her life was, and longed to get away from her society self. She wondered if Sir Charles' opinion would give her the chance. But the fashionable physician's advice would not pay her debts, and it was almost out of the question to leave London till some of the more pressing creditors were satisfied. Adela wondered, too, if she might not be able to do something with moneylenders. Doubtless a score of these gentlemen would be only too willing to oblige her. But this would be obtaining money by false pretences, even if at usurious interest, and she knew if she fell into their clutches there was only one way out.

She must go somewhere to think the situation out. She would not go home to lunch, because Callader had promised to call, and she shrank from meeting him at present. She would lunch quietly at the Savoy, and perhaps, once in a way, might snatch an hour to herself.

She ordered a simple lunch, and, as she turned her attention to it, there was a sudden rush of customers into the restaurant, and Adela found herself surrounded by chattering frivolous women. Three sat down breathlessly at the same table as herself.

"Wherever have you been?" one asked. "I never saw you this morning. Wasn't it splendid?"

"What?" Adela asked vaguely.

"Oh, Nita Courtfield's evidence. Did you ever know anything so audacious? It was splendid to watch the way she fought Rupert. But that bit of evidence as to the half-burnt letter was fatal. Do you think she will be tried for perjury?"

"I wasn't there," Adela said indifferently.

The three frivolities, rustling in their silk and chiffons, screamed excitedly:

"Not there? I can't understand what you are thinking about. I wouldn't have missed it for anything. It was better and more actual than a play. You will come after lunch, of course?"

Adela excused herself. Was it impossible to get away from this rush and rattle? The whole world seemed full of it, and it might be her turn next. These silly creatures might soon be discussing her, and watching her in the dock. They would be none the more friendly and more merciful because they had undertaken a score of times of her boundless hospitality. In imagination she pictured them watching her as she stood up to face her trial. Anything was better than this. She would go back to her flat and rest. She could send Mark Callader away under the excuse that she was suffering from a severe headache. She felt utterly tired and worn-out, and must have sleep. A curious fluttering at her heart every now and then alarmed her. On reaching home she was informed that Mr. Callader had come and gone. He had stayed to write a note and then left, saying he had important business to attend to. But a man was waiting in the dining-room, who had declined to go away. He refused his name, but declared he must stay, because it was most important that he should see Miss Burton. Another creditor, no doubt, Adela thought; she would have to get rid of him somehow.

But it was not a creditor; it was the diminutive Max Cordy, self possessed and amusingly insolent as usual. Vexed as she was, Adela could hardly repress a smile, for Cordy was arrayed in a grey frock-suit of perfect cut. He appeared to be especially proud of his patent-leather boots, and held his glossy hat at quite the correct angle. He was pleased to see Adela and labored under the impression that she was equally glad to see him.

"What do you want here?" she demanded. Cordy winked slightly.

"I think you can guess," he said. "I was sent by the old 'un. He desires me to say he is much better and the danger is off for the present. But he has got to get away from London. He thinks that a month or two in the country will do him good. Still, we can't take any risks, and that is why we want your help."

"I will do what I can," Adela said wearily. "You have come to make some proposition. What is it?"

CHAPTER XVII

A RESPITE

Max Cordy sank gracefully into a chair, hitched up his trousers and crossed his legs. Without asking permission of Adela he proceeded to light a cigarette. She could have boxed his ears, but behind her annoyance was a sense of amusement, perhaps even of admiration, at the little man who seemed so completely at home. He no longer looked like a boy, but like a young man on whom fortune has smiled.

"Well, it's like this, miss," he said, leaning forward confidentially. "We'll manage, for the present, at any rate, to keep out of the way of the police. The old 'un don't say much, but he knows he can trust me; in fact, I shouldn't dare do anything contrary to his instructions, because there are little episodes in my own past which—well, we won't pursue that. But when men choose to play their own game at the guv'nor's expense, somehow or another things never seem to go well with them again. Bless you! You needn't be afraid to speak candidly to me. I know nothing. I don't even know who you are, though I expect you are some relation to the guv'nor. I know he's a swell, right enough—connected with the peerage, and all the rest of it. Still—"

"Hadn't we better get to the point?"

"Of course; I am sorry. But, you see, I don't often get a chance of talking to a lovely lady. As I said, the old man wants to get away from London. It isn't quite safe for him to travel in the ordinary way, nor leave the Borough in our motor. Now, what's to be done is this. You must go off for a ride this afternoon in your car by yourself. It won't be the first time you have done such a thing, will it? Go by way of 'Ampstead, and 'Endon, and when you get near the Welsh 'Arp, I shouldn't be surprised if you found the guv'nor waiting for you. Then you can take him as far as St. Alban's, after which he will know what to do. I think that's all, miss. If you should 'appen to be somewhere about there at four o'clock this afternoon the guv'nor will take it very kind."

It was on the tip of Adela's tongue to refuse. Her impulse was to turn this preposterous little criminal out of the room, and tell him sternly not to come any more. But she was too deeply in the toils for that. To put it bluntly, she was as much involved as Samuel Burton himself. She was just as great a criminal. She had not actually picked pockets, but the beautiful dress she was wearing was not paid for, nor was it likely to be. The bubble to her romance was pricked. She now knew what Samuel Burton was. Why, she was actually dependent upon the trades people for the very food she ate. Moreover, her debt to Samuel Burton was a heavy one, and she could not go back on him at present. She would have to wait another opportunity.

"Very well," she said wearily. "It shall be as you say. I will be there at the appointed time."

She changed her dress for something dark and plain and made some excuse for dispensing with her chauffeur. The man expressed no astonishment; he was too used to his mistress's vagaries. Besides, Adela could drive well, and had often been out alone in her car. Bowling along, leaving the familiar streets behind, she grew less restless, and less discontented as the fresh sweet air of the afternoon blew upon her face. Then, a little later, she caught sight of the familiar figure of Samuel Burton strolling slowly along the road. He had cast off all signs of his recent illness, walked with an easy jaunty air, had resumed his moustache, and was unmistakably well dressed. As the car pulled up, he jumped in, and Adela set the great motor going once more.

"Are you better?"

"I am feeling almost myself again. To tell you the truth, adventure is meat and drink to me. I am only happy when I am in danger, and I have been in danger lately. The strange thing is that the enemy I have most to fear is the man you are going to marry. But I think I shall be able to close his lips now. Let me congratulate you, my dear. I read all about it in the papers—a marriage has been arranged, and will shortly take place between the Honorable Mark Callader and Miss Adela Burton, the beautiful heiress to the wealth of Samuel Burton, esquire, the American millionaire. Ah, how I laughed at it! There were a lot of paragraphs about me, too, all of them, between ourselves, absolute lies, my dear."

"Why not?" Adela said wearily. "Your whole life is a lie, and so is mine, too, for the matter of that. I am getting so dreadfully tired of it. I meant to have used the last money you gave me to pay my creditors, and then disappear from London altogether, but I couldn't do it."

The old man by Adela's side chuckled.

"Shall I tell you why? You couldn't do it because you hadn't money enough. You thought what I gave you would be sufficient, but it wasn't. Idle and extravagant people never know how much they owe. And so it's all gone, and you want some more, my dear? Well, you shall have it. You needn't be the least afraid of that. I have one or two little schemes on hand which I couldn't perfect in London. I am going into the country where I can be quiet and think matters out. I want to have a horse to ride, and a garden to walk in, to go to bed at ten, and breakfast at eight, and that's why I have taken a furnished house not very far from the village of Callader. At St. Alban's another car will meet me, and take me north. These motors are excellent things from my point of view. When you go into a railway station you never know who is watching you; you can never tell what detectives are prowling about; but in a car you can put on a mask and goggles, and nobody can tell you from Adam; except that, poor man, he didn't motor."

Adela was only listening vaguely. She had her own painful thoughts to occupy her, but was glad to know that Samuel Burton would be out of the way for some time to come. She was not likely to have any more unpleasant visits from Max Cordy, and, perhaps she would get sufficient money to clear her most pressing liabilities. When that was done, she knew exactly what to do. Her spirits began to rise with the swift motion of the car. She found it hard to believe that the man sitting by her side was a hardened criminal. He did not look like it in the least. He might have passed for a distinguished military man or a member of the aristocracy, clean-living, and basking in the sunshine of prosperity. She could not help being struck by the fact that the neighborhood which Burton had chosen for his rustication was within a short distance of Callader Castle, Mark Callader's home, and she ventured to remark this to her companion.

Burton stroked his moustache and smiled.

"My dear child," he said blandly, "this is no mere coincidence. In a career like mine there are no such things as coincidences. If we are careless enough to permit them, we find that they invariably lead us into trouble. I am going to Callader for a purpose. What that purpose is does not matter to you so long as you benefit by it; and you will benefit by it, and to a material extent, too. By the way, have you heard anything of a house-party which Callader's getting up for the race-week? I think I saw something of it in one of the society papers. It is a magnificent place, Callader Castle. I stayed there more than once during the life of the late Lord Kempston; in fact, I used to do a lot of shooting there; but in those days I was not called Samuel Burton, and I had not brought the hair of my relatives in sorrow to the grave. I was a model young man then, and, upon my word, my dear child, when I come to think of it, I wish that I had remained one. But there is a wild strain in our blood somewhere. Some people can't be honest and straightforward, and I suppose I am one of them. I don't think I ever did a kind and disinterested action in my life except when I adopted you, and really, that was more of a fad than anything else. I hope it is true that Callader is getting up a party, and that he will ask you to join it. It is a glorious old place, and its art treasures must be worth a million of money."

"I have never been there," Adela said indifferently, "and I'm not particularly anxious to go. How much further do you wish me to take you? Is there any point where you would like me to put you down?"

They were approaching the outskirts of the town, and at a sign from Burton Adela pulled up. He jumped from the car lightly and kissed his hand to Adela as he strode along the road. Then Adela swung her car around and headed for London. She was glad to be rid of her responsibility, and hoped she would have a little time to breathe now. It was not much past five when she returned. No one had called in her absence, and she was glad to think that she had nothing pressing to do that evening at least, nothing which she could not postpone, with the assistance of the 'phone, and a wire or two. She would dine at home, and go to bed early. There was a book she wanted to read which she had not had time to look at. She tossed aside a mass of correspondence, which would keep till the morning. As she turned the letters over, she found the note which Mark Callader had left for her. Perhaps he would call for an answer! At any rate, she tore open the envelope.

"Sorry I didn't see you this morning," the message ran, "but I couldn't wait. I wanted to tell you that I have made arrangements for a house party at Callader for the races. About a score of people are coming, all of the right sort, and the Duchess of Southampton has consented to act as hostess. She and I will go up together this day fortnight, and, of course, you will come too. The rest of the guests will arrive next day. It we have decent weather, and any luck, we ought to have a real good time. Yours ever, Mark."

Adela tore the note into fragments with an angry gesture. Was she never to have peace and quietness again. No sooner had she got rid of Samuel Burton than Fate conspired to bring them together again.

"I am fortune's fool. There are trouble and danger here, I can see. Why can't I take my courage in my hands and end this cruel farce before?"

CHAPTER XVIII

ON THE WHEEL

Adela, however, could not snap the chain for the present. She would have to drag it along until the time came when the fetters could be struck off. The more she thought of it the more hopeless the prospect seemed. A month or two ago she would have thought it incredible that she could have desired any change at all. She had appeared to be born for the part which she filled so readily. She was trying to think how it had all begun. What was the first step she took towards the dazzling position she occupied to-day? She had always been told that she was rich. Even at school she had been courted and flattered. She had started life with an easy-going chaperone, who had allowed her to do exactly as she pleased. Her education in society affairs must have been a gradual process, and all along the way there had been nothing but lavish and criminal waste of money.

Adela had never met with anything in the shape of a rebuff. She had experienced no moral or physical tonic, none of the cold douches of adversity which give tone and vigor to the system. To carry the metaphor further, Adela's bath had always been a marble one, always warm and always scented. For as long as she could remember she had been wrapped in the choicest wool, and the softest and most yielding silks. Indeed, there had been something almost Oriental in the splendor of her course. With her means she could command the best of everything, could arrange the clock of time to suit her lightest convenience. Everything seemed to run on oiled wheels. She had only to express a wish, and it was accomplished. Whatever she took a fancy to she procured heedless of the Day of Reckoning.

Small wonder, then, that with her beauty, and her splendid talents, with a her large means, she should find herself occupying the position in which she stood to-day. There had never been any other life, but had there been another she had not the least desire to try it. Occasionally she may have allowed her thoughts to dwell upon the existence which other women led. She was aware, of course, that the drapers, milliners and dressmakers who ministered to her wants had to work long and hard to keep body and soul together. And now she was finding herself envying these people, actually comparing herself with them to her disadvantage. The weight and pressure of her life were beginning to weigh upon her. It seemed to tighten across her chest like an iron hand. At times she would have been too glad to quit it, but she could not see her way to make a bold bid for emancipation. To begin with, she lacked sufficient ready money. She was appalled to think how swiftly the notes Burton had given her had gone. She had received only that morning a polite intimation from her bankers to draw no further cheques until her account had been put on a more satisfactory footing.

Well, she must go on for the present, but there was no reason why she should remain pending her departure for Callader Castle. Her secretary should paragraph the press that she was suffering from a slight breakdown. She would withdraw to Maidenhead, and pass a few days in strict seclusion. By this time, the cottage garden would be a thing of beauty. The tender green would be trembling on the larches, the white lilac would be soft and fragrant, and in the wood behind the house, where in summer she swung her silken hammock, there would be a waving golden carpet of daffodils. The birds would be singing, too, and as Adela thought of it all she had a wild longing to be away at once, where all was peace, and worry and care would not intrude.

It was good to get away from the town with its unending round of gaiety, its dust and noise and meretriciousness, to the sanity and purity of the country. The sun was shining as she drove along. She could see the tender caressing green of the bursting buds and there was a smell of wood violets in the air. Adela could have wished the atmosphere of the cottage had been a little less artificial. It struck her for the first time that the pictures and carpets and elaborate furniture were strangely out of place. She felt they were all in bad taste. The cottage was showy and fussy and ostentatious. In the drawing-room the faint smell of the Turkish cigarettes still hung about the curtains, and playing cards littered one of the side tables. Adela flung open the windows and let in the fresh sweet air. She was feeling better already. She was losing that strange, haunting feeling that something was about to happen. The tightness about her heart was gone. For the rest of the day she rambled about, and slept that night as she had not done for months. Yet at the end of the second day, she began to feel bored again. The sense of ennui came upon her with a force in that was strong and unpleasant.

"I hope I shall not be always like this. I wonder if I shall ever enjoy anything again? I wonder if life is over? Perhaps I have crammed all my pleasures into small compass. What is the matter with me? I want to be alone. I have a horror of these people, and yet I am almost afraid of being left by myself."

But there was no answer to her musings. There was nothing for it but to wait and see what a week's absolute quiet would do. The fourth day was dragging slowly on. The primrose twilight was falling, and Adela sat before the fire making a faint pretence of reading a book. The very peace and silence began to oppress her. She longed for something in the way of excitement and she got it. For she could hear the rush and fert of a car as it scrunched the gravelled path. Then she heard another and another. A door burst open and the lounge hall was filled with mirth and laughter. Adela knew that laughter only too well. It was the high false note peculiar to her set, the sort of screech which hears a faint resemblance to honest jollity.

They were all there, or so it seemed. Their perfume filled the house. Without rising from her chair Adela could see them all, could almost tell how they were dressed. Only a few minutes before she had been longing for human company, now she shrank from it as if she had done something wrong, as a hunted stag might shrink at the baying of the hounds. But there was no time to think, for the whole glittering mob flocked in, men as well as women. Perhaps a dozen or more swooped down upon Adela with infinite noise and screams and chatter more or less meaningless. One or two of her visitors bore names of historic interest, and one or two were plutocrats, whose money was the only passport into what passes for society.

It was some little time before Adela could find out what it meant. Then one voice, thriller and more strident, rose above the rest. It was that of a woman who had recently been a star of the American music hall stage, and was now the wife of a Russian, Baron Lapariski, who enjoys a vast fortune of his own making.

"Let Topsy explain," one of the men said. "It was her idea and she may as well have the credit of it."

But Topsy, otherwise the baroness, shook her yellow curls, and showed her teeth in a dazzling smile. She was pretty in a saucy way, and Adela detested her beyond any of her acquaintance, though outwardly they appeared to be on the friendliest terms.

"Well, it was like this," the Baroness drawled. "We were bored for want of something to do, so it occurred to me that we might motor here, and give you a pleasant surprise."

"You certainly have," Adela said.

"That's right," the speaker continued. "I just knew you would be glad to see us. You must be moped to death. So we got out our cars, and here we are. Thinking you might not be prepared to entertain a large party, we brought our own supper with us. They used to do this kind of thing when I was a girl. A surprise party we call it. We wait upon ourselves, and each one puts his or her contribution on the table. It will be something for the papers to talk about."

Adela smiled faintly; she had no doubt the necessary notoriety would follow, and could imagine how other people would copy the foolish example. But there was no help for it. She could not turn these people out of the house, but now that they had come she longed more than ever to be alone. Meanwhile the Baroness was rattling on in her quick, stacatto fashion, whilst others of the party were producing dainty-looking packages bearing the imprint of a famous restaurateur.

"Some more are coming presently," the Baroness went on. "We asked Douglas Denne, but he said he was afraid he couldn't get away, but he half gave his word that he would motor down. We tried to get Mark Callader as well, but he had got a prizefight or something of that sort on. By the way, Adela, have you made up your party for Callader Castle? Have you room for another one?"

There was no mistaking what the speaker meant. She put the question eagerly, and looked Adela straight in the face.

"Really, I don't know anything about it. It was Mr. Callader's idea, and he didn't consult me as to who was to be asked. But I fear—"

The Baroness clicked her lips together.

"That's all right," she exclaimed. "I guess I'll ask Mark myself. I'm just dying to spend a week at Callader Castle. They tell me it is a lovely place."

Adela wished she had been firmer, and declared finally that the party was made up. In no case would she have the woman at Callader's; on this point she was emphatic. She would see Callader without delay, and if he were foolish enough to ask the Baroness, she would herself decline to go.

"I know you don't want me," the Baroness laughed half-hysterically. "But I am going and don't you forget it. You can't keep me out when I've made up my mind. Now, what do you say to supper."

CHAPTER XIX

AFTER SUPPER

Though to Adela the eccentric supper was intensely wearisome, her uninvited guests enjoyed themselves. She marvelled how they could find anything interesting, or amusing, or pleasant in such a puerile frivolity. She forgot that she had herself participated in a hundred things equally extravagant, that she had invented or prompted a score of silly fads for senseless people. She laughed and smiled at her guests, and joined in their conversation, but she was the skeleton at the feast.

She glanced furtively at the clock from time to time, and was surprised it was yet barely ten. She might consider herself fortunate if they left before one or two o'clock.

After supper a move was made to the commodious hall. Cards were called for and in a few moments they were all seated at bridge. The place echoed to inane laughter and talk. The pictures on the walls grew dim behind the clouds of cigarette smoke. Would society ever tire of bridge? Would they play to all eternity? She was aghast to see how keen and anxious and eager they were. But had she not herself been a slave to the same tyranny?

To-night she had disclaimed any desire to play, had asked to be allowed to sit out. But circumstances were too strong for her, and she found herself by and bye at the same table with the Baroness, and two white-faced dissipated youths, both of them apparently bent upon unloading a handsome property in the shortest possible time. Adela knew that she was playing with three of the most reckless gamblers in the room. But always accustomed to high stakes, she raised no objection when one of the young men proposed a limit which made even her uncomfortable. For a hand or two she played listlessly, and then the gambling fever fired her blood. She forgot all her good resolutions and put everything aside in the excitement of the hour. They were playing grimly and in earnest. Nothing could be heard at their table beyond the murmur of the scorers, and the gentle flutter of the cards as they slipped over the cloth. When Adela glanced at the clock again it was just past twelve, and the Baroness was reminding her, with a bewitching smile, that she had won just over a thousand pounds.

"So much as that?"

"I think it is a bit more," her partner said coolly. He seemed to be rather proud of his extravagance. "Shocking bad luck we've had, Adela, haven't we? I'd like to go on, but I must get back to town by half-past one. I am going to Paris to-morrow. Send my account to me to my place, and I'll tell my man to send you my cheque."

"I should like a cheque, too," the Baroness laughed. "I have had a terrible time lately, and the money will be most awfully useful. Now, Adela, pay up."

Adela tried to smile in her turn.

"I am afraid I can't to-night," she said. "I'm not sure that I have a cheque book with me, and I couldn't draw on my account for so much if I had. You must wait for at least a week, perhaps longer."

The Baroness' smile was not so pleasant. She pushed the cards away and lighted a cigarette. The two young men had vanished in the meanwhile, and the other players were deeply engrossed in their own games, so Adela and her companion were practically alone. The Baroness reclined in her chair.

"It doesn't much matter," she said slowly. "Take a month, if you like, though I really am frightfully hard up. But I won't press you, if you behave nicely. Of course, you know gambling debts must be paid on the nail?"

The hot blood flamed into Adela's face.

"My dear Baroness," she said, "really you need not trouble yourself to give me elementary lessons in one's social duties. I must have learnt them all when you were playing in the second row of the chorus with a travelling opera company."

The Baroness laughed easily.

"Oh, yes, we've both come on since those days. But, my dear child, don't let us quarrel. Forget the debt, if you like. Put it off as long as you please. It really doesn't matter, but, of course, you were joking just now when you said the house-party for Callader was filled up. What difference will one or two people make? Mark and myself are such good friends, too. We'll call that settled."

There was no mistaking what the speaker meant. She spoke in silky tones, and her stereotyped smile was very much in evidence. But it was a threat, as Adela very well knew. This vulgar, pushing creature was striking a bargain with her. She was offering to make things easy for Adela and avert scandal in return for an invitation to Callader Castle. If she did not get it society would learn in a day or two that Adela Burton had contracted a debt of honor she could not pay. It is the social crime that society does not forget or forgive. She might cheerfully break every commandment of the Decalogue and nobody would think a pin the worse of her.

Not only could Adela not pay, she had not the slightest idea when she could discharge the debt. Nor could she plead any excuse. She had sat down to the table with her eyes open. She had been a consenting party to those high stakes. She was not only morally wrong, but in her present financial position she had acted with downright dishonesty. She would have given five years of her life to be able to draw a cheque for the full amount, to tell the Baroness with polite bitterness what she thought of her, and forbid her to enter her house again. But all she could do now was to smile in a noncommittal fashion, and hope for the best. The Baroness dropped her cigarette on the ash tray, and laughed none too pleasantly. She seemed to know almost by instinct what was passing through Adela's mind, and Adela was painfully aware of the fact. She rose and walked over to the fireplace, whilst the Baroness crossed over to another table where they were needing one to make up a game, Adela stood gazing thoughtfully into the glowing fire. She did not seem to know that someone was addressing her. Then she turned to see Douglas Denne by her side. She held out her hand with a smile, and was genuinely glad to see him. He was different from most people she knew. His strength and manhood attracted her.

"How long have you been here?" she asked.

"Oh, not very long. I don't know why I came. Perhaps it was because I wanted to see you again, or perhaps because I was bored and had nothing else to do. One always gets some amusement at your house. I was interested to watch and hear the little comedy between the Baroness and yourself. I tried my hardest not to listen, but the talk was forced upon me. Don't you think it was foolish to put yourself in that woman's power? You know as well as I do. She is daring, ambitious, dishonest and unscrupulous, and you have actually gone out of your way to give her a weapon with which she will carve her way into Callader Castle. Why do you play cards for more money than you can afford?"

Adela was not offended. Somehow she never resented the directness of Douglas Donne's speech.

"Why do we do all sorts of foolish things?" she asked. "Why did I sit down to play when I didn't wish to? However, I have lost what I can't pay, and the Baroness means to have her price. I don't know how I can prevent her from going to Callader Castle, but it will be easy at the last moment to make some excuse for my not going."

Denne shook his head severely.

"Ah, that will be weak. Tell me, how much money do you owe her? A thousand pounds? As much as that! I gather you haven't the means to pay her—don't know when you will have. It's a tight corner, very. But whatever happens you must not be under any obligations to the Baroness. You must borrow the money, if necessary."

Adela laughed wistfully.

"That sounds easy to you, I daresay. But I begin to realise my folly, and to find that though I have troops of acquaintances, I have no friends. Is there one amongst all the people I know who would lend me that money—or even half of it? There isn't one."

There was a peculiar smile upon Denne's lips as he gazed into Adela's face.

"You take too sombre a view of the situation. There is one who would lend you the money; in fact, I know one who will do so. You are going to borrow it from me."

A faint pink flush crept over Adela's face. She looked up with grateful eyes, but shook her head resolutely.

"I cannot do it. You must see how impossible it is that I can do it. What would people say?"

"But people will not know, and are not likely to. Now, don't allow false pride to stand in your way. You must not accept any favor from a woman like the Baroness. Besides, my offer is only a business transaction, after all."

"Indeed it isn't; it is an act of great generosity and kindness. If you only knew how tired I am of this wretched life, if you only knew how I long to get away from it! It is killing me; I don't know how I stand it. Don't you feel the strain?"

"I do not, for the simple reason that I keep out of it," Denne replied. "Honestly, I haven't the strength. You society women are a perfect mystery to me. Why, on three nights a week, at least, I am in bed by ten, and I take a lot of healthy outdoor exercise. If I acted as you do, and attended to my work as well, I should be in an asylum in twelve months. I take a certain interest in society because I am obliged to, and, to tell you the honest truth, I get a lot of amusement out of it in exchange. Moreover, I was not always in the position I occupy now. I was poor and struggling enough at one time. Ah! you look pale. Perhaps you feel it close here?"

Adela shook her head.

"Come out into the porch," urged Denne. "Throw something over your head. These feather-brains won't miss us, and it is a lovely night. I am not often talkative. Communicativeness is a luxury I seldom indulge in."

CHAPTER XX

THE PRICE OF FORTUNE

Denne stood in the porch looking out in the moonlight, thinking and wondering, wondering. Was it worth while? What was he to gain by embarking upon a sentimental enterprise like this? Adela Burton was the most beautiful woman he had ever seen, certainly the most intellectual; a self-respecting man was bound to feel some contempt for a woman blessed with wealth, and health and beauty, who frittered her life away as Adela was doing.

Denne was trying to take an entirely cynical view of the matter and was honestly attempting to make himself believe that he would not have given Adela a second thought if she had not become engaged to Callader. Moreover, he was not at all sure that the woman by his side was worth the trouble Philip Vanstone had said she was, but people with temperaments were not as a rule good judges of these things, and Vanstone was carried away by admiration for Adela's personal charms. For all Denne knew to the contrary Adela might be as heartless and selfish as any of her friends. That she was not too scrupulous upon occasion Denne had proved. Yet he could not keep away from her, could not put her out of his mind. For her sake he was launching upon a dangerous enterprise, for her sake he was laying a snare for Callader, which might land himself in serious difficulty. But though he was rapidly reasoning the matter with himself he was not making a conspicuous success of it. He was in love with Adela, of that he had no longer any doubt, and his passion and admiration had been whetted by knowing that she was engaged to somebody else. These thoughts flashed through his mind as he stood watching the play of the moonlight upon the tender green of the trees. What a contrast the tranquil beauty of reposing Nature offered to the group of roues in the hall.

Outside, was the calm loveliness of the landscape, sweet and wholesome, and refreshing; inside, set in an atmosphere of perfume and cigarette smoke, was the quick sharp outline of faces, hard and keen with greed, as the players bent over the tables.

"One gets it all here," Denne said at length; "every side of the argument. I suppose this is what people call the 'simple life.' The simplicity lies in the people, not in the life at all. Now tell me honestly, do you enjoy this kind of thing?"

It was like Denne to put the matter so directly,

"Well, then, I don't," Adela confessed. "I am beginning to hate it. Mind, I didn't ask these people to come here this evening. Indeed, I was not in the least pleased to see them. I came from town because I am not well. My doctor told me I was overdoing it, and warned me of the consequences. But what slaves are we to habit! After the first few hours I felt utterly miserable, tired of myself and everything else. Like a man who gets into the habit of drinking brandy, there comes a time when he loathes the stuff. Yet he cannot keep away from it. Of course, it is easy to moralise, to see how hollow and heartless it all is. But we go on doing it all the same."

"Yes, we are all alike," Denne smiled. "We are all so hopelessly vulgar. Personally, I can't see the slightest difference between the most exclusive set and this. Her Grace sneers at the man who is proud of his new fortune, who tells everybody what he gave for his house, and what his carpets cost. But she is no better herself. She gives great entertainments, or goes to the opera smothered in diamonds while nine-tenths of her tradesmen remain unpaid. She doesn't care whether they are paid or not. Her pomp, vanity and ostentation may differ in degree, but it doesn't in kind. My withers are unwrung because I am a man of simple tastes. My hobby is art, and yet, I, in my own way, I suppose, am as vulgar as the rest of them. I like to feel my power. I like to feel that men watch and follow my lead. Our fathers believed that knowledge was power; to-day money is power. I value money accordingly. I suppose I am like Cecil Rhodes in that respect, but in my young days I was much happier with a gun or searching for a rare bird's nest. I often wonder what my father would have said if he had lived to see what I have come to. He was a simple country parson, perfectly contented with his three hundred a year, and out of that he always found money for charity. My mother was just the same. And what I have developed into—a mere money-making machine, a man with a commercial instinct, and the knowledge how to apply it. I don't suppose I have ever done anybody any good in my life; I don't remember ever considering anybody but myself, and the consequence is that, despite my success and my good health, I am not in the least happy. I don't know why I tell you these things, unless it be that there comes a time when a man wants to confide in a woman, and you happen to be that woman. But I am afraid I am rather late in the day."

"You surprise me," Adela answered. "I never took you to be that kind of man at all. Still, isn't it in your power to right matters? You are not bound to go on making money, you know. Why not go out of business and take up sport, or Parliament. If I were a man, there are plenty of things I should like to do."

"I used to think so at one time," Denne said, "but you get caught up in the machine. You have no idea what power it has over you; you simply can't get away from it. There are thousands of men, ostensibly rich, who would be comparatively poor if they had to realise everything to-morrow? Do you know what would happen if I tried to do it myself? I should create a panic on the Stock Exchange! Scores of honest men would be ruined and scores of shady financiers would make fortunes. So, you see, I must go on. If I could find the right woman, possibly I might—"

Denne ceased to speak. He looked out across the landscape with a troubled expression in his eyes. He might have said more had not at that moment one of the parties had broken up with two of the players strolling out into the porch. Frivolous chatter ensued, and jokes and quips and personalities which at another time would have brought a smile to Adela's lips gave her no pleasure. She resented the intrusion. Never had these friends of hers seemed so silly, so inane.

"I had no idea it was so late," she said. "It is getting chilly. Mr. Denne and myself have been discussing money matters. I have been learning things."

"Lucky people," one of the visitors remarked. "I never have any occasion to worry about money. I haven't any."

Adela did not stop to listen, and returned into the hall. Most of the card tables were deserted, and several of the guests openly and avowedly yawned. The surprise party had lost its novelty, and they were anxious to get back to London. The hum of a car was heard outside, and from the porch there emerged the thick-set figure of Mark Callader.

"Sorry to be so late. But I thought I would run down on the off chance of catching you here. Been enjoying yourselves? Hallo! what are you doing here, Denne?"

There was challenge in the speech, but Denne ignored it.

"Oh, I am following the fashion," he said; "I don't like to be out of the movement altogether."

Callader muttered something, and stalked over to Adela with that half truculent, half-bullying air of possession which set Denne's teeth on edge.

"What have you been doing?"

Adela shrugged her shoulders and laughed drearily.

"What do we always do? We chatter and cackle for a time, and then with one accord sit down to that dreadful bridge."

The Baroness's high-pitched laugh rang in the roof. She came forward smilingly, but the glint of battle lit up her eye.

"We always talk like that when we lose," she exclaimed. "When we win it is different. Don't tell anybody, Mark, but Adela has had a most awfully bad night. Between ourselves, I believe she has gambled the rest of her fortune away. She dropped a cool thousand to me, and wants time to pay."

Callader turned inquiringly to Adela.

"What's Topsy mean?" he growled.

"I thought her words were plain enough," Adela said wearily. "I owe her a thousand pounds, and it isn't convenient to pay her this evening. I don't know what steps she will take. She can post me if she likes, and then I shall disappear from Society altogether."

The Baroness laughed softly.

"Did anyone ever hear such nonsense?" she screamed. "Just as if I should do that. Of course, I can wait. I am not so hard up as all that. You can pay me, my dear, when we meet at Callader Castle. And, by the way, Mark, where are your manners? Don't you know that I have not had my invitation yet? But, of course, that is an oversight."

"Nothing to do with me," Callader said in his brutal fashion. "I have asked a few people, but I left Adela to look after the rest, and between ourselves, my dear Topsy, I really don't think you would hit it off with the Duchess. She is a bit old-fashioned, and your playful ways would not be to her taste. However, I don't care. You can settle the matter with Adela."

"The matter is already settled," Adela said solidly. "I have made up my party, and there is no room for anybody else."

Most of the other guests were listening with some interest. They could see that a duel was being fought between their hostess and the Baroness, and they waited with zest to see the finish. The Baroness laughed cheerily, showing her perfect teeth.

"As you please," she said. "And as to that little cheque?"

She paused significantly. Adela stood cold and silent, and forced the tears back in her eyes. Was her courage leaving her? As she glanced round at half-smiling faces, she saw Denne signalling to her. She knew that he meant well, and for a moment she paused, suspended as it were, between pride and poverty.

CHAPTER XXI

A FRIEND IN NEED

Adela did not hesitate for long; the present temptation was altogether beyond her strength. It offered her the means of getting rid of this woman, of triumphing over her, of letting her know she was only in the house on sufferance. She gave a grateful glance at Denne, and turned upon the Baroness.

"Really, you are making a great fuss about a trifle. Are we a set of impecunious tradesmen that we cannot trust one another for a few days? Is it the first time that either of us has won or lost money like this? I did not say I could not pay you. I said it was not quite convenient. However, it is far more inconvenient to go on owing this sum, and if you will wait I'll see if I have got a cheque-book here."

Once more the Baroness smiled. This must be pure bluff on Adela's part. There was not the slightest chance of her finding the cheque-book. The Baroness was sure of her ground; she would prevail. Already in imagination she was deciding what dresses she would take to Callader Castle.

"Oh, don't trouble," she said, sweetly.

But Adela had already left the room.

She hastily tore out one of the oblong pink slips, and scribbled the amount of her indebtedness upon it. With a smile that was bland and sweet as the Baroness's own, she handed the paper over. Then the Baroness's expression changed.

"That's one to Adela," a guest whispered to his neighbor. "Doesn't the Baroness looked charmed? Just like one of those money-lending fellows when you call to take up a bill which they expect you want to renew. I bet you six to four Topsy doesn't see the inside of Callader Castle this year."

"Thanks awfully," the Baroness murmured. "Sure it doesn't inconvenience you, dear? I suppose it will be all right when it comes to be presented. This isn't one of your little jokes?"

"I don't feel in a jesting mood," Adela said, "and as to Callader, you will see that I can't alter my arrangements now."

Adela walked to the fireplace. It was a signal for dismissal, and the party took it as such. They crowded round their hostess to say good-night, and passed noisily out into the night. There was a rattle and purring of cars, then, gradually, silence fell on the cottage. Denne came up and shook hands with Adela in his easy natural fashion, nodded curtly to Callader, and vanished discreetly.

Mark had thrown himself into a chair by the side of the fire and lighted a cigarette. There was something in his heavy, dogged face that Adela did not like. She was longing to be alone, for she was tired and weary, and not up to anything in the nature of a scene. A week ago she could have handled Callader easily it would have been child's play to her then. But she had had a very trying and exhausting night, and was not either mentally or physically equal to hostilities.

"Don't you think you had better be a going?" she said. "It is nearly two o'clock, and I am worn out."

Callader showed no sign of taking the hint, but sat worrying at his cigarette as a dog worries at a bone.

"I'll go presently; there's no hurry. Meanwhile, I want to know what's the game?"

"Game," Adela cried contemptuously, "what game?"

"You know perfectly well what I mean. This game over that cheque. You are a proud girl, and would do a good deal rather than be under an obligation to the Baroness. You dislike her, and she would never come here it she didn't happen to be in your set. Where did you get the money?"

"Where do I generally get my money?"

"I know all about that. We are all hard up at times, and if you had had the money an hour ago you would have given the Baroness a cheque then. You borrowed it from Denne."

The color flamed into Adela's face.

"You have no right to say anything of the kind. Mr. Denne was good enough to offer to be my banker when he saw how that woman pestered me, and was trying to extort an invitation to Callader. If you had asked her to come I should have declined to be present. Of course, I refused Mr. Denne's offer; indeed, I could do nothing less."

"Of course, of course," Callader sneered. "But Denne renewed the offer when he saw you were in a tight pace, and you accepted it. Now, I won't have it. If you are in a mess you must get out of it without Denne's help. I am sorry I asked him to Callader. When the party breaks up there I will tell him a thing or two. And you will have to tell him that I will not have him hanging about you. Sit down and write to him now."

Adela rose slowly to her feet. For the moment her weakness had left her, and she was filled with a passionate contempt and courage which were born of overwhelming anger.

"You coward," she cried, "you contemptible coward! Do you think because I have promised to marry, you that you have the right to treat me in this degrading fashion? I have told you I refused Mr. Denne's offer, and with that you will have to be content. Must I call my servants to turn you out of the house?"

This scornful outburst left Callader untouched. He laid two strong hands upon Adela's shoulders. She could feel the intensity of their grip. Possibly Callader was not aware he was using any force. A dull red glow gleamed in his little eyes, and his face was dogged and cruel.

"None of that play-acting," he said. "Don't try me too far, or, by Heaven, you may be sorry for it. I am not responsible for myself after a certain stage."

"I am not afraid of you," Adela retorted. "Remove your hands at once. I am not Mrs. Mark Callader yet."

Callader's hands fell to his sides. He was evidently putting a great constraint upon himself; his red face shone and the big knotted veins stood out on his forehead.

"Very well," he growled. "We will say nothing more about it at present, only, mind, I mean to have my own way, and you shall drop Denne after the Callader party is over. In the meantime—"

"And in the meantime I shall be glad to be alone. I came here for peace and quietness. I am not well. The life I am leading is telling upon me. Come tomorrow, and let us thrash this matter out. Now, please, leave me."

Callader sullenly pitched the end of his cigarette in the fire. In spite of his dull, suspicious wrath, he felt a grudging admiration as he looked at Adela. She stood white and cold and set, but full of spirit and resolution, qualities which, to him, counted for more than grace and physical beauty. He turned without a word and closed the door behind him.

Adela heard his car humming in the distance. The luxury of solitude was upon her, and she dropped into a chair and covered her face with her hands. There was a hard lump in her throat, an icy feeling at her heart which seemed to melt suddenly in a rush of tears. As her tears fell, the dry, hard pain which for the last few hours had been throbbing in her brain vanished. It was good to know she could cry. It was pleasant to feel she was still yielding to a natural womanly weakness. When she wiped her eyes and looked up, she saw Douglas Denne regarding her gravely and critically. There was an apologetic touch in his manner which she had never noticed before, and he spoke in gentle tones.

"I know it is wrong of me. I ought not to have come back. I ought not to have watched you. But I had to return because we had to transact a little business. You were wise to accept my offer, though I did not put it into words the second time, and I am glad you scored off that woman. But she will probably present your cheque immediately, and if we don't take steps to meet it the draft will be dishonored. You must give me the name of your bankers, so that, the first thing in the morning, I can pay in a sum of money through my firm, and make the whole thing look like a business transaction."

"I cannot sufficiently thank you."

"I want no thanks at all. I am only too pleased to be able to do you this little service. I'll copy the name and the branch of your bankers from your cheque-book, if you don't mind. There is another matter I wish to mention. I believe Callader has an idea of what has taken place. Those thickheaded people are nearly always suspicious, and nearly always observant at the wrong time. I didn't like the expression of his face, nor the dogged way he sat down after your guests had gone. If he has anything to say to me, I ought to know how far you have confided in him."

"You think of everything," Adela said gratefully. "In point of fact, Mark was suspicious. He accused me directly of borrowing money off you to pay this debt, and I was obliged to say that I had refused your offer. It is idle to disguise the fact; I lied to him."

Denne smiled as he held out his hand.

"Well," he said, "now that I know how things stand I need not stay any longer. Good-night, once more."

But Denne was troubled in his mind as he drove homewards. He had done everything possible in the circumstances, and yet he was haunted with doubt whether the woman was worth it. What would his friends say if they knew that he was carrying on a platonic friendship with Adela Burton? Where and how was the thing to end? At all events there was plenty of time to think it over. He would have ample opportunity of studying the situation during the coming visit to Callader Castle.

"Is she worth it? Is she worth it?" still rang in his ears as he fell asleep.

CHAPTER XXII

THE EDGE OF THE CLIFF

The daffodils were breaking into rippling waves in the orchard behind the cottage, a nightingale had been heard among the shrubs, but Adela took no heed of such things. Time was when she had enjoyed the country; indeed, the furnishing of the cottage had afforded her one of her few pleasures of recent years, but now, like Gallio, she cared for none of these things, for she was engrossed in her own woes and miseries. In a measure she was better, was benefiting by the regular hours and simple food. She did not lie awake so long at nights, but her face was pale and drawn, and there was just the suspicion of a purple shadow under her eyes. Above all, she could not throw off the fear of impending disaster—that dread of nameless trouble which is far worse than trouble itself. This feeling was with her day and night.

In truth, she had enough to worry about. The more she thought over her situation the more desperate did it seem. She had time to look her affairs in the face, nor did she flinch from the ordeal. Her assets were the furniture of her cottage and flat, and a certain amount of jewellery, which would not realise anything like what it cost. Adela had never spent much on personal adornment. She was almost sorry now she had not. If everything were disposed of she might manage to scrape together some ten thousand pounds to meet her creditors.

At the outset she had comforted herself with the reflection that this would be nearly enough. It was only when she came to examine her enormous pile of bills, to reckon up her liabilities and put them down in black and white, that she realised what a black deficit there was. Her only course was to wait until Samuel Burton's schemes matured, and then, perhaps, she would have funds sufficient to pay everybody. But, on the other hand, there was the bitter reflection that Burton's money was the fruit of fraud and dishonesty. She could no longer disguise the fact that she was as callous and as reckless an adventuress as any woman who figured in the criminal courts. Burton might be a gentleman by birth, but he was a hardened old scoundrel, and she was practically an accessory after the fact.

She was helpless, tied hand and foot; it was idle to blind herself to the fact. Everything conspired to point to marriage with Callader as the safest, if not the sole way, out of her difficulties. What his resources were she did not know, and had never inquired. But he had the appearance of being a rich man, and Burton had said that in course of time he would become Marquis of Kempston. There was a young heir in the way, but when that fact had been pointed out to Burton, he merely smiled. Was there some hidden family scandal here? Samuel Burton was not the man to make such remarks at random; he must have had justification for them.

But to marry Mark Callader! Adela trembled when she thought of it; but she was prepared to take the risk; there was no other way to save herself from something worse than disgrace. Nor was she under any delusion as to what her life would be. Callader was a cold-blooded brute with no instincts of pity, and no feeling for anyone. He lived hard; it was his constant boast that nothing hurt him. He ate and drank with the best, and yet never seemed to be out of condition. The redness of his face and the network of veins in his cheeks told their own story. But Callader bragged that he had never known an ache or pain in his life. Despite his knowledge of art matters, and his feeling for such things, his tastes were low; he was always uncomfortable in the drawing-room, and infinitely preferred the bar parlor of a sporting public-house, especially when the details of a prize-fight had to be settled. With these men he was quite at home. 'Bookies' were hand-in-glove with him, and pink-eyed journalists who called him by his Christian name. Moreover, he could ride the maddest horse that ever stepped. Adela had seen more than one exhibition of his cruelty in this regard.

No doubt he was proud of her in his way. He would take a pride in her beauty, as he did in his china and pictures. But he would be harsh, callous, and brutal, and she had seen that he would not scruple to lay hands upon her if necessary. Adela had met other men like Mark Callader. She was on intimate terms with the wives of two of them, and knew what the shrinking glance and the white face and timid gesture meant. Samuel Burton knew it also. If not, why should he have told Adela that he would give her a weapon to keep Callader in order when she married him?

There was no help for it. Adela was as much a prisoner as if she had been undergoing a term of penal servitude. She was bound to the wheel of circumstance. She had looked over the edge of the cliff, and the abyss below had been darker and uglier than she had expected.

She would just have to dress her best. The day came for her journey North. She smiled bitterly as she discussed her dresses with her maid. As she drove towards London in her car she had ample evidence that people took her at her face value. The car was a gleaming mass of crimson and black, and burnished brass. There was not a woman in the whole metropolis more beautiful or better dressed than herself. People turned to look at her as she stood on the platform. She saw eyebrows raised enquiringly, and heard one man telling another that she was Miss Adela Burton, the great heiress. A little milliner with a box on her arm regarded her with a mute homage which would have been gratifying at any other time, but now the girl's gaze filled her with self-contempt.

Everything was being made smooth for her. She had the obsequious attention of the railway servants, a carriage to herself, and was surrounded with the latest books and papers. She had luncheon and afternoon tea on the express; these intervals broke the tedium of the long journey. She left the train for a car, in which she whirled through keen, pure air. Presently the car turned in between two lodge gates with the Callader arms carved in stone on each pillar. She drove up a magnificent beech avenue, winding through the park for some two miles, the grand old trees fluttered in their tender spring dress, the bracken was dappled with the faint yellow stars of primroses. There were shadows here and there in the undergrowth where the deer moved along, and across the park was a distant prospect of the sea. Presently the house loomed in sight, a long, grey stone building with smoothly-shaven lawns in front, a perfect blaze of spring flowers, while the larch-woods behind broke the sky-line with varied contour. Adela thought it a grand old place, which indeed it was, being one of the finest ancestral homes in England. Here for four hundred years the Calladers had flourished and held sway. From the Castle had emerged a succession of soldiers and statesmen whose names were writ largely in history. Adela detected herself wondering—not without a blush—what the dead and gone Calladers would think if they could see their two descendants of to-day. But she could not give play to such speculations, for the great doors were thrown open, and Adela was conducted to the beautiful old hall, with its lantern overhead, and its stained glass in the pointed windows. Everything seemed to be planned on the same lavish scale. Here was space and breadth and beauty, and all the array of art treasures which made Callader Castle celebrated.

Adela came down to dinner presently. There were a score or so of guests in the drawing-room. She knew them all; they seemed just the same as when she had parted with them a fortnight ago, except that they were differently dressed. To all intents and purposes it was a replica of the London mode—even to the cackle, the silly laughter, and inane jokes. Douglas Denne towered above the rest, quiet and observant as usual, with a hint of cynicism on his lips. Callader came forward, bent down, and pressed his lips lightly to Adela's cheek. She could feel her face flaming. The touch seemed to sting and burn her. Yet she had to smile, to listen to the feeble jokes, and return them in kind. She would have liked to pass out on to the wide stone terrace, to watch the sunset, but to express such a desire would have been pronounced eccentric.

"What shall we do to-morrow?" Adela asked.

"What do you suppose we are going to do?" Callader retorted. "We shall be racing for the next four days. That is what we came for. There is nothing else to do in a hole like this."

A murmur of approval followed. Adela felt isolated, as if she did not belong to these people, as if she were here on sufferance. She had this curious sensation all through dinner, and was glad when the long, elaborate meal was over, and they were back in the drawing-room again. Denne dropped into a chair by her side. He could not fail to notice the pallor of her face, and the faint purple under her eyes.

"I hope you are better," he said. "I can't say you look it, but I hope I am wrong."

Adela shrugged her shoulders.

"I am sleeping better, and have a better appetite, but I am not enjoying myself. Everything bores me, and I shall be glad to get back to my cottage. I think I shall take a long tour abroad. I have a fancy for a walking expedition. But don't talk about me."

Denne murmured that he could not conceive a more fascinating subject. It was not in his way to pay compliments, and the speech on his lips sounded foolish. In fact, he had been thinking constantly about Adela. He had not solved the problem that was uppermost in his mind; could not bring himself to make a sacrifice that might end in disastrous failure. That he cared for Adela, he no longer tried to disguise from himself; he knew he loved her. He had even dared to believe that his affection was returned. But was she worth it? That was still the question. Was she a woman to whom he could tie himself for life, whom he would have to consider almost to the exclusion of everything else. She was out of sorts now, weary of the empty artificiality of her existence. But how long would that feeling last? As his wife she would have the command of almost limitless resource. Would she think of nothing beyond the spending of his fortune and the ambition of being the best-dressed woman, and the leader of the smartest set in Society? The problem still baffled him, yet he found it as much as he could do to hold himself in hand. He did not realise that he was not the first man ready to sacrifice everything for a woman.

CHAPTER XXIII

AN UNSHEATHED SWORD

Here was another familiar picture. Adela had seen it over and over again. Sometimes it was called Ascot, sometimes Goodwood, sometimes Epsom. There was only a change of scene—a hill there, a glimpse of the sea there, a group of trees yonder to vary the monotony. Here was the shouting crowd, the raucous yell of red-faced bookmakers, the long parallel lines of white railings, and a huge stand at the back of the paddock crammed with an excited, eager multitude, to whom the absolute sport of racing was the last consideration, and an ingrained love of betting the first. Yonder were the people drawn from the whole countryside, and here was the well-dressed crowd chattering and laughing, and making their bets on the chief race of the day. The Rokeby Park meeting was very similar to a score of others. It had precisely similar attributes, and produced similar excitement. This excitement was not shared by Adela Burton. Of course, she had made her bets as usual, but she was supremely indifferent whether she won or lost. She surveyed the crowd through her glasses. She looked over the paddock to the rails beyond which the coaches and carriages had drawn up in line. Most of her own party were off somewhere, and Denne stood behind her with that peculiar halo of aloofness which always surrounded him like an atmosphere. Adela turned suddenly and handed him the glasses.

"I wish you would look at those people next to General Manton's coach," she observed. "I have an absurd idea at that I can see Mr. Burton, and a still more absurd idea that the Baroness Lapanski is with him. It is ridiculous, but I should like to hear you assure at me that I am mistaken."

Denne turned his glasses in the direction indicated.

"You are not in the least mistaken," he said. "That is Mr. Burton beyond a doubt, and, equally beyond a doubt, the Baroness is with him. But surely there is nothing remarkable about it. There is no reason why Mr. Burton should not go racing, and no just cause or impediment why the Baroness should not accompany him."

Adela had forgotten that Burton had taken a house in the village. Possibly his temporary abode was close to Callader Castle, and this might be part of some deep-laid scheme of his. She took the glasses from her companion's hand, and gazed at the carriage long and intently. Burton was immaculately dressed in grey frock-suit. His glasses were slung over his shoulder, and he seemed to be intensely amused at his companion's talk. Even at that distance Adela could see the Baroness' yellow hair and flashing teeth, and take in all the details of her toilette. By and bye the pair left the carriage and strolled across to the paddock. Adela looked for them again more than once during the day, but without success. The incident in itself was nothing, and yet it filled her with a sort of vague alarm. She was glad when the last race was run, and the Callader Castle party turned their faces homewards. It was a beautiful spring evening, almost summer-like in its balmy heat, so that tea was taken in the great stone hall, with the doors and windows wide open. There was still plenty of light after dinner, and some member of the party, wiser and saner than the rest, suggested a stroll out of doors. The guests broke up into little groups, Adela leading the way with Callader. He had not said much to her that day; he had appeared sulky, as if she had incurred his displeasure. At a distance Denne followed, accompanied by Vanstone, who was of the party. They turned into a rose-lined alley.

"It is beautifully quiet here," Vanstone suggested, "let us sit down a bit. What a treat it is to get away from the chattering mob! I often wonder why I visit these people at all. I sometimes wish I had been born poor, so that I should have been compelled to work. Besides, I want to talk to you."

"On a lovely evening like this?"

"Why not? Such a night invites confidences. How fresh everything smells, and how delicious the silence after the roar and noise of the racecourse! But never mind about that. What I want to know is, what are you going to do in the matter of Adela Burton?"

"My dear fellow, what can I do?"

"You know what I mean. I have not got over the shock I had when I heard she was engaged to Callader. That cad is not fit to have the care of a woman. He is sure to neglect her after a bit, and I should not be surprised if he used personal violence towards her. You promised me—"

"My dear Philip, I don't think I did. I was rather careful not to make any promise. You were interested in the subject, you made a psychological study of it. You thought that Miss Burton was worth saving, and asked me to take a hand in the problem. Now, I am not quite convinced that she is worth saving. That is the crux of the whole thing."

"But you admire her, Denne?"

"Oh, I go farther than that, Philip. I am in love with her. I am as much in love with her as if I were a sentimental ass of twenty-three or a dreamer and poet like yourself. I am unpleasantly aware that there are two sides to my nature, though I thought I had subdued one of them long ago. Perhaps you appreciate the difficulty I am in? Is it worth my while to give the reins to my fancy? May I look forward to a happy future, or is there not a serious chance of Douglas Denne, the individualist and financier, becoming known as the husband of Mrs. Denne, with the privilege of footing her bills. I have studied this set long enough to know how heartless and frivolous it is, and how impossible it is for any good to come out of it. Mind, I haven't come to any decision; there is time enough for that. Now, please, don't say anything about being tried in a fiery furnace, or washed in the waters of adversity, or anything of that kind, because in ninety-nine cases out of a hundred that is pure nonsense."

"You are wrong," Vanstone said vehemently. "I tell you that girl is worth all the trouble. I am certain of it, and you know it, too. If you would only give your better nature a chance. But, come what may, Adela Burton must not marry Callader. If we allow that to be done, we shall be as guilty of murder as if we calmly watched a child drowning in the lake here."

Denne flicked the end off his cigar.

"Make your mind easy on that score. Mark Callader will never marry Adela Burton. I have taken steps to prevent that catastrophe. I am not sure that I haven't done a foolish thing. I may even have put myself within the grip of the law. But Callader is a scoundrel as well as a bully, and when I lay certain facts before him, I fancy he will take his punishment lying down."

Vanstone was about to reply when the people under discussion came in sight. Callader was walking moodily by Adela's side, his hands thrust deep into his pockets. Adela carried her head high, and her face was pale and scornful. They went down a side path, and had not noticed Denne and his companion, who could still see the ill-assorted couple. Callader paused and took hold of Adela's arm. He twisted her around as a keeper might have done who finds some loafer poaching in his woods. There was less in the incident than in what it suggested. It was all over in a moment, and Callader had his hands buried in his pockets again. Vanstone turned to Denne—a curious light shining in his eyes.

"What do you think of that? It is only a foretaste of what is to follow."

Denne said nothing. He passed his tongue over his lips, which had become suddenly dry, but wild rage filled his heart. It might have gone hard with Callader if the two had met at that moment. A minute later and Callader turned aside, walking rapidly towards the house. Adela stood motionless as a statue, looking out over the park in the direction of the sea.

"I'll get you to excuse me for a while," said Denne, rising; "I want to speak to Miss Burton."

Vanstone nodded; he was discreet enough to say no more. He wished the episode they had witnessed to saturate Denne's mind, so to speak; for its moral was evident. Moreover, Denne had undertaken to use his best efforts to prevent the marriage.

Denne walked up to Adela, and made some commonplace remark. Her face was deadly pale, though there was no suggestion of tears in her eyes, and she was breathing rapidly as if she had walked far.

"It is nice to be alone sometimes," Denne said.

"And yet one gets tired of it," Adela replied. "I was longing for someone to talk to. I have offended Callader, who has left me to go back to the house by myself. But I am not in the mood to listen to their idle chatter. Let us go round by the lake, and walk up the avenue. We shall be able to manage it before dark."

Denne was nothing loth. He had got the better of his fury, and made no allusion to the incident which was uppermost in his mind. They strolled along side by side, enjoying the peace and harmony of the evening, until they reached a charming little house, half-timbered and ivy-covered, which was accessible from the park by means of an old gate of hammered iron.

"That is just the place I should like," Adela said. "It is big enough, and yet not too big, and such a long way from everywhere. I suppose it belongs to the family. Probably it was built for the use of some of the Callader spinsters in the old days. Did you ever see such a beautiful lawn? I wonder who lives here now. I must ascertain."

Adela lingered admiring the spring flowers in their spreading beds. Then a figure appeared, the figure of an elderly, well set-up man in evening dress. He looked singularly handsome and prosperous, like the best type of military man with his white hair and carefully trimmed grey moustache. As he approached the iron gate, Adela gave a little cry as she recognised Samuel Burton.

Apparently he heard the exclamation, for he hurried forward, his manner easy and debonair. He nodded in friendly fashion to Denne and held out his hand to Adela.

"A most pleasant surprise," he said. "I have taken this house for a few weeks from the tenant, who has gone abroad. Nice place, isn't it. I saw you at the races, but I didn't want to interfere. I have a little house-party of my own. Baron Lapanski and his wife are here, and the latter is so good as to act as my hostess. Come in and see the place. You will get back in plenty of time for bridge."

CHAPTER XXIV

THE DESIRABLE ALIEN

Burton spoke in his most charming manner. He might have been a man of means and position. To look at him one assumed that money was probably the last thing he thought of. He stood with his hands behind him, admiring the beauty of the evening, and puffing a cigar, with a sense of exquisite enjoyment. Adela had forgotten her companion; she was so staggered by Burton's audacity as to think of nothing else. It was the height of folly to put his head in the lion's mouth. Adela knew that Burton had to thank Mark Callader for his recent peril, and here he was deliberately settling down under the very walls of Callader Castle. It could not be a coincidence, because Burton had told her that he knew all about Callader, and that the house had been open to him in his younger days.

"You must be mad," she exclaimed, "mad!"

She regretted the speech almost as soon as it was uttered, for she saw Denne looking at her with a curious expression—half-questioning, half-suspicious, on his face. But nothing disturbed the even tenor of Burton's serenity. He took it all as a matter of course, laying his hand upon Adela's arm, and patting it gently.

"It is very good of you," he said, "to be so anxious about an old man like me. It isn't often, Mr. Denne, that you see young people so thoughtful for their seniors. You need not be afraid, Adela. You are concerned about my distressing cough. You think me foolish to come so far north at this treacherous season, but, perhaps, you don't know that I am a north-countryman, and that this is my native air."

It was spoken so naturally that even Denne appeared to be disarmed. Adela was lost in admiration of Burton's presence of mind and resourcefulness. Without a moment's hesitation he had made her indiscreet speech sound quite harmless and proper.

"But you had better come in," Burton went on, "if only for a few minutes."

Adela had no objection to offer, and Denne was entirely in her hands. They walked across the beautifully kept lawn, into the hall, where half-a-dozen people or more were playing pool. In his quiet, observant way, Denne noticed the Baron and his wife. He smiled faintly as his eyes fell upon Felix Marner, who, with his wife, was also of the party. Baroness Lapanski was seated in a big chair watching the game, but she came forward and shook hands in the friendliest possible fashion with Adela, entirely ignoring the latter's coolness.

"I told you I should be here," she said, "do you know any of these people?"

"They are strangers, excepting Mr. and Mrs. Marner and your husband," Adela replied. "American, are they not?"

The pool players were too absorbed in their game to heed what was taking place, for the Baroness had led the way to a large bay window some distance from the billiard-table. At a sign from Burton, Baron Lapanski joined the group. He was a short, enormously fat man, with heavy features, and dark moustache and beard, the sort of person that never says much and thereby gains a reputation for wisdom. Who the Baron was and whence he came nobody knew or cared. He was supposed to own great estates in Siberia, and, for the rest, his operations on the Stock Exchange were on a large scale. At any rate, he entertained lavishly and liberally, though no man in that set enjoyed himself less than did Baron Lapanski. He was always bored, always suggested the tame bear on the end of a chain. He sat silent and moody at his own parties, unless, perchance, he had some financier to keep him company. Denne thought the Russian came forward reluctantly. There was something in his sombre eyes that implied that he was waiting for a lead from Burton, at whom he glanced furtively from time to time. He was obviously puzzled and feeling his way.

"You are right about their being American," the Baroness said gaily. "Ah, they are not of our world to-day, but they will be to-morrow, and between ourselves, my dear, they are the queerest zoological set I ever sat down with. That is one of the drawbacks of being on friendly terms with a financier like Mr. Burton. You never know who you will meet at their houses. But all these people are tremendously rich. They have made their money in oil, or pigs, or timber, and some other quaint trade known only to Americans. I am sure if they knew you were here they would throw down their cues at once to make your acquaintance. Shall I announce you, my dear?"

"I would much rather not. By the way, how long are you staying?"

The Baroness shrugged her plump shoulders.

"I can't tell you," she said carelessly. "It lies entirely with Mr. Burton. We shall be here till after the races, and I believe Mr. Burton and my husband have a big deal on with these funny-looking men who are trying to play pool. You will come over and dine with us one night this week, I hope, and I trust Callader will ask us in return. You can tell the Duchess I am not such a fearful person. I don't suppose she would mind meeting me at dinner once in a way. There is no reason why she should recognise me when next we meet. You see what a forgiving soul I am?"

Adela said something appropriate, for to some extent the Baroness was mistress of the situation. She was acting as hostess to Burton's guests, and it was clearly within her province in making these suggestions.

"Now say you'll come," she said genially.

"I'll ask Mark," Adela said coldly. "I should think he would rather like it. Those people look just the sort of men he would be fond of—especially the one with the red moustache. But what are Felix Marner and his wife doing here?"

The Baroness laughed gaily.

"Oh, studying types, of course," she said. "Felix Marner is a great man. He has left his mark on his generation, as the literary men are so fond of saying. He is the authority upon art. He lives in a world of his own. It is so seldom that he condescends to come down to our level that we sit at his feet and sip wisdom, just as Ruskin's disciples used to do. But, my dear, it is only a pose after all. Despite his picturesqueness and his mediaeval flavor, Felix Marner is as fond of the good things of life as we are, and his perfect house in Frogmore-street has to be kept up. It is amusing to hear his dissertations on art, and how that raw crowd listen open-mouthed to him. But, if I am not mistaken, before we leave Felix will have sold them a score of pictures, and a lot of china and furniture, quite as a favor, of course, and, incidentally, put a few thousand pounds in his pocket. Between ourselves, Marner is as big a humbug as anybody else, and we all know it."

Burton appeared to be amused at this sally.

"We are all humbugs," he said airily, "are we not, Baron? What do you say?"

The Baron lifted his heavy eyes to Burton's face. He looked like a dull boy watching his master.

"I suppose we are. If you say so it must be true. We are all humbugs."

"Including Mr. Denne?" Burton asked.

Lapanski shifted uneasily from one foot to the other. Apparently the conversation was a little over his head. Adela thought it odd that one so dull and stupid and heavy should be looked up to as a leading light in the world of finance, but she had an instinct that Burton was playing with his guest. Lapanski gave her the impression that he was under his host's thumb. She would have found it difficult to give her reasons for this impression, but she had formed it, and, moreover, the Baroness was looking somewhat anxiously, if impatiently, at her husband.

"I am afraid it is true," Denne smiled, "But you mustn't take away the reputation of Felix Marner. Don't forget that he is an institution, that there are thousands of earnest students on both sides of the Atlantic who hang breathlessly upon his lightest word. I should very much like to see Marner sitting down to the same table with your other guests, Burton. Don't you think, Miss Burton, we could persuade Callader to invite our friends to dinner?"

"An inspiration," Burton cried. "I thank you for the idea. Positively it will be a new sensation, and my friend, the Baron, shall come out in his true colors. He will show us what a comedian, what a judge of character he is; like Yorick he shall set the table in a roar, eh, Baron?"

Lapanski grinned uncomfortably. A sullen red spread over his face, and he echoed Burton's words mechanically.

"I will set the table in a roar," he said.

Adela wondered what hold Burton had over this man. Why was he treating him with such merciless contempt? It was not usual to spurn a financier in this way. In the world in which Adela moved there was only one thing that inspired respect, and that was money. What, then, was the secret of Burton's hold upon his guest? She was still pondering this question when the game of pool was finished, and some of the guests came forward, obviously waiting for introductions. Half an hour later Adela found herself in the garden again, accompanied by Denne and Burton.

"There, you have seen him for yourself," the latter said gaily, "Prosperity as well as adversity makes us acquainted with strange bedfellows. As a financier, Denne, you must be aware of that."

"Oh, I am," Denne said drily. "In the course of my business experience, I have met with some of the choicest scoundrels the world has produced. They afford an entertaining study, even at the present moment—"

Denne stopped significantly, and Burton laughed as if some joke amused him.

"I know what you mean," he said. "Upon my word, I have a good mind to come as far as the Castle with you, and leave my guests to their own devices for a while. They will be safe in the capable hands of the Baroness."

"Would it be wise?" Adela asked indiscreetly.

"You are very thoughtful," Burton replied. "'But a mild evening like this cannot do me any harm."

CHAPTER XXV

A MUTUAL UNDERSTANDING

Adela said no more. Burton would have his own way, and seemed so sure of his ground, so absolutely certain of his reception, that she could offer no further opposition. He strode gaily along by the side of the others, chatting in his light and clever way. It was almost impossible that this well-dressed, well-spoken, light-hearted old man could be the broken-down, desperate creature whom Adela had gone to visit in a London slum on that eventful night which she was not likely to forget. She was feeling the vague dreamy sensation that had come upon her on the night when she had first met Samuel Burton. Could this man be the penniless, desperate adventurer, who required all his mother wit to escape from the toils of the police? She wondered whether Denne knew anything, whether he had guessed at the truth. But Denne was talking to Burton as he would have talked to an equal. There was something almost respectful in his manner. Still, it was hard to infer anything from Denne's inscrutable face; whether winning or losing, he always looked the same. No one had ever seen behind his mask.

They came to the Castle at length, and walked through the open door into the great hall, now blazing with scores of electric lights. One or two men were smoking, and the click of the balls could be heard from the billiard-room. In a room beyond three or four tables were set out for cards. Burton was expatiating on the beauty of the house, and the fine proportions of the hall, when Callader appeared. He stood in the doorway regarding Burton with a malignant scowl, apparently petrified by the intruder's audacity.

"What are you doing here?" he asked, pointedly.

Burton turned round with his most engaging smile.

"A most natural question, my dear fellow," he said glibly, "a most natural question. You thought I was a long way off, didn't you? In point of fact, I am quite a near neighbor. I have taken a charming house on the edge of the park for a few weeks. My friend, the Baroness Lapanski, has been good enough to act as my hostess. You see, I wished to give my adopted daughter a surprise, and she found me out this evening, by accident. But how are you, my dear fellow?"

Callader muttered something under his breath. His dull, heavy face flushed, and there was an angry light in his deep-set eyes. Adela, apparently quiet and indifferent, watched the scene with a breathless eagerness that set her heart beating and caused her limbs to tremble. She knew by instinct that Denne was watching, too, but she did not dare to look at him. She was waiting for the inevitable outbreak. She wondered what form it would take. The only one of the group who was quite at ease was the unwelcome visitor himself. He smiled pleasantly, caressed his grey moustache, and yet, at the same time, kept his eyes steadily fixed upon Callader with a challenging glint which was not to be mistaken.

"Did you want to see me?" Callader asked.

"Of course I did, my dear fellow," Burton went on in the same easy style. "I walked over on purpose. I have not seen you since the little dinner at the house of our friend Denne. The Baroness hopes that she and her small party may be privileged to dine here one night this week—quite an informal affair, not more than eight or ten of us altogether. I have six prize Americans, immensely rich, exceedingly simple, and all ready to purchase art treasures by the cartload. They would be glad to meet you. My dear sir, it is an opportunity not to be neglected."

Callader made no answer at the moment. He was no match for his keener-witted antagonist and was obviously puzzled. In his slow way he was struggling to see what the latter was leading to. He was only sure of one thing, and that was that Burton appeared to be standing on perfectly firm ground. At last Callader clumsily mumbled what sounded like an assent to the suggestion. He proffered refreshments, and was evidently doing his best to make himself agreeable.

"Nothing for me," Burton said. "I never touch anything except at meals. You might walk as far as the end of the avenue, and we can fix up an evening."

"Very well," Callader said. "If you are ready let us start at once. I can't leave my guests long."

"They will have to be desolated by your absence for a little time," Burton remarked. "I daresay they will manage to survive it."

The words were thrown at Callader much as a biscuit might be thrown to a dog. Burton turned and kissed his hand gracefully, picked up a cigarette from a silver box on the table and lighted it. As he passed from the porch into the garden Adela could hear him dilating on the beauty of the evening. He did not appear to have a single trouble in the world. He resembled a simple-hearted gentleman of clean life and clear conscience. But when he and Callader were beyond earshot his manner changed.

"What the devil are you driving at?" Callader asked.

Burton was hard and stern now.

"It won't pay to take that tone with me," he said. "You know what happens when flint and steel strike together over a barrel of gunpowder. Now if you live in the same glass house as I do, you can't blow up my part of it without shattering yours at the same time. I know what I have to thank you for. You intended to put me out of the way and were fool enough to think you could save yourself at my expense. You'd have been comforted to feel that I was safe in a place where I should be compelled to pass the rest of my days. Meanwhile you would have the spending of Sam Burton's money. A very nice arrangement, especially to a gambler who hasn't two shillings to jingle together. But if you try that on again the consequences will be disastrous. I don't wish you any harm, though you haven't played the game. But I don't mind telling you that if you make another attempt to prick my bubble you will find yours vanish into thin air at the same time. I have made all my arrangements. Within twenty-four hours of my finding myself in trouble, you will find yourself in similar circumstances. Don't say I haven't warned you. I would have shown you before long what it was to play with me, but, unfortunately, I could not do so without injuring my adopted daughter. It may strike you as being very strange, that I want Adela to marry you. I am anxious to see her Marchioness of Kempston; and that is why—"

"Oh, stop your fooling," Callader said sulkily. "You know there is little chance of that. A robust young life stands between me and that, and he is likely to outlive me."

"In the ordinary course of things, yes. But I know what I am talking about. I have lived amongst singular people and heard strange things in my time, and, by a judicious use of this knowledge I have made money. I won't tell you everything now. Some day, and that before very long, you will know what I mean when I say that there is every possibility of Adela Burton becoming Marchioness of Kempston. Adela will make a most charming widow."

"I think you must be demented."

"I have counted all the chances," Burton replied airily. "I should say that at the end of four years Adela would be mistress of Callader Castle with an enormous fortune to keep it up. By that time you will be out of the way. You are the sort of man that dies early. You eat enormously, turn night into day, and it is your boast that nothing you drink does you any harm. I understand that in certain circles, you have a high reputation for these accomplishments. They say that long after the rest have collapsed, you carry your liquor like a man. My dear sir, it is just people like yourself that go off in the most unexpected fashion. Those big veins on your forehead, and those little red lines in your face tell their own story. I have known a hundred of similar cases. Some men envy you and point at you admiringly. But one day it goes round the clubs that poor Mark Callader has had a stroke, and the next thing one hears is that he is dead. If I were a betting man, I would wager against your living for another four years. It was the same with your father and grandfather before you. I knew them both."

Callader shuffled along uncomfortably by his companion's side. He knew enough and more than enough of Burton's past, but as yet he was not aware of the old adventurer's identity. He would have given a good round sum for enlightenment at that moment. That Burton was a man of birth and breeding was apparent on the face of it, but that he was a scoundrel in spite of his wealth, Burton was also aware. He did not guess that Burton's money was a myth, and that he did not know which way to turn for a hundred pounds. But there was no suggestion of this in Burton's manner.

"I think we begin to understand one another," the latter went on. "You are going to marry my adopted daughter, so I must be easy with you. If I were you, I should be more careful. I met a man a day or two ago who was asking me pertinent questions. There is no occasion to give the man a name, but he is an art dealer in a large way of business, and he is beginning to get a little nervous over one or two transactions he has had with you lately. It was lucky he mentioned the subject to me, because I was able to allay his fears. But I should drop it, my dear Callader, if I were you, because if you don't, sooner or later it will land you in trouble."

Callader's face turned a shade redder and, though he muttered something under his breath, he gave way to no outburst of indignation. He realised that his antagonist was far too adroit for such a clumsy attack as his.

"Take my warning," Burton said in a fatherly way. "Hold your hand for a bit longer, at any rate. It will be time enough for that when you are Marquis of Kempston."

"What rot!" Callader growled. "What do you mean? It is impossible."

"My dear sir, there are no such things as impossibilities. I know what I am talking about, and when I tell you that my girl Adela will be Marchioness of Kempston in a year or two, I am merely speaking the truth. I won't tell you more at present. When I am dealing with a blackguard, I am bound to keep a card or two up my sleeve. Good night. By the way, didn't we agree to dine with you on Thursday evening? All right. Au revoir."

CHAPTER XXVI

GOLDEN YOUTH

The house party rolled back to Callader Castle in high good humor. It had been a veritable backers' day at Rokeby Park, and they all returned with a great deal more money than they started with. Besides, it was pleasant to contemplate one's shrewdness, and to be assured that, for once, at all events, one had got the better of what one called the 'pencillers.' They dashed to the hall door in carriages and motors, and the women clamored for tea. The Duchess of Southampton was as unlike the wearer of the traditional strawberry leaves of fiction as it was possible to imagine. For her grace was short and stout, not to say muscular. She was dressed in the plainest of plain Norfolk jackets, her skirt was short, and her well-polished brown boots eminently serviceable. She wore a grey Trilby hat tilted to the side of her head, and a beautifully tied stock ornamented with a diamond horse-shoe pin. Her good-humored face was round and red, and her very hair was cut short like a man's. To use her own breezy expression, she had been reared in a racing stable, and in her heart of hearts the stud books and the racing calendar were far more important than Debrett.

But, nevertheless, she came of a remarkably good stock, and though her manners were free to the verge of familiarity, she never forgot herself or her position, as many a parvenu could tell. She viewed her present companions with good-natured contempt. Her opinion of Mark Callader she never disguised. But then, he was a Callader, and that counted for a great deal.

The Duchess sank down in a chair just as she was and called loudly for tea. She had no occasion to go upstairs to change first, for she was a law unto herself, and did as she pleased. She flung her brown leather racing-glasses aside, and pitched her gold mounted betting book on the table.

"The best day I have had," she exclaimed, "since Rainbow won the Ascot seven years ago. I must have netted seven thousand, I think, and, goodness knows, I want it, for my stables at Randwick are falling to pieces."

Her voice was big and resonant. She drank a cup of tea with zest, and the others crowded around her asking questions, and the whole place was a babel of talk. The servants glided about the hall listening greedily, though appearing to hear nothing. No subject was discussed besides racing. Talk was still proceeding with undiminished animation when the first dinner-bell rang.

"Let's see," the Duchess said, "haven't we a lot of people coming to dinner to-night. Didn't you say something to me about American freaks, Mark, and the Baroness Lapanski. Well, I am not particularly anxious to meet her, and you had no business to ask her without my permission. Still, I know how to deal with that sort of woman, and will put up with her for the sake of meeting Mr. Samuel Burton."

The sun was shining brightly, the flowers in the garden formed masses of glowing colors, the woods behind the castle were blithe with the song of the birds. The stained glass windows in the hall trembled in the gorgeous sunlight that put to shame the feeble twinkling of the electrics high up in the carved oak roof. It was a shame, an outrage, Denne thought, to shut out an evening of such splendor. He was one of the first to make his appearance. He threw himself down in a big chair in a corner of the hall, and picked up a cigarette idly and placed it between his lips. He was joined presently by Vanstone. It wanted half an hour or more to dinner-time, and most of the guests were not likely to make their appearance till the last moment.

"Why are you obliterating yourself like this?" Vanstone asked. "Why this modesty?"

"I am a mere looker-on," Denne answered. "To tell you the truth, I prefer to watch the fun. If society wasn't a comedy, I should never trouble it."

"A cheap amusement," Vanstone suggested.

"Cheap! You call it cheap? I admit it is far more amusing than the theatre, but it is the reverse of cheap, Philip. One way and another it costs me the best part of twenty thousand a year. Still, there are moments when one feels the money is well laid out, and this is one of them."

Vanstone smiled at his friend's caustic humor. From their dim corner they saw Adela cross the hall and stand by the spacious hearth, gazing thoughtfully at the fire. She needed not to go as far as the drawing-room, for the guests would be received here; in fact, it was the custom at Callader to await the announcement in the fine old hall. It gave a greater air of freedom, and enabled the men to smoke their cigarettes till the last moment.

Adela was quite unconscious that she was not alone. A slanting beam of golden light from one of the stained-glass windows fell across her, and threw her pale, beautiful face into high relief. The light trembled on her white lace dress. She looked almost ethereal, like some thing apart, and out of keeping with the place, save that the setting was worthy of the picture.

"I am right," Vanstone vowed. "I am sure that woman is worth saving, Denne. Look at the expression of her face. There are thousands of women who envy Adela Burton, and yet I feel sure she is so unhappy she would change places with any of them."

"You may be right," Denne admitted. "I wish to goodness I could make up my mind. But, whatever happens, she shall not marry Callader. I am afraid I am a bit like the dog in the manger. I cannot decide whether I want her or not, and at the same time I won't let anybody else have her."

"Were I in your place, Denne, I shouldn't hesitate."

Denne made no reply. Another figure now appeared in sight, and crossed the hall jauntily. He walked gently up to Adela and laid his hand on her shoulder. Sitting there quietly watching, Denne felt that the simile of the stage of a theatre was more apropos than he imagined. Samuel Burton possessed certain of the attributes of the theatre. He looked very much like Wyndham in certain parts—Wyndham, as a well-groomed gentleman, with an absolutely perfect knowledge of the world. And beside him, too, stood the beautiful heroine, in need, as beautiful heroines generally are, of advice and assistance.

The beam of yellow light fell on Burton's face, and touched his glossy shirt front, revealing the beautiful symmetry of his tie, and seeming to turn the ends of his moustache into gold. There was nothing smiling or cynical about him now, and his glance was one of pure, disinterested affection. He might have been a proud father, rejoicing in the sweetness and grace and beauty of his child. Hard and worldly as he was, Denne beheld the couple not without emotion. This old scamp, after all, had one soft spot, one spring of feeling untainted, by rascality or selfishness.

"I thought I'd come early, on the off-chance of a few words alone with you. The Baroness will be here later with the rest of the menagerie. I believe they are being personally conducted by that prince of cicerones, Felix Marner. How are you, my dear child?"

Adela's answer did not reach the listeners. Vanstone whispered to his companion that he was not feeling comfortable; their position was too like eavesdropping. They would have to disclose themselves a minute later, but further embarrassment was saved, for out of the stillness of the evening came a cackle of voices, and the Baroness Lapanski entered, followed by the rest of the guests. She had not waited to ring the bell, nor did she deem it necessary to stand on ceremony. She merely came in smiling, as if quite at home, while, at the same moment, the Duchess of Southampton and Callader appeared.

"I am glad they came," Denne muttered. "I, too, was beginning to feel it decidedly awkward, but we shall be all right now. Pass the cigarettes, Phil. I think we may have a bit of fun before dinner. It will be worth the journey here to see the meeting between the Duchess and the Baron."

Her Grace of Southampton politely surveyed the newcomers through a pair of long handled glasses with the interest of a naturalist regarding a new specimen. She was beautifully dressed now. There were diamonds about her throat, she had discarded her 'horsey' manner, and looked to the full what she was, and that was a great lady, indeed, She ignored the Baroness's outstretched hand, and embraced the whole of the party with a comprehensive sweep of her head.

"I hope you are quite well," the Baroness said sweetly.

"I am never anything else," the Duchess answered. "I live too healthy a life, and, as a rule, make it a point to be in bed by eleven o'clock. My only weakness is that I am a trifle short-sighted. I find it so difficult to recognise acquaintances when I meet them again. I always tell them this because it frequently saves a great deal of pain."

The Duchess turned aside and began a conversation with one of the guests staying at the house. Denne looked on with a smile of amusement. The dash of comedy appealed to him, and rendered life more tolerable.

"That was cleverly done," he said to Vanstone. "The Duchess is a many sided woman. There is nothing so enjoyable as to see one society woman being rude to another without being vulgar."

Burton walked easily across the room towards his host. As he drew near, Denne noticed that the Duchess regarded him with flattering attention. She turned to Callader and demanded an introduction, which Mark made in his clumsy way.

The great lady drew aside the skirt of her dress, and motioned Burton with a glance to sit down beside her. She looked a little disturbed and uncomfortable, but her shrewd grey eyes stared Burton intently in the face.

"So you are Samuel Burton," she said in a low voice. "I am an old woman, and have seen much of the world and I have learnt to be surprised at nothing. What are you doing here? Aren't you afraid of being recognised?"

"I am not," Burton replied. "Besides, there are very few of my contemporaries left. But there was never any deceiving you, Hilda. I am in your hands, and throw myself on your mercy. But, please, don't let anybody know. Let it pass that I am Samuel Burton, the millionaire; upon my word, my dear creature, I believe I am as respectable as the majority of my class."

CHAPTER XXVII

THE SAXON CUP AGAIN

The dinner, an elaborate meal served by half a score of servants, dragged its slow length along. Priceless pictures hung on the walls of the vast dining-hall, each standing out in its frame against the carved oak, illuminated with its bulb of electric light beneath. Here were examples of Rembrandts and Velasquez, Reynolds and Romney, and the rest, which went far to represent the pictorial treasures belonging to the house of Callader. Otherwise the hall was in darkness, excepting that the table was one soft radiance of green light gleaming from between banks of flowers. The American guests were properly impressed. Neither flamboyant nor self-assertive, they had fallen under the glamor of their mediaeval surroundings. For the most part the men were typically American, tall and lean and clean of limb, restless of eye and quick of hand. The women were beautifully dressed, and quite at home.

The conversation was less sparkling and less personal than usual, perhaps because it was felt that most of it would be over the heads of the visitors. Burton sat next to the Duchess, with whom he held friendly intercourse. At the other end Felix Marner expatiated on art in his most academic manner. The subject of his talk was the Velasquez which hung at the end of the dining-hall over the carved fireplace. Dinner was ended before the discourse, and after the ladies had retired, Marner walked down the room and stood in front of the fireplace with the Americans around him.

"I suppose this is the finest specimen of the master's manner," he said. "Like so many of Velasquez's paintings, it has a history of its own. I understand it came into the Callader family in very curious and romantic circumstances. As you see for yourself, it is the portrait of a Spanish lady. I believe that in the artist's time an adventurous Callader was attached to the Court of Madrid; indeed, he was in the service of the State. He is supposed to have married the daughter of a Spanish Don. Tradition says that he ran away with her, to the anger of her family, who swore vengeance. Two of the lady's brothers set out to pursue the runaway couple, and the lady's horse fell over a precipice in Granada, and she was killed on the spot. I fancy that Callader afterwards fought a three handed duel with the brothers, but what was the upshot, I don't know. At any rate, the Callader I am speaking of was able to do Velasquez a service, and the artist painted the unfortunate lady's portrait from memory. It was brought to Callader, and hung in the hall here, where it has remained ever since. Few know of it, and still fewer imagine it has become extremely valuable; indeed, apart from the romance, the picture is one of the greatest works of art in the world."

"What is it worth?" one of the Americans asked.

Marner smiled faintly at the question. He looked as if he had expected something of the kind. He replied vaguely that it was impossible to reduce the value of the painting to prosaic dollars, but at auction it might fetch fifty thousand pounds. A reverent hush fell upon the small group of plutocrats. Their knowledge of art was exceedingly slight, but they could appreciate the solid fact that this was something which might realise two hundred thousand of their beloved dollars in the open market. Denne strolled over to the little company, and watched in carefully disguised amusement. Two of the visitors were eagerly asking questions of Callader, who shrugged his shoulders, as if the subject had no interest for him

"A fine picture," Burton said, taking his cigarette from his lips to speak. "Marvellous coloring, too. A little yellow, perhaps, but the high-lights are perfect. But, after all, what is Art? And who are we that judge? Don't you think a future generation may throw all our treasures on the rubbish heap? I daresay if we came back in five hundred years we should discover that our treasured masters were considered to be no better than sign-painters. Of courses that is putting the case flippantly, but fine as that picture is, I know a man who could copy it so faithfully that you could not tell the difference between the replica and the original."

"What do you mean by that?" Callader asked.

"My dear fellow, I mean exactly what I say. If I could borrow your picture for a fortnight, I could replace it by one similar in every respect. Then I could sell the original at my own price, and the connoisseur who came here would fall down and worship the copy. It has been done."

An ugly scowl crossed Callader's face.

"I don't like jokes of that sort," he muttered.

"Do you like any jokes?" Burton retorted. "My good man, I am only giving you a tip. In these hard times, when a man in your position has to keep up appearances he sometimes is driven to resort to ingenious expedients. Upon my word, when I think of your opportunities, I marvel at your self-restraint. This old place is shut up for ten or eleven months in the year. Your dull-witted servants never notice anything. What is to prevent you from removing the best of these pictures, and replacing them with copies? You would be perfectly safe. They are all heirlooms, and can never find their way into the sale-room. So long as they are the sacred pictures of Callader Castle, the question of their genuineness would never occur to anyone. In fact, there might be a serious risk to cast a doubt upon them? What do you say, Denne?"

Douglas was enjoying the scene immensely. He knew what the rest of them were ignorant of—that a deep and subtle meaning lay behind Burton's innocent words. He watched Callader shifting about uneasily, and noted the moody frown on his red face. Felix Marner, too, was rather disturbed. He had lost his usual picturesque sang froid, and, for once, was not posing.

"Mr. Burton is joking, of course," Denne answered. "He is giving play to his imagination. All millionaires are men of imagination; they couldn't be millionaires without it. Callader evidently thinks the joke has been carried too far."

"I do," Callader muttered sullenly.

"Then let us leave Northumberland," Denne said. "It is clear these gentlemen cannot hope to do any business with Callader. Most of them will do better to call upon Mr. Marner at his charming house in London. Hardly anything that is really valuable comes into the market without passing through his hands. I myself saw something in Frogmore-street not long ago that enchanted me. It was a gold Saxon Cup, not very much to look at, perhaps, but exceedingly valuable. I wonder whether you still have it, Marner; if you have, I am sure these gentlemen would like to see it."

"Yes, I have it still," Marner said in his stately fashion. "I should very much like to keep it for myself, but my limited means preludes any such idea. As I am going on to Scotland from here to show it to a collector of old plate, I brought the Cup with me. If you gentlemen would like to see it, I shall be only too glad to fetch it."

Great virtuoso and artist as he was, Marner never lacked an eye to the main chance, and this was an opportunity for making a handsome sum which was not to be neglected. Immediately upon hearing of the advent of the Americans, he had written to his bankers for the Cup, and it had arrived by special messenger that morning. He walked quietly out of the room, as if he were conferring a favor upon the other guests, and returned after a while bearing the Cup in his hands. It passed from one to the other admiringly. The Americans bent over it with awed reverence. It was the kind of thing that stirred their imagination, the kind of treasure that no millionaire could afford to be without. Vanstone came eagerly forward, and asked if he might inspect the treasure. He turned it round, held it up to the light, and then looked questioningly at Denne. But the latter made no sign, and looked as if he were tired of the whole thing, and desirous of getting away to something else.

"May I ask you where you got this?" Vanstone said.

"I would rather not say, if you don't mind," Marner replied. "You see, a good many people are compelled by circumstances to sell these things, and they don't like to have it talked about. You understand."

"I beg your pardon," Vanstone said politely.

"Oh, not at all, not at all, my dear fellow. Naturally one would give the pedigree of the Cup to any purchaser; you may be interested to hear that it is valued at six thousand guineas. I beg Callader's pardon for mentioning it, and, indeed, it is hardly necessary to say that I did not come here to do business."

The words fell from Marner's lips quite casually. He smiled in his own gracious manner, as he wrapped the Cup carefully up in its tissue paper again, and walked out of the room with it. He was far too clever a man of business to appear eager, to try to quicken the pace, for he knew that in a day or two more than one of his hearers would make a bid for the Saxon Cup.

The group scattered, and Denne moved away to the smoking room. Vanstone detained him a moment.

"One word," he said, "What does this mean, Denne? Is this some deep laid scheme of yours?"

"In what respect?" Denne asked.

"Oh, you know. Why are you always beating about the bush. Don't you recollect my coming into your house one night as Paul Lestrine was going out? He left behind him on the table a piece of marvellous workmanship in gold, which, I understood you had bought. You didn't show it to me at the time, but I could see what a perfect thing it was. Now, don't tell me it wasn't the Saxon Cup, because I know better. This being the case, why do you allow Marner to pass it off as it it belonged to him? Surely you haven't turned dealer? You would not demean yourself to play some of the tricks of that trade?"

For once Denne looked uneasy, and led Vanstone by the arm to one side.

"You are quite right," he said, "but I have not tried to deceive you. There is a pretty little conspiracy on foot here, and I am making use of it for my own ends. But I will ask you to keep the knowledge to yourself because it is not wholly a personal affair. I may tell you, however, that on this depends the happiness of a lady in whom you are deeply interested—Adela Burton."

CHAPTER XXVIII

AN EXPERT OPINION

"I don't like it at all," Vanstone said uneasily.

"What don't you like?" Denne asked. "Anybody would think I was doing something heinous."

Vanstone shot a glance at his companion. The poet's thin, sensitive face wore an expression of worry. Like men of his temperament, he was something of a hero-worshipper, and ranked Denne high in his estimate of contemporary humanity. Most men, to his mind, were commonplace, sordid, ambitious, and had a keen eye to the main chance. But Denne was different, though rich beyond the dreams of avarice, he had a magnificent contempt for money for its own sake. He had grown wealthy because he was cleverer than his fellow-creatures, but Vanstone knew that he had lofty ideals and a limitless horizon. Denne would do great good with his wealth some day, of that Vanstone felt assured.

Thus it was that Denne's present policy disturbed him; it looked as if his friend were contemplating something mean and discreditable.

"I think you understand me," Vanstone rejoined. "I don't like to see you do what smaller men do. I don't think it is worthy of you."

"What isn't worthy of me?" Denne asked.

"Why, such a scheme as yours; it sounds contemptible. I hope you won't mind my plain speaking. I am afraid that I often try you."

"You are quite right," Denne smiled, "and that is one reason why we are such good friends. Most people seem to stand in awe of me, or rather to respect my money, which comes to the same thing. Don't you know what is at the back of my mind? Didn't you ask me to save Adela Burton? Do you wish her to marry Callader? Do you want to see that fine-natured woman tied to such a brute? I promised to save her if I could, but you must allow me to do it in my own way."

"Still, there is another method," Vanstone ventured to say. "A man so rich and powerful—"

"Ah, there we get back to the old thing again. I thought you had a bigger soul, Philip; and, besides, the fact that I have all this money handicaps me seriously. Oh, I know what you think. You think that I should be a powerful rival, that if I were to pit myself against Callader, he would have very little chance with me. Unfortunately, I know that too well. This is not egotism. It is merely an unpleasant truth. The longer one moves in Society the more this comes home to one. What girl of our acquaintance would say 'No' to the spending of my fortune? Not one, and you would not have me put my head in a noose like that. My position resembles that of the heroine of a novelette—I mean, the rich heroine who dreads lest she be wooed for her wealth alone. She pines for the right man, and eventually he comes, and all is happiness. But then, you see, that is fiction, and this is stern reality. I don't doubt that Adela would throw over Callader if I asked her to marry me, but, foolish as it may seem, I hope to find a wife who will value Douglas Denne for his own sake. That is why I hesitate, why I am forced to meet Callader with his own weapons."

"I wish I could convince you that Adela is really worth all the trouble and more."

"My dear fellow," Deans said with some impatience, "I believe she is. I am rapidly coming to that conclusion. I am getting sentimental about her. The romantic side of the situation appeals to me, but I have my doubts, and must not throw away my future happiness recklessly. I have pledged my word that Adela shall not marry Callader, and the only way to deal with a man like Mark is to frighten him. He must realise that he is in my power, and that, if this thing goes on, I shall expose him. In this instance exposure would mean disgrace, and probably a long term of imprisonment. For some time I have suspected what was going on, and to-night have proved it. I laid a trap for Callader, and he walked into it blindfold."

"That is just what I complain of," Vanstone persisted.

"But why, my dear follow, why?"

"Because it isn't worthy of you; it savors of conspiracy. And to carry it out you have taken Paul Lestrine into your confidence. I don't like that man; I believe he is a wolf. He only sticks to you for what he can get out of you, and if it were worth his while he would betray you without the slightest hesitation. You may strike Mark Callader's guns, but take care you don't come to grief. I have forgotten most of the law I learnt when I was called, but I know that judges take a very stern view of conspiracy. If your plot came to light you might probably get imprisonment yourself. But what is Callader doing?"

Denne pondered before he spoke.

"There is a good deal in what you say. Your point of view had not occurred to me. I see I must be careful, but there is no other way. Like most bullies, Callader is a coward at heart, and will be too anxious to save his own skin to think much about me. But have you no idea what he has been doing? I only found it out a short time ago. Callader is an extravagant man. He spends money freely, yet is not very much in debt; has no occupation, inherited little from his father, yet lives with the best of us. Have you never asked yourself where this cash comes from?"

"There are so many mysteries in our set," Vanstone answered. "I could point to a score of younger sons with slender allowances who appear to be in possession of unlimited means."

"Butterflies bred on the hotbed of credit. But Callader really has the money. Didn't you notice how angry he was when that old scamp Burton suggested how easy it would be to raid the family treasures, and replace them with forgeries. You see wow the fraud came to be worked. The pictures have been here for generations. They are never likely to come under the hammer, and so long as they are here, no one is likely to question their genuineness."

"I begin to understand," Vanstone admitted. "But I confess I am puzzled about the Saxon Cup? That belongs to you."

"Well, it did. But suppose it happened to be unearthed here amongst the family treasures and that no record of it could be found anywhere, Callader could make a few thousand pounds with impunity. He only has to hand the thing over to Marner, who is one of the cleverest salesmen I know, and a deal is practically accomplished. When I discovered that the Saxon Cup had made its way from Callader Castle to Frogmore-street, I knew for a fact what I had long suspected. I knew that Callader was removing the art treasures here and replacing them with forgeries. I have learnt that this has been going on for a considerable time. If I remain silent, it will never be found out, and Callader has hit upon an ingenious method of putting a quarter of a million or so into his pocket. The fact that he spends it as fast as he gets it does not affect my argument. Now, my dear friend, you see how I hope to prevent Callader from marrying Adela Burton. I am not proud of my scheme, but it is the best I can think of."

Vanstone shook his head sorrowfully; the more he thought over this plan the less he liked it. The two were still in the dining-hall; the table had been cleared, and the servants had departed. It was a singularly unfitting scene for sordid criminality and cheap detective work. It was extraordinary to gaze upon the marvellous creations on the walls, and to know that they were remarkable but deliberate forgeries. Vanstone passed from one to another, looking at each long and carefully. Denne, with his back to the fireplace, watched his friend with a slight smile on his face. At that moment Burton came into the room. He wanted his cigarette-case, had anyone seen it? He found it presently on an old oak cabinet, and strolled over to Denne. He stood by the capitalist's side, debonair, comfortable and quite at home. It was impossible to associate such a man with anything sordid or contemptible.

At the same time, there was a touch of cynicism in his smile as he nodded towards Vanstone.

"Does your friend know anything about pictures?"

"He has a feeling for them," Denne replied. "Vanstone has the artistic temperament. We were talking just now of your theory that it would be easy to remove these pictures, and substitute copies for them."

"Oh, it was only a passing fancy," he said. "I have heard of such things being done. To my knowledge it happened some fifteen years ago in Germany. The culprit was a serene Highness who was trustee for some large properties, and there was a fine hullabaloo when the thing came to be known. Of course it was hushed up. They manage those things better in Germany than they do in England. All the priceless treasures were lost, most of them turning up in the galleries of an American millionaire. Some ingenious swindlers afterwards discovered what had happened, and compelled the Yankee to disgorge. He, poor man, took them to be connected with the German Court, and parted with the treasures without questions asked."

"A very interesting story," was Denne's comment.

Burton did not say that this was a personal reminiscence. The moral of the narrative would not have been affected if he had. He inspected the Velasquez over the fireplace, and laid his hand upon a flaw in the panelling in which the painting was embedded.

"Now look at this," he said. "The picture has been here for two centuries at least. During that time, I understand, it has never been removed. But if you will examine this woodwork you will see that a screw has been removed quite recently. Far be it from me to suggest anything wrong. Our young friend Callader bears too high a reputation for that. Still—"

Burton broke off significantly and smiled to himself as he left the room.

"That is very strange," Denne observed. "I wonder—well, it is no use wondering; I must find out for myself."

CHAPTER XXIX

A LEAF FROM THE PAST

Burton returned to the great hall with a self-satisfied air. He had not dropped the hint to Denne for nothing. It was part of the scheme he had in his mind. He found Felix Marner in the hall expatiating to the Americans. It was doubtful whether they understood half of what he said, but they followed him with none the less interest because he had as high a reputation in the United States as he had in Europe. It would be the correct thing to say they had met him. Moreover, every genuine American is fond of a lecture. For a moment there was suspicion of a sneer on Burton's face as he paused to listen. The hall was large, and he caught only the faint murmur of Marner's voice. In a distant corner a trio of vacuous looking youths were discussing tomorrow's racing programme. They had a litter of sporting papers and guides before them, and weighed up the chance of this or that horse with an earnestness which spoke volumes for their folly.

Callader was nowhere to be seen; probably he was in the billiard room playing with some of his guests. Burton could hear the click of the balls and the shrill sound of laughter. In one of the small drawing-rooms the lights were low, and a dozen persons were bending with concentrated interest over the bridge tables.

Adela came through a curtained doorway presently, and sat down, looking white, jaded and tired. Burton's heart smote him, and he crossed over and took a seat by her side. He patted her hand gently.

"You don't look at all well," he remarked. "You ought to be happy."

"I ought to be," Adela said, "but I am not. Oh, why should there be any pretence between us? I wish you had never come back. I wish you had left me to my own resources. I have tried to break away from this, to free myself, but it is impossible. If I could only get enough money to pay—"

"My dear child, you are not worrying over that!" Burton exclaimed. "You will have plenty of money soon. In a week or two I shall be in funds again. Besides, before long you will marry Mark, and be mistress of Callader Castle. Yes, I know you think there is an obstacle, but that will be removed."

"When can I have some more money?" she asked.

Burton was most sanguine. There were grand schemes in hand, he said. They were more or less certainties, and before long Adela would command more wealth than ever. Burton had all the shallow hopefulness of the born gambler and adventurer, and always pinned his faith to the morrow. But Adela listened with sinking heart. It was hateful to touch this money. It was different when she was ignorant of its source. Now, she would have liked to decline any further assistance from Burton, but she could not do it yet. She would keep her own counsel, and say nothing to anybody, and, when the golden stream began to flow again, she would clear off her liabilities, and disappear. She had ample excuse; she was run down; her physician had been imperative as to her need of a thorough change. She would take it, and in a year be forgotten. In twelve months, if her name was mentioned, people would ask who she was.

With this comforting thought uppermost in her mind, she sat gazing into space. She saw nothing of Burton's concern and affection, nor heeded the paternal note in his voice. The Duchess of Southampton spoke twice before Adela was conscious of her presence.

"You are wanted in the billiard room," she said. "Now, run away and make yourself agreeable. I want to have a chat with Mr. Burton."

Adela vanished, and the Duchess took her seat, and turned upon Burton with grim directness.

"I have been waiting nearly all the evening for this opportunity. I want an explanation. What are you doing here?"

Burton smiled with perfect equanimity.

"What a question!" he said. "In the first place why shouldn't I be here? Don't you know that I am Mr. Samuel Burton, the American millionaire. It doesn't matter how I made my fortune. Nobody asks such questions in the States. The new man simply crops up, startles Wall-street by his daring operations, and the press does the rest. Within a day or two the papers are teeming with the story of his millions. He takes a suite of rooms at one of the best hotels, gives out that he is building a five-million dollar place on Fifth-avenue, and the thing is done. Meanwhile, it is possible that he has not got a single dollar. But, then, the American papers like to add another to their list of millionaires—they think it enhances the importance of the nation. They imagine it makes Europeans jealous. And that, my dear Hilda, in a nutshell, is the story of Samuel Burton's fortune."

"Are you a millionaire?"

"Oh, that is quite immaterial. Do I look like a poor man? Does my adopted daughter look like a poor man's child? You know what she has been spending the last few years. I never indulged in undue extravagance at any inconvenience to myself."

"That is true," the Duchess said candidly. "I never met a man in my life so cruelly callous and selfish as you. You were the same even as a boy. You ruined your friends without the least compunction. You broke your mother's heart, and your father's suicide was directly attributable to you. You left the army in disgrace. If you had not belonged to a great family you would most assuredly have been prosecuted. You took advantage of your young brother officers' ignorance to rob them at cards. Everybody who knew you was glad when you disappeared from England. It was a load off the mind of your acquaintances. We all thought you were dead."

"Or hoped so," Burton said coolly.

"Well, yes; except one or two foolish women. Like most scamps you were very handsome and fascinating. You are a handsome old man now, and strangely enough you don't bear the least trace of one who, for the best part of his life, must have been rubbing shoulders with the scum of the earth. Your appearance would be security for anything in reason."

"I suppose it would," Burton said with a smile.

"And now you come back as if the past were extinguished. I can quite understand when I look at you again how you have not been recognised, and I see you possess your old fascinations. If anybody had told me I should be sitting here to-night talking in this friendly way to Samuel Mostyn, I should have laughed the idea to scorn. I should have said at once that if he dared to address a word to me I would instantly have exposed him, and had him turned out of the house. But I have done nothing of the kind, simply because, forty years ago, I was weak enough to be fond of you, and would have followed you to the end of the world. I didn't have the chance, however, which was a good thing for me."

Burton listened good-naturedly, and the under-current of bitterness in his companion's speech did not touch him at all.

"My good soul," he said, "isn't this ancient history? But I am glad we met to-night, because I want to talk to you about Adela. You may not believe it, but I am very fond of that girl. When I met her first she was a tiny child, and I was in a position of great danger."

"From the police?"

"My dear Hilda, I could never tell a lie to an old friend like you. I have never actually been in gaol, but I should have been incarcerated on this particular occasion if Adela had not helped me. I had a long spell of prosperity afterwards; in fact, I have been more or less fortunate ever since I made Adela what she is. I took her out of the slum in which she was living after her mother died."

"I thought she was a lady," the Duchess interrupted.

"So she is. You have only to look at her to see that. On her father's side, at any rate, her pedigree is all right. Her mother was a dancer, a brilliant dancer, a brilliant beauty, who was a great favorite amongst certain men. Now I am coming to the point. I daresay you wonder why I am so anxious to see my adopted daughter married to Callader."

"It is a marvel to me," the Duchess said drily.

"I thought it would be. But you see, when I am finished—and the need is much nearer than people imagine—Adela will have little or nothing. I make enormous sums of money, but I am no millionaire. I shall leave nothing. But if Adela marries Callader, I can pass away with the comfortable assurance that her future is provided for. When she becomes Marchioness of Kempston—"

"My good man, what are you talking about? You forget young Guy stands in the way."

"No, that is precisely what he does not do. I am going to tell you a secret, because I can trust you. You know what a wild fellow the late Marquis of Kempston was. You know that five and twenty years ago it was considered discreet for him to disappear to America. I met him in the States In some very shady company indeed. I introduced him to Sophie Letolle, and was present at their wedding. Adela was the only child of that union. Please don't interrupt me for a moment. You are going to say that this makes no difference because Kempston married again at home, and had a son, Guy. But he parted from Sophie after twelve tempestuous months with her, came home to England, and married under the impression that she was dead. He didn't know that his first wife was alive, or that she had borne him a child. I couldn't inform him, because he broke his neck in the hunting field soon after Guy's birth. I am able to prove all this, and can show you the necessary documents if you like. It will be hard upon Guy to oust him in this fashion, but the fact remains that he is no more heir than I am and that the real heir of the family is Mark Callader."

The Duchess swayed her fan backwards and forwards. For once in her life she was too astonished to speak.

CHAPTER XXX

"BEWARE OF ENTRANCE TO A QUARREL"

"Samuel Burton had dropped his easy debonair manner, and was speaking with unusual earnestness. He sat with his hands folded between his knees, and his looks declared his anxiety. For once the Duchess was utterly astonished, though she had frequently plumed herself as being proof against any sensation whatever.

She knew Burton's character, and that, as a rule, his word was not to be trusted. But it never occurred to her to disbelieve him in this instance. There was no reason why he should fabricate such a story, and so far as her grace could see, Burton would not benefit by the fraud.

"Now, is this true?" the Duchess inquired at last.

"Yes, really, and I will help you to prove it. This card contains the name and address of a man who can give you chapter and verse for everything I say. I ask you as a favor to take this matter up, and go through with it. Unfortunately, I shall not be here to lend you any assistance."

"Are you going away?"

A peculiar smile hovered on Burton's lips.

"Yes, I am going away," he said with strange gentleness. "But my journey is not of the kind you are thinking of; it is the journey which we must all take, and from which we never return."

"My dear Samuel, do you mean that you—"

"Precisely; that is exactly what I mean. I have known it for some time past, and have had more than one imperative warning which is not to be disregarded. The next attack will be the last, and it may come at any moment. You can't lead the life I have been leading for forty years without paying the price. The anxiety is killing, and when you people say that scoundrels like myself have no heart or conscience, don't believe it. We suffer as other folks do, and our anxiety is far greater. One does not go into a bold scheme without the imminent risk of gaol as one's sole reward in the same way as one sets out for a fortnight's shooting. I don't know why I am talking in this strain; perhaps it is because you believed in me once. Anyhow, you are one of the few friends I ever had, and I know I can leave the future of my girl in your hands. I have worked and schemed for her as if she were my only child, and I wish her future to be assured. What I could do for her has practically been done already; I am near the end of my resources. But she will be provided for if she marries Callader and becomes Marchioness of Kempston. In any case she will be entitled to some income out of the estates—perhaps two or three thousand a year—as the Lady Adela Callader, daughter of the late Marchioness of Kempston. Of course, Duchess, there is no occasion for immediate hurry, and we may have opportunities of discussing this matter again. On the other hand, we may not, and that is why I mention it now. I shall be found dead in my bed some morning, if not to-morrow, some other day—and it will be soon."

The Duchess was moved in spite of herself. She was a woman and the romance and pathos of the thing impressed her. She would have said more, only Adela came up at that moment, and Burton walked away, as if in search of recreation. The party in the billiard-room had broken up, for Callader lounged heavily in the hall, frowning as if displeased. Possibly he had been losing, and he was a bad loser. Possibly he had been drinking, too, for there was a dully, crimson flush on his face, and the veins on his forehead stood out a brilliant purple. Adela fancied he was trying to pick a quarrel with Denne, for Douglas talked in what Callader found an irritating fashion.

"What is the matter?" the Duchess asked.

"I haven't the remotest idea," Denne said. "I have incurred our host's displeasure. Perhaps he can explain; I am sure I can't."

"He knows all about it," Callader growled. "There are more ways than one of telling a man you consider him a fool."

"Did I insinuate that?"

"Need you ask?" Callader retorted. "I am getting tired of it. If you intend to stay here, I'll thank you to be more civil in future. Upon my word, you moneyed men think you can do and say anything. There was a time when people in society—"

"Don't you think you are going too far?" Adela said gently. "I am certain Mr. Denne can have said and done nothing to offend you intentionally."

Callader lifted his heavy eyes to Adela's face.

"You are like all the rest of them. If a man has plenty of money he can do no wrong. As if money were everything. We are going too far in worship of the dollar. It is all money nowadays. When I was a boy, in my uncle's time, a man like Denne would have been only too glad—"

Denne laid a hand on the speaker's shoulder. His lips were rigidly set, and there was a steely glint in his eyes. Adela hoped he would not lose control of himself, and even the Duchess was uneasy at the turn things threatened to take. She addressed a sharp reproof to Callader, but this only added fuel to his wrath.

"I think I had better go," Denne said. "Callader imagines some grievance which will have vanished in the morning."

"Say I've been drinking!" Callader exclaimed.

"I should have a very poor regard for the truth if I said anything else," Denne replied.

He turned on his heel and walked quietly away, leaving Callader speechless with rage. He was breathing heavily, and gave out an aroma which resembled whisky more than it did eau de Cologne. The Duchess of Southampton turned her back upon Callader, deeply offended. Adela must stay and hear what Callader had to say. She had some idea, too, of what was passing through his mind. She knew that he was jealous of Denne, and that, perhaps, he had some cause for this feeling. Her heart was hard and bitter, and she protested silently that this tension could not possibly continue. That she had promised to marry such a man humiliated her. Nay, it appeared absolutely incredible that she was going deliberately to tie herself to Callader for the rest of her natural life. She ignored his strength and his manhood, and only dwelt on the innate brutality of the man who could so far forget himself as to insult a guest under his own roof.

"Why do you do these things?" she demanded. "Why do you behave in such a disgraceful fashion? This is not an assault-at-arms or a turn at a music-hall. I never felt so ashamed of myself before."

Callader dropped heavily into a chair and gazed moodily into the empty grate. He was in one of his sulky moods, and Adela knew what that meant. With a gesture of contempt, she turned and left him. From the billiard-room and card rooms beyond came the noise of chatter and laughter. No one appeared to miss Callader. None regretted his absence.

The American party departed presently with Samuel Burton at its head, and the Duchess palpably yawned as she made her way upstairs. The door leading from the hall to the terrace was still open. It was very tempting, and as Adela desired to be alone in the fresh air and the darkness so that she might be at peace to think over the near future, she went outside, and paced up and down the terrace. She could see through the open windows into the ball, and in the stillness of the night every word was audible. Denne had evidently returned, for she saw him standing in front of Callader, apparently to afford the latter a chance of explaining himself. Denne's expression was hard and cold, and he seemed to be taking quite another attitude from that he had adopted so long as the Duchess and Adela were present.

Though she knew it was improper to listen, Adela was fascinated, and seemed rooted to the spot. She could not but hear Donne, and saw Callader rise to his feet and stand before Denne in a threatening position.

"You mustn't do that," Denne said crisply and clearly. "You mustn't take that tone, now we are alone. If you wish me to leave, you have only got to say so, but be careful, please, how you make an enemy of me. I am amused to see you posing as the master of Callader. Why, I could ruin you by lifting my finger. If I only said a dozen words you would be expelled from your clubs, and stand in the dock, answering a criminal charge. You imagine I don't know what is going on here? Do you think I don't know where you get your money? You may hoodwink some, but your new scheme for amassing wealth suddenly isn't clever enough to deceive me. What would Miss Burton say if she only knew?"

"That's it," Callader said thickly, "that's it. I knew you were jealous. You haven't got much of an opinion of me, but I can see as far as most people. You are jealous, because the girl prefers me to you."

"Are you sure she does?" Denne asked quietly.

Adela felt the blood mounting into her cheeks. Something in the question set her tingling from head to foot, and it went home to Callader, too, for he clenched his fist and drew back his right arm menacingly. Denne merely smiled.

"Have a care," he urged, "have a care. Remember that I am your guest. Still, if you like to defy me, you can. But you won't do that, for the simple reason that you are afraid to. I know too much, and the consequences would be too serious. But whether we are to be enemies or not, one thing is certain, you shall not marry Miss Burton."

Once more the blood flamed into Adela's face, and she glanced through the window in expectation of a violent outburst from Callader. But none came. On the contrary, Callader flung himself back in his chair again, and laughed harshly.

CHAPTER XXXI

A COUNTER-PLOT

Adela withdrew to her room and dismissed her maid for the night. She longed to have what she called a 'good think.' She sat before her dressing-table looking vaguely at her reflection in the glass. Was this white-faced woman with the rings under her eyes the Adela Burton whom people professed to find so beautiful and fascinating? She smiled with self-pitying contempt. Was any woman in England more miserable than she? What a sham and fraud she was—moving amongst the salt of the earth, in the exclusive circles which were at once the envy and admiration of those beneath them!

From the outside it looked a veritable fairyland of beauty and wealth and pleasure that never palled. Her name for it was Whited Sepulchre.

Adela felt that, though she was surrounded by every luxury and comfort, she was little better than a criminal. She was tied to the wheel, and must go on to the bitter end, whatever that end might be. There was no snapping of the fetters, no prospect of freedom or peace or happiness in the future. She must marry Mark Callader, and then confess to him that she was only a pauper. On her part she must suffer him to the end of her days.

Yet there was comfort and consolation in the enigmatical remark Denne had addressed to her affianced husband. She had never analysed her feelings towards Douglas, although she knew he cared for her. He was a clean-living man of good report of whom any woman might be proud. If Denne had asked her to marry him, Adela would have done so, primarily for his money, but, at the same time, counting herself fortunate amongst women in that Denne was a fine personality apart from his wealth.

But why did he make that remark? It was made in no boasting spirit, but rather as an intimation of clear and undoubted fact by a strong man who knew his mind, and realised what he said. On the face of it, it seemed ridiculous, but Denne had weighed his words, and had spoken with a full sense of responsibility.

What did he mean by it? Why had he set out to accomplish this end? Why had he spoken so contemptuously to Callader, as if the latter were only a dishonest clerk detected in a petty theft? He had roundly accused Callader of being a thief. He had spoken of proofs which would infallibly lead to Callader's arrest if they were made public. Adela smiled bitterly; there was hardly a soul about who was honest and upright. Ah! but if it were practicable to release her from her promise to Callader? An intense longing to know the truth came over her, and she was impelled to see Denne and learn what this mystery was. It was not too late to go downstairs. She heard voices below as she stood on the wide landing. She heard the click of the billiard balls.

Descending very quietly, she paused at a turn of the wide staircase, for she saw at a lower stage Callader and Marner in intimate conversation.

The latter lay back in the depths of an armchair, his legs crossed, the tips of his long, slender fingers pressed together, and spoke in his cool, deliberate way. His delightfully clear enunciation enabled Adela to hear quite plainly. Doubtless he was under the impression that he was alone with Callader, and could not have known even a whisper carried in the resounding hall.

"This is a serious matter," he was saying, "My dear sir, I don't think you realise how serious it is. Do try to pay some sort of attention."

"This is the second time to-night," Callader said in his thick voice, "that I have been accused of—"

"The truth isn't always palatable," Marner replied. "And besides, it is no reproach to you. I have just been talking to a man who has come all the way from London on purpose to see me. He told me certain things which caused me a considerable amount of anxiety. I wonder if you ever met a man called Lestrine?"

"I know him," Callader muttered. "Italian, isn't he? One of the best judges of objects of art I have ever known, wonderfully clever in unearthing rare curios, especially those of historic interest which have been lost sight of."

"Such as the Saxon Cup?" Marner murmured.

"Eh, what? The Saxon Cup? Why, that belongs to us. I found it myself. But you know the history of the find."

"You were looking among a lot of old rubbish in a chest, and discovered the Cup. You showed it to me, and I pronounced it to be the genuine thing. It is the genuine thing beyond a doubt, but that is not exactly the point I want to arrive at. Let us suppose that you have an enemy, and that that enemy has acquired certain information which might land you into trouble. We'll say, still, for the sake of argument, that you have been disposing of the family treasures and pocketing the proceeds."

"Hush! hush!" Callader said hoarsely. "Suppose anybody should hear."

"There is no fear of that. We are alone, and I am speaking very quietly. To continue, suppose you have been doing this kind of thing for years. You could make a very handsome income."

"You know I have," Callader growled.

A pained expression came over Marner's face.

"My dear fellow, you wound me," he said softly. "I know nothing. How should I? We do business together, and when a man in your position brings anything to me to dispose of I will not insult him by asking him where he got them. I am merely putting a suppositious case."

"Go on, you old fox," Callader exclaimed. "Upon my word, as you sit there, the picture of respectability, I begin to wonder whether I am dreaming or not. I begin to doubt the evidence of my senses, and my knowledge that you are the greatest scamp of us all."

Marner sat perfectly unmoved. His pose was unaltered, save that he shook his head sorrowfully, and muttered that it was impossible for a man to do business, and indulge his taste for intoxicants at the same time.

"Humbug me if you like, Marner, I believe you are capable of humbugging yourself, too."

"Then we will resume our discussion," Marner went on in his even tones. "We will suppose that your enemy is in a good position, and commands unlimited money. He suspects what you are doing. He is naturally anxious to prove it, because he wants to get you in his power. Afterwards he will be able to dictate terms, to make you do just as he likes. He might even prevent your marriage. He has his own way of getting at the bottom of things. We will suppose that he sends a confidential messenger to the Continent to search for some unique art treasure. We will suppose that the messenger succeeds in procuring an article of rare historic interest, let us say, the Saxon Cup."

Callader started from his seat. He was betraying more than a sullen interest in the conversation.

"Do you mean to say," he demanded, "that Denne had the audacity—"

"My dear sir, I mention no names. But if this Cup were deposited among your family possessions in such a way that you were bound to find it, and it was eventually handed over to me to dispose of, your enemy would have proof positive that his suspicions were correct. Now do you see the situation? Now do you realise the position in which you will be placed."

"But," Callader protested, "he never told anybody where the Cup came from. In any case, you must have been a fool—"

"My dear sir, why be so impetuous? How could one possibly tell that this adroit conspiracy was on the tapis? How could one know that the Cup had actually been placed where it should he found, and that your enemy should stand quietly by, enjoying the comedy, when the Cup was submitted to certain American gentlemen for examination? If you ask why I didn't think of this before, I answer, how could I? But this is how the matter stands, and at the present moment your position, is not—"

"Our position, you mean,"

"Oh dear, no, your position. I beg to state that I had nothing to do with it. The Cup was handed to me by you for disposal. I propose to forget this conversation before I go to bed. If I had to give evidence in a court of law, I shall be unable to recall a single word of it. Make your mind easy on that point, Callader. But if trouble arises, and there is any—hem—litigation, you will have to conduct your case single-handed. On the other hand, if you care to be diplomatic, and place yourself entirely at my disposal, I think I can show you a way whereby you can turn the tables and make a good round sum of money at the same time. There is such a thing in this country as a law against conspiracy. That interference with the liberty of the subject is peculiarly obnoxious because it is little better than blackmail. You may be all your enemy takes you for, but this move of his is a criminal offence, and if you only had pluck enough—"

"No man ever questioned that," Callader interrupted. "Don't worry about my pluck; I can take care of that. How did you learn all this?"

"I learnt it from Paul Lestrine. He came down here to-night to see me. He must leave England at once; his doctors tell him he cannot possibly spend another winter here. He is a poisonous scoundrel and has behaved very badly to Denne, who has been a very good friend to him. But that is by the way. He wants ten thousand pounds, and I think I have shown him how to get it. You will have to pay the money, but that won't matter, since you'll get it back fifty-fold from Mr.—, I forget your enemy's name. Would you care to see Lestrine, and talk it over with him? He is in one of the alcoves in the garden, smoking cigarettes."

CHAPTER XXXII

Adela had no scruple in deciding to follow the matter up, whether she were guilty of eavesdropping or not. She felt a real concern for Denne; indeed, she had not hitherto realised how deeply she was interested in him. He had been a very good friend to her; with the exception of Samuel Burton, perhaps the best she had ever had. Moreover, he admired her, which naturally counted with her as a woman. It was gradually dawning upon her as not improbable that this alleged conspiracy on Denne's part was connected with his intention to prevent her marriage with Callader.

But if Denne had really done anything to compromise himself legally, he must be saved from the consequences of his rashness. Adela might be impecunious, and her position be desperate, but that was no reason why she should not help her friends. She might learn something to-night which might prove of inestimable value to Denne later.

She waited until the way was clear, then quietly stepped out on to the terrace. The night was warm and pleasant, and fairly dark for the time of the year. At the end of the terrace was an elaborate alcove with comfortable seats, and a table in the middle, and Adela made out Marner and his companion from the glowing tips of their cigars. Walking on the grass she was able to draw near without attracting notice, and presently went to the side of the alcove and looked through the latticed windows.

"Show a light," Callader said impatiently.

"Is it necessary?" Marner asked, in his smooth voice. "Surely it will be far safer to stay as we are."

"Nobody will see us. Who is likely to come at this time of night? I prefer to look at the man I am dealing with. I am not so confoundedly clever as you are. There's a switch somewhere behind you; turn it on."

A soft light glowed in the alcove from a pair of electric bulbs in the roof. It was not a powerful light, but it served to render the darkness outside all the more intense, and Adela could listen at the window in absolute safety. She saw Marner and Callader standing, and seated in one of the chairs was the sinister figure of Paul Lestrine. He gazed from one to the other with an inscrutable smile in his eyes. An astute observer would have known at once that he was the real master of the situation.

"I am glad to see you," Lestrine said in his quiet way. "I have been talking to Mr. Marner, and I see you, sir, have been talking to him also. You have a proposal to make—"

"I am not sure of that; it all depends upon circumstances. What do you want?"

But Lestrine refused to be drawn. He sat quietly smiling; he felt his power, and evidently he would know how to use it when the time came.

"I would like to hear you speak first. You see, I am a poor man. I have not the nerve I used to possess. Mr. Denne is not to be trifled with."

"What's the use of all this infernal diplomatic nonsense?" he exclaimed. "Why don't you come to the point? You are a rascal, Lestrine, and the sooner you realise it the better. You want me to make a bargain with you, and I am prepared to do so if it is worth my while. What is your figure?"

"Oh, gently, gently," he said. "My dear Callader, we shall never get to business if you begin in this fashion. There are preliminaries to settle. Of course, if you like me to withdraw, and leave you to discuss this matter with Lestrine, I shall be willing. It is no concern of mine."

"Oh, isn't it?" Callader rejoined in his brutal way. "You can't detach yourself like that, my friend. You may be devilish clever, but if I choose to speak, I can tell a few strange stories. Why not have this thing settled in a plain manner? We are three rascals, and it would be hard to say which is the worst. So far as I can see, Denne has some hold over me and Lestrine has come to show me a way out of the mess. To do that, and betray his master, he wants ten thousand pounds. If he can show me how he proposes to earn the money, I am willing to pay it. Now, go on, Lestrine, and no more beating about the bush."

"Well, it comes to this," Lestrine began, "I have to leave England almost at once. My doctor tells me I am threatened with consumption. It is imperative, he says, that I should try a warmer climate. I must not stay in England later than September. That is unfortunate, because I have many projects on hand, for, after all, there is no country like this for the making of money."

"You must have made a great deal," Callader observed.

"Oh, I have. But, then, you see, I have the sanguine temperament. I cannot resist a speculation. Therefore, directly the money comes to me, it melts away like snow. At the present time I have practically nothing—nothing but a great scheme which I propose to keep to myself. For that scheme I need at least ten thousand pounds. With so much money I can go to the South, and work there what you call it—like a mole in the ground. It will be for you, Mr. Callader, to give me this money. It is not very much I ask."

"A mere trifle!" Callader sneered. "And how are you going to earn it? That's all I want to know?"

"I would earn it this week," he said. "I would prevent you from being ruined by Denne. Why he hates you I neither know nor care; it is no business of mine. I cannot tell whether he is right when he charges you with breach of trust in selling the family pictures and other treasures. I do not even say that such is the case, but Denne thinks so, though he does not honor me by taking me into his confidence. But such are his suspicions, or he would not have instructed me to purchase a Cup we know of, and hide it at Callader, where you would be certain to find it. Am I not correct? Was not something of the sort discovered? Was it not shown to-night to certain guests of yours in Denne's presence? You need not answer the question. You see, if Denne follows this up, if he makes it public property, there are many awkward questions—"

"Yes, yes," Callader exclaimed, "but get on."

"I am nearing my point. I can show you, I think, how to turn the tables upon Denne. We will suppose that you and Mr. Marner take me by surprise, and force a confession out of me. We will go further, and assume that I sign the confession. I need not elaborate it. I have only to tell the plain, unvarnished truth, and you have in your hands a weapon wherewith you can stab Denne to the heart. Armed with such a document, you could go to the nearest magistrate, and apply for a warrant for Denne's arrest. It will make a pretty story, won't it? You have facts enough to secure a conviction, and if the defence accuse you of illegally selling the family treasures the monstrous charge will be laughed out of the Court; nobody would believe it. You see, no one's interest would be jeopardised; who cares whether the accusation were true or not. And as to the Saxon Cup, I will give you the name of the Castle where it came from, and prove that I bought it on behalf of Mr. Denne. Now do you begin to see?"

"To a certain extent," Callader said after a long pause. "But there is one weak spot in your scheme. When you come to give evidence and are cross-examined—"

"Ah! that is the point. I will not be here. I shall let it be assumed that the confession was forced out of me, and that I signed it to save my own skin. When the police come to look for me I shall have vanished, and the authorities will search Europe for me in vain. Then, behold, you will have everything your own way; you will have evidence which nobody can refuse, and be able to do with Denne as you please. You cannot deprive him of his millions, but you can ostracise him, and cause him to be shunned by all who know him. Why, if you like you can go to him with this paper in your hand, and compel him to buy it from you at your own price. Of course, a gentleman in your position would not do that sort of thing."

"Never mind that," he said, "that is no concern of yours. The question is, when will you sign this paper, and when do you want the money. But if you play me false—"

"How can I play you false?" he asked. "When this confession is signed, I am in your hands. If I stay in England, and proceedings are taken, I shall be arrested at the same time as Denne is. Besides, I want this money, for I must get away as soon as possible. I will come to-morrow night, and sign anything you like to put down on paper."

"Better wait till Saturday," he said. "If you will come then about the same time, your money shall be ready."

CHAPTER XXXIII

LIFE'S FITFUL FEVER

After the little group of conspirators had broken up, Adela retreated to her room, locked the door, and sat down to think the matter out. She had a fair notion of their plot, and her duty gradually became clear. Of course, she never supposed that Denne was actuated by any criminal motive when he tried to get Callader into his power. Beyond all doubt, his suspicions about him were correct. Mark had taken advantage of his position to remove some of the finest pictures and treasures from the Castle, and replace them with copies. Moving in the set she did, Adela was well aware that Callader's lavish expenditure had formed the subject of much idle gossip. She began to see where this money had come from.

But why was Denne so interested? Why had he taken these enormous pains, and incurred this great expense simply to prove that Callader was a thief? Although she was alone, Adela felt her features suffused with a glow of pleasurable warmth.

But this was by the way; Denne was in imminent danger, and he must be warned. It was possible, as Lestrine had hinted, that Callader might not go so far as to take proceedings. He was much more likely to use Lestrine's confession to extract a prodigious sum of money from Denne. Still, it was never safe to take anything for granted in dealing with a man like Callader, whose lust for revenge might outweigh his lust for money, in which case in the inevitable exposure Denne's character would be shattered. Those who knew the inner history of the case might understand. Women would instinctively divine there was something to be said in Denne's justification. But the world was not made up of women, and if this thing were made public, Denne would be socially ruined. She would acquaint him with this danger early next day.

With this thought in her mind, Adela retired to bed, but the hours passed in fitful sleep, and unpleasant dreams. She woke finally with a racking headache, and lassitude in all her limbs. It was impossible to lift her head from the pillow and drink the cup of tea which a sympathetic maid brought her. She lay half-asleep, half-awake, far into the afternoon, rebelling at her helplessness, and deploring that fortune should have deserted her at this crisis.

She contrived to get downstairs about teatime, grateful to find that the house party had gone racing. They returned after five, excited and exuberant, over another good day in the ring. Callader alone was sullen and savage. He crossed over to her side, and asked her graciously enough how she felt, but a certain hard suspiciousness in his manner gave her to understand that he did not believe that there was much the matter with her.

"Have you had a good day?" she asked languidly.

"Infernally bad! Everybody has made money but me. The luck of those people! They plunged on anything that turned up, and simply could not lose, while I, with some of the best information I have had for years, am thousands out on the day's racing."

All this was vouchsafed in Callader's worst style. Of course, Adela said something sympathetic, but it was obvious that she was not seriously interested. She looked about her to see Denne, but he had not put in an appearance. Callader detected the glance, and divined its meaning.

"You needn't worry about Denne," he said; "he has gone, and, so far as I am concerned, I much prefer his room to his company. He said he had a telegram this afternoon, and went straight from the course to the station. I am sorry to disappoint you, but you have almost seen the last of Denne."

"What do you mean?" Adela asked.

"Oh, wait and see," he said, "some men, you know, go up like a rocket, and come down like a stick, and Denne is one of them. How many capitalists have you known come into Society, cut a dash, and then vanish to avoid trouble. Not that one minds that sort of thing, because many of these fellows are interesting, and for that reason I was disposed to take up Denne for a time. The airs that fellow used to give himself! He talked to me yesterday as if I had been an under-servant in my own house. However, he won't trouble us any more. Should you see him, you can tell him that he is not wanted. Do you understand?"

"I cannot do what you want," she said. "Strange as it may seem, I like Mr. Denne."

"Like him!" Callader sneered. "Is that all? Say you prefer him to me, and have done with it."

"Is there any need?" Adela asked. "Would not any woman in her senses prefer Mr. Denne to you? I am too ill to carry on a discussion like this, but you force me to speak plainly. I thought we had come to some sort of arrangement. You have done me the honor of asking me to be your wife, and I have, well, I have acquiesced. It would be sheer hypocrisy to speak in any warmer terms, but it was quite understood that we are not to interfere with each other's affairs. You can go your own way, and you will hear no word from me about your friends, but I will brook no interference with mine. Mr. Denne is a friend of mine, and likely to remain so. He is a gentleman, and it is refreshing to talk to him after meeting the brainless men one sees in what, for a better word, we call Society."

"Make the most of your opportunities; I can take Denne in my hand and crush him like an eggshell. I can throw him into gaol, and if he comes near me, I'll do so. There are other means of getting even with that fellow, but there are times when revenge is far sweeter than mere—"

Callader paused, and caught his lip between his teeth. Adela knew exactly what he was going to say, and the word had passed her lips before she was conscious of speaking it.

"Than mere money," she said.

She regretted the speech the next moment, for there came into Callader's eyes a look that was positively murderous.

"What do you know?" he asked hoarsely.

"Oh, nothing," Adela replied. "There are only two things you care about, and money is the other one."

As she stood there watching Burton a fresh idea struck her. Why not take him into her confidence? Why not let him know what had happened? He was far cleverer than she and far better versed in the ways of the world.

"I must speak to you," the girl whispered. "Something very unexpected has happened—in connection with Callader and Mr. Denne. I can't tell you here. Can you invent an excuse for coming over later in the evening?"

"Is it so very pressing?" Burton asked.

Adela nodded emphatically. Suddenly the pleasant smile left Burton's face, which turned a strange unearthly grey. He pressed his hand to his head, then drew a handkerchief from his pocket, and placed it to his lips. How it came to pass, Adela could not tell; it was all a kind of misty dream, a horrible minute or two of suspense, and then Burton lay on the floor, an inert heap of brown and grey and white, a thin red stream trickling from his lips.

"He's dying," Adela cried; "dying."

CHAPTER XXXIV

STRESS OF CIRCUMSTANCES

For the first time in her life Adela stood face to face with death. Everything had hitherto been made smooth for her, so that the sudden tragedy came upon her with a peculiar and unexpected horror. She did not need anyone to tell her that this was the end of poor Samuel Burton. She saw it in the ashen pallor of his face, in the twitching lips, and the thin red streak trickling down the old man's shirt front.

With it all she was cool and collected, and she had the curious sensation of having expected the catastrophe. The contrast between this dying man and his luxurious surroundings was appalling. His race was run, and not all the wealth of Croesus could save him or prolong even by a few short hours that wasted life. It did not need the authority of a doctor to pronounce that nothing could be done, though this evidence was speedily forthcoming. Most of the guests had vanished by the time that Burton was carried upstairs, and laid upon a bed. He was still breathing faintly, but no hope was held out that he would ever regain consciousness. "It will be over in a few minutes," Adela heard the doctor say to the Duchess of Southampton, and a blinding rush of tears filled her eyes as she heard the verdict.

She was surprised to see that her companion, too, was softly weeping. It might not be prudent to inquire too closely into the past of Samuel Burton but she had been Adela's friend, and she would have been less than human had his passing not greatly affected her. She began to comprehend that he had entertained for her a truly genuine affection. No father could have been more fondly extravagant, no parent could have lavished more upon an only child.

"I don't know what to say," her grace remarked. "This must be a great shock for you, my child."

"It is very kind of you to come to me," Adela replied. "Positively you are the only one who has thought of me. I suppose most of Mark's guests look upon this as an intolerable nuisance."

"I am afraid they do, my dear, and, I daresay, you are wondering why I should feel it so much, I will tell you a secret, Adela. But, tell me, first, do you know anything about Mr. Burton's past life? Did he ever tell you that his was an assumed name?"

"I know nothing," Adela answered. "In fact, until quite lately I was more or less a mystery myself. I had not the faintest idea who my benefactor was, all my money being paid to me through a firm of solicitors, whose sole reply when I pressed for information respecting my adopted father was that I should know everything in due course. Then Mr. Burton came back from America, and told me something about myself and my circumstances. But who he was or where he came from, I haven't the remotest notion. He knew me as a child, and it was his whim to bring me up in the lap of luxury. I understand my mother was a woman about whom the less said the better. I am telling you these things because I know you are different from the rest of the people here. There come times when woman craves for sympathy, and this is to me one of them. People look upon me as the most fortunate of girls, and all envy me, but there isn't a maid in the Castle I wouldn't change places with. But we don't want to talk about that—at least not just yet. May I ask whether you know anything?"

"About what?"

"My benefactor?" Adela said.

"You have been candid with me," she said at length, "and I shall be equally candid with you. I suppose I must have known him for at least forty years, but when we were young people he was not Samuel Burton but Samuel Mostyn. He was a son of the late Marquis of Castlestray, and it is no scandal to say that there never breathed a man who caused his family such black and bitter trouble. He was a handsome, clever boy, and had a frank, open, fascinating face, which made him a general favorite. I know there are some who say you can always tell a degenerate by certain signs, but don't you believe it, my dear. Never was a man yet who looked less like the rascal type than Sam Mostyn. He could look upon you straight in the face, so that you believed every word he said, and yet through and through he was a selfish, heartless, unfeeling wretch. I was foolish enough to be very fond of him; even after I had found out I cared for him just the same, and but for a fortunate chance he might have broken my heart as he did scores of others. He robbed his father, narrowly escaped prosecution several times, and was turned out of the army for disgraceful practices, and even then women would have been glad to follow him to the end of the world. Though I got over my trouble in time I never cared for any other man. When I met him the other night I recognised him at once. I ought to have bidden him leave or exposed him. I ought, well, I didn't. Because, though people say I am masculine, and strong-headed, I am only a woman, and the recollection of old days came back to me, and I did nothing. Besides, one is always ready to find an excuse for people one is fond of, and I was glad to discover that Samuel had a weak spot, and that he was sincerely fond of you. He told me all about that, and several things besides. Now, what are you going to do? You will be a rich girl—"

"No," Adela said quietly. "I shall not lave a penny. I only knew that quite recently. Burton was not a millionaire, and made his money by methods which I'd better not discuss. He told me that if anything happened to him I should have to look after myself in future. In point of fact, Duchess, I am deeply in debt."

"I am glad to find you so frank," she said. "I had more than a hint of this. Our poor dead friend behaved well according to his lights, but he did not understand the cruel position he placed you in. You know what people will say. There is Callader, to begin with."

"I am glad you mentioned him," she whispered. "For the moment I had forgotten. Now you know what I am—shall I say a penniless adventurer imposing on society? It is not my fault, but the fact remains. When Mr. Burton came to me he was flying from the police. What he had done I do not know, but he was in desperate circumstances, and to a great extent had to thank Mr. Callader for his perilous position. Mark is still under the impression that my benefactor was a millionaire, and still believes that if he doesn't behave himself he may lose the chance of spending my fortune. On the other hand, I am certain that Mr. Burton knew something seriously to Mark's discredit. He told me that he did not mind my marrying him because he could enable me to keep him in due order. What that meant I never learned, and I don't suppose I ever shall know now!"

"I think you will," the Duchess said quietly. "Samuel took me into his confidence, and I shall be able presently to examine his papers. But something is troubling you, besides fear of Callader. Tell me what it is. I will be your friend if I can."

Adela told her story fully and fairly, setting down nought in malice, and extenuating nothing. She did not spare herself, and every detail of any consequence was related. She spoke freely of the enmity between Denne and Callader, and how the former had declared that she should never be Mark's wife, and gave a particular account of the fateful meeting in the alcove at the end of the terrace. Nor could she complain that she lacked a sympathetic hearer.

"I am glad you have told me this," the Duchess observed at the close. "What an extraordinary story! What will you do? How can you protect Mr. Denne from the consequences of his own folly? It is incredible that so shrewd a man should have so far forgotten himself. Surely, he might have learnt in some other way, whether or not Callader was selling the family treasures. But when men are in love they do extraordinary things."

"What do you mean by that?" Adela faltered.

"Oh, my dear child, the thing is plain. Douglas Denne has fallen in love with you. I suppose he didn't realise it till your engagement to Callader was announced, and then he deemed it too late; but he loved you nevertheless. Probably he dreaded being married, not for himself, but his money, which was a very natural suspicion for a wealthy man like Denne. What I have seen of him I like amazingly. He is a visionary, too, and I know did not despair that some day a girl might love him for his own sake alone, as the novels say. No doubt he adopted his own method of getting a hold over Callader, but I can see that he stands in a serious position. Still, so long as Callader thinks you are a great heiress—"

"He must think so as long as may be," Adela said. "He must not know that I am a pauper, and that—"

Adela paused, conscious of an unusual expression in the face of her companion. Then she looked round and saw Callader standing behind her, with suspicion in his deep-set eyes.

CHAPTER XXXV

FOR HONOR'S SAKE

In many respects Adela had never had a high opinion of Callader's mental capacity. She believed he was dull and slow of comprehension, and she hoped that she had not done him any injustice, for a man of alert intellect would have no difficulty in piecing together her remarks. However, Callader's face did not indicate that he had gleaned much. He stood in his usual, heavy, sullen way, like a man who is uncertain of his welcome. Yet it was very necessary to discover how much he had heard. Adela put a question or two to him, but his replies gave her no help, and he strolled over to the fireplace and took a cigarette-case from his pocket.

"What are you going to do about this affair?" he asked.

"What can one do?" the Duchess retorted sharply. "We must bury the poor man decently. I suppose you didn't know his name wasn't Burton at all?"

"Oh, yes, I did," Callader said coolly. "His name was Samuel Mostyn. I met him years ago in New York. In fact, we did business together, and I don't mind admitting that I got the worst of the deal. I daresay it will hurt your feelings, Adela, but Samuel Mostyn, alias Burton, was one of the choicest scamps. That doesn't seem to count for much nowadays, and in this regard, I understand Burton was highly respectable."

As to-morrow would be Sunday she would have to leave for London that very evening. She must contrive to see Denne without further delay, and warn him of his impending fate.

It still wanted an hour or so to dinner-time, so that Adela had time to walk down to the village post office, and wire to a friend asking for a reply calling her to town at once. This hackneyed expedient had been utilised repeatedly, and was, in fact, the normal method resorted to for getting away from a house which might prove undesirable, and in the existing circumstances it served. At eight o'clock the reply came and Adela sent it up with a few pencilled words to Callader's dressing-room. A quarter of an hour later she was hurrying across country in a motor-car to catch the London express at a Junction some twenty miles away. It was broad daylight by the time she arrived in town. She went straight to her flat and lay-down on her bed as she was, and slept the sleep of utter exhaustion. She woke at one o'clock, and refreshed herself with a bath. Then she immediately began her search for Denne. It would not be altogether easy, she knew, for he was sure to be out of town for the weekend. Still, a telephone was available, and by four Adela discovered that he was spending the time with bachelor friends up the river. This was a cause of annoyance in itself, but Adela determined that it should not stand in her way. The cottage by the river could be reached within an hour's run from town, and after a hasty dinner at seven Adela set out on her uncongenial errand.

She cared little or nothing what might happen. It made no difference to her what her chauffeur thought. It was possible, however, that she might steal this interview with Denne without anybody being the wiser. She left her car in the town, and walked towards the cottage. She had already written a letter, and loitered in the road for a minute or two, waiting for a probable messenger.

He came presently in the guise of the human boy, whistling blithely to himself as he walked along. Adela placed the note and a shilling in his hand.

"The shilling is for you, if you earn it," she said. "You are to go up to that cottage and ask for Mr. Denne. You must put the note into his own hands, and he will give you a message, 'Yes' or 'No.' When you come back to me, I will give you this shilling and another one as well. Do you understand?"

The boy nodded and winked slowly. He was acquainting Adela with the fact that he quite appreciated the situation. She waited eagerly for his return, conscious of a strange trembling nervousness, the like of which she had never experienced before. Usually she was ready enough to laugh at the silly affectations of the woman of her set which were given to prattle of their nerves, but she was beginning to know what they meant. The boy returned with a grin of satisfaction on his face.

"I saw the gentleman," he said. "He is coming now."

"Why this mystery?" he smiled. "I thought you were still at Callader Castle. But something has happened. I never saw you so pale before. What is wrong?"

"Let us go somewhere where we can talk a little," she said. "What must you think of my coming all this way, and forcing myself upon you in this fashion? What will your friends say?"

"I don't think we need trouble about them," Denne assured her. "Your note was brought to me as I was dressing. The other men were in their rooms. If we go through this little gate into the grounds we shall be safe in the rose garden for half an hour. You mean to say you came here to see me all alone?"

"I was bound to. I could not possibly tell anybody else. I made an excuse to leave the Castle. They think I am spending Sunday with a friend who is ill. I drove here in my car and left my man in the village."

"Now," he said, as he led the way to a seat. "No one is likely to interrupt us. Tell me why you took all this trouble for the sake of a humble person like myself. You must have had a great deal of worry during the last few days. So your fairy godfather turns out to be Lord Samuel Mostyn."

"Did you know that?" Adela asked.

"Well, I had some sort of idea," Denne admitted.

"We can come to that presently," Adela went on. "There are many questions I want to ask you when you have heard the reason of my errand. I have been finding out strange things lately, and now the strangest of all is the knowledge I have obtained about the history of the Saxon Cup."

"What do you know about that?" he asked.

"I think I may say I know everything," Adela answered. "Paul Lestrine obtained it for you in Germany. For reasons best known to yourself, you contrived that the Saxon Cup should be deposited at Callader Castle where Mark Callader found it, and naturally came to the conclusion that it formed part of the family heirlooms. But why did you put it there? How did you discover Mark was selling paintings and works of art, and replacing them with copies?"

"Pardon me," he said. "Let me ask you a question before I answer yours. How did you learn that I had any hand in this matter? Where did you hear the name of Paul Lestrine? I am certain he never told you he was engaged in this transaction. I beg you to be candid—"

"Have I shown any inclination to be otherwise?" She demanded. "Do you suppose that I have taken this risk and compromised myself from any personal motive? Oh, can't you see that I am only too anxious to save you from the consequences of your stupendous rashness. I know that Lestrine is mixed up in this affair because I overheard him tell Callader and Marner so. He has betrayed your interests and sold you for money. If you will only listen I will tell you everything."

"I spoke in haste," Denne answered at once, "and shall be only too grateful to hear your story."

CHAPTER XXXVI

SO VERY HUMAN

Resolutely, Adela put aside all sense of conventionality. It fell from her shoulders like a disused garment. She was just a woman inspired with the hope of saving this man from what she believed to be dire and imminent peril. She had already gone a long way to rescue him, and had done so at great trouble and risk to herself, for she had absolutely nothing to gain. But never had she been more thoroughly in earnest before.

No longer did she blind herself to the truth. She knew she was not animated by sentiments of ordinary friendship, but was actuated by deep and genuine love for Douglas Denne. Curiously, too, now she seemed to have loved him from the first. He had, indeed, become more or less reconciled to the fact that she was the promised wife of Mark Callader, but she knew now that nothing would induce her to keep her word. What were Denne's feelings to her she knew not, for of actual direct avowal of anything approaching to love, not a syllable had crossed his lips. But if she lost Callader without winning Denne, that did not concern her. She would work for her daily bread rather than marry Mark.

Nevertheless, subtle instinct informed her that Denne cared for her as much as she cared for him. He had not told her so in as many words, but she cherished the look he had cast upon her when he met her to-night, when her visit could not possibly have been expected. A similar train of thought and hope doubtless passed through Denne's mind. He could not gaze into her white, pure face, and doubt her loyalty, and the generous impulse which had prompted her to do this deed. He had always admired her daintiness and beauty, but these carried another charm now—the charm of sincerity and naturalness, and a deep abiding affection. Adela did not realise how far she had acknowledged the natural sway of her heart. She did not know that she was looking at Denne as a mother might regard a child on the brink of terrible danger. As Denne grasped all this, he recollected that Philip Vanstone had never wavered in his declaration she was a woman worth the saving. In spite of his danger, in spite of the knowledge that he had done a rash thing, he was conscious of a buoyancy of spirits to which for many years he had been a stranger. He had found what he had been looking for with an ardor which he did not realise till this moment.

But this was not the time to speak. He could not take the shrinking girl in his arms, and cover her face with kisses. His natural innate delicacy prevented him from so theatrical an issue.

"It was more than good of you to come," Denne said. "Now let us discuss this affair from a business point of view. You say that Paul Lestrine has betrayed me?"

"You may take that for granted," Adela replied. "I heard the whole conversation. It began, in the first place, between Callader and Marner. It was rather a shock to me in a way, because I had always regarded Mr. Marner as a great man in every sense of the word. I can hardly bring myself to believe that he is little better than a felon."

"Oh, he is certainly all that," Denne said with a dry smile, "and an exceedingly clever one. I have known this for some time. There is a gang of expert thieves who deal exclusively in valuable works of art. They have been carrying on operations for years. The prime movers keep themselves in the background, and the most brilliant of them all is Felix Marner. But his career is at an end. That business of the Saxon Cup will wreck him. The presiding spirit of the combine lives in Paris. He has posed for a long time as a man of great wealth and a prominent philanthropist. I heard by telephone this afternoon that he had been arrested and thousands of pounds worth of missing pictures discovered in his house. Mark my words, Marner will be missing in a day or two. This will be a fine scandal for the papers to exploit. So you see, we need not worry ourselves about Marner. In any case, I know he will take care to obliterate himself, so far as any charge against me is concerned. But please go on, I have interrupted you."

"What was I saying?" Adela asked. "Oh, I remember. Mark Callader and Mr. Marner were talking in the hall, and I listened. I ought not to have done so, but they were talking about you, Douglas, and I listened. Then I heard the whole scheme. Lestrine had come down to Callader to see Mr. Marner, and had offered, for a large sum of money, to sign a confession of the part he had played in the matter. Callader was very much upset at first; he has no resourcefulness and evidently thought he was done. Then Mr. Marner pointed out a way by which he could blackmail you—I think blackmail is the proper word. They decided that with Listerine's signed confession they could apply for a warrant against you on the ground of conspiracy."

"So they could," Denne said coolly. "There is not the slightest doubt about that. I suppose the idea was to offer to stay proceedings for a hundred thousand pounds. Am I not right?"

"That was it exactly. Then they went out into the garden and had an interview with Paul Lestrine, and I followed. I am not ashamed to say that I heard every word. It appears that Lestrine is suffering from consumption, must leave England at once, and wants money very badly."

"He ought not," Denne muttered. "Goodness knows, I have paid him well. But he has the gambler's temperament. I suppose he has lost it all in play."

"So he said," Adela went on. "He would sign this confession for ten thousand pounds. No doubt he has had the money by this time, because the appointment was for last night. Lestrine's idea was to disappear, and never be heard of again. Now, you know why I came to warn you of this terrible danger. Can you do anything to save yourself?"

Adela looked up imploringly into Denne's face as she spoke, laid a trembling hand on his arm. She had never been so earnest or so moved in her life. In Denne's glance there was a certain something that comforted her, and thrilled her with elation at the same time. She had naturally expected to see some change, some sign of annoyance or alarm on his part; but if he felt this, there was not the slightest trace of it in his features.

"I shall know how to thank you presently," he said, "for the moment, I don't feel particularly alarmed. I daresay I should have managed to circumvent Callader in any case, and yet I might have gone to work in a better fashion, I think. It was a dangerous, not to say stupid, thing to do. But we all make mistakes at times, especially when we allow our hearts to rule our heads."

"Did you do that?" Adela asked innocently.

"Why, of course I did," Denne smiled. "You don't suppose I should have been guilty of such rashness otherwise. Will you believe me if I tell you that I embarked upon this enterprise solely for your sake?"

"I believe you if you say so," Adela murmured.

"And now let me tell you something. All my life I have been a lonely man, and not the less so because so many people sought my friendship. When I was poor and struggling I was comparatively happy, because the men I knew best then valued me because I was only Douglas Denne. But my uphill fight lasted long enough that real friends became extremely rare. Ah! a true friend is the gift of God. When I made my fortune, and came to London, I had learnt to discriminate between the gold and dross at a glance. I daresay I should have been a good deal happier had I not been somewhat of a poet as well as a capitalist, for I had the artistic temperament, which is not an unmixed blessing. You would be surprised to learn what dreams I have had and how I have tried to reach the ideal existence. Nobody ever heard me talk like this before, but you will know later why I am telling you these things. You see, I was looking for a woman who would marry me without a thought for my money. I had discussed the matter over and over again with Philip Vanstone, who is the only man in whom I have fully confided, and when I asked him to name such a woman, he did not hesitate for a moment, but told me who she was. Can you guess?"

Adela shook her head.

"Do I know her?"

"Oh, yes, you know her well. When I heard the name, I was amazed. One has to make an allowance for poets, but Vanstone stuck to his point. He begged me to see more of this woman, and study her for myself. I did so, and, to my great amazement, found that Vanstone was right. He has a far better insight into woman's nature than I have. The astounding part of the whole business was this: that the girl in question appeared to be one of the most frivolous of women. As the acknowledged leader of one of the smart sets, there was no end to her extravagance and folly. Studying her, I mixed much in her set, until a habit was formed, and became part and parcel of myself. What originated as a sort of psychological recreation grew to be the outstanding occupation of my life. Gradually I began to see that this woman, like most of us, was but the slave of her environment, for only one man or woman in a million can get away from his or her surroundings. Sometimes Fortune is kind, and takes matters into her own hands; sometimes what appears to be the greatest blow turns out to be the direct intervention of Providence. But why do you look at me with that puzzled expression? Can't you guess whom I am talking about? Surely it is quite obvious?"

A wave of color rushed over Adela's face. She had followed Denne with rapt attention, and until this moment his parable had puzzled her. Now she was beginning to understand, to see how closely his description fitted her. She might have been offended; indeed, his outspoken candor had offered every excuse, but she was not hurt at all. She saw that he was paying her the highest compliment in his power, that he recognised in her something which was worth the winning. It had been worth his while to interest himself in her. It had been worth his while to rescue her from a future into which she was venturing deliberately and with open eyes.

"Oh," she stammered, "if you really mean—"

She paused and started back. Then someone in the distance was heard calling Denne, and the smile faded from his face.

"You had better go," he said; "I will see you to-morrow."

CHAPTER XXXVII

"OUTRAGEOUS FORTUNE"

"What was spoken in whispers gathered volume as it was circulated, and in a few days everybody knew the story of the man who had chosen to call himself Samuel Burton. The older generation in society recollected him perfectly well; and regaled younger men with stories of his hot youth, and of the black circumstances in which he left the army. He had made his money in his lifetime in some dark and mysterious manner known to himself, and had maintained his adopted daughter in every luxury; but the fact that he had left her entirely penniless was an open secret now. Men speculated in their idle, gossiping way on what Adela would do, and laughed over Mark Callader's disappointment. As for Adela, no one seemed to care a pin. Others as fortunately situated as herself had gone under, and society had forgotten them in a week.

But certain people were not in the least likely to forget the unfortunate girl. She figured largely in the books of many tradesmen and shopkeepers in the West End, who took alarm at once. Though it was barely luncheon time, Adela already felt the sting of it. Had she opened the many demands for instant payment that every post had brought she might have been at least forewarned. She had been annoyed by seedy-looking men who had thrust documents upon her in the streets, but these she had thrown aside contemptuously. When she came down late to lunch she had to face one harsh aspect of her altered circumstances. For a man was waiting to see her who would take no denial. He was civil enough, but his manner was so persistent that she felt her heart turn cold within her as she asked his business.

"Well, miss," the man began. "You see, it is quite a matter of business. I don't suppose you will understand what I mean, but I am here on behalf of Maurice and Co., of Hendon-street. It is just over eleven hundred pounds altogether."

"But I will send you a cheque," Adela said haughtily.

"Bless you, miss, a cheque won't do. I am sent here by the sheriff. But I shall be very glad to take cash, hard cash. I won't trouble you for a moment after that. I am responsible to the sheriff; I am what is called a sheriff's officer, if you know what I mean."

Adela was beginning to understand; she had heard of such things before; indeed, she recollected seeing a play once which was called the 'Man in Possession.' Gradually it dawned upon her that this grimy person would stay on her premises till the debt was paid. The indignity of it struck her like a blow, and she crossed over to the bell, and rang it passionately. She rang it again and again, but nobody replied.

"I expect they've gone," the man in possession said meekly. "They probably guessed my business. I've been in swell houses before, and the servants nearly always vanish like this."

Adela stood with her hand on the electric bell. She could hear it trilling away in the distance, but there was no response. The tears rushed into her eyes, but she managed to hold them back. She was at the mercy of the world; she had not a friend to hold out a helping hand.

"But what can I do?" she implored. She had lost all her haughty manner. "Must you stay here till the money is actually paid. Can't you take my word?"

The man shook his head resolutely.

"More'n my place is worth to leave you, miss," he said. "You'll have a week or so to find the money."

"And if I don't find it?"

"Then, in that case, you'll be sold up. You'll excuse me for saying it, miss, but you was very foolish to let things go so far. When you had the writ you ought to have gone to your solicitor, and he would have gained time for you."

Adela sighed hopelessly; she was not sure she knew what the man was talking about, and wondered what a writ was. Was it one of those papers which had been thrust upon her in the street? Yes, that must have been it. As she stood grappling with her perplexity she heard the front-door bell ringing almost incessantly. No doubt this was one of her frivolous friends come to find out how the land lay. With her lip between her teeth Adela walked into the hall and flung open the door. Despite her anxiety she could not restrain a smile as she beheld the diminutive figure of Max Cordy. He was beautifully attired in a grey frock suit. His boots were glossy with varnish, and he took off an elegant silk hat with a demonstrative flourish.

"I hope I have got here in time, miss," he said. "Yes, I know all about it. This is just the thing that Mr. Burton was afraid of. Now, you let me come inside, and I'll soon get rid of your unwelcome visitor. Leave him to me, and if any questions are asked, refer to me, for I am your solicitor."

Adela was inclined to let everything pass, and wondered whether she would wake up presently to find this an uneasy dream. She stood aside for Cordy to precede her. He walked into the dining-room and laid his hat upon the table.

"Now, my man," he said in a tone of ineffable patronage, "I am Miss Burton's solicitor. I only heard of this business this morning. Of course, it isn't your fault. The only question is, how much?"

The man in possession quoted his previous figures with unction, but was not in the least sanguine that the money would be forthcoming. However, in the most businesslike way Cordy placed his hand in his breast pocket, and produced a parcel of notes. These he counted into the hands of the bailiff along with a sovereign or two and some odd shillings. Almost before Adela knew what had happened her visitor had departed.

"But you ought not to have done this," she protested.

"Oh, it isn't my money," Cordy said. "It belonged to Mr. Burton. There is a bit more where it came from, but not much. You see, there would have been a good deal if the governor had not died. I've lost the best friend I ever had."

"You had known him long?"

"Oh, dear, yes. I have been with him all over the world. I have known him ever since I was a boy. You need not smile, miss, I'm a lot older than you think. I know I look young. Why, put me in an Eton suit and I would pass for fourteen. That is where I was so useful to the poor old governor upon occasion. I could look so very innocent."

Adela asked no further questions. She had no wish to hear more of the seamy side of her benefactor's life, and indeed would be only too happy to come out of her artificial existence and go to some quiet spot where she would know peace and comfort. This little fellow meant well, but something about him grated on her horribly. Even his look of undisguised admiration filled her with disgust.

"You had better go," she said quietly. "I am most sincerely obliged to you, though I am afraid you have wasted your money. For there are others who will hunt me down like wolves. I daresay that's one at the door at this moment."

Cordy darted off to answer the ring, and returned with a woefully changed countenance, looking like a boy who has been detected in an unsuccessful raid upon an orchard. He was followed by a man who, in many respects, was the counterfeit of the person who had not long since departed. Max Cordy dropped into a chair and groaned aloud.

"Here's a pretty business," he exclaimed; "here's a pretty business. Oh! miss, why ever didn't you take someone into your confidence. I am afraid there is nothing for it but a trip to Holloway."

"I didn't know," Adela faltered, "but what does this mean? What does this man want? Surely, it can't be any worse than the last affair."

In the depths of his chair, Cordy writhed with anguish.

"You tell her," he said to the man. "It's your business, and I haven't the heart to do it."

"Well, you see, it's a Committal Order, miss," the intruder said hoarsely. "There is nothing to distrain upon here, and somebody else is already in your cottage at Maidenhead. It is about nine hundred pounds altogether. If you can't find the money, I am afraid I shall have to get you to come as far as Holloway Gaol with me."

It seemed almost incredible, something beyond the wildest dream. Yet the man was speaking quietly and rationally. Adela recollected that a similar thing had happened in the case of one of her own friends. It had been the theme of a spicy scandal at the time, and had afforded an outlet for many a frivolous jest. Adela was now conscious of the grim reality of such an experience. She shot a mute glance at Cordy, who tapped his breast-pocket, and shook his head despairingly. There was only one thing to be done, and every drain of pride in Adela's nature revolted against it. She crossed to her desk and hastily dashed off a note, which she handed to Cordy.

"Take that to Mr. Denne at once," she said. "You must find him. There is no immediate hurry for this? If I can get the money in an hour or two, I suppose you can wait?"

The bailiff had some of the milk of human kindness in his nature, for he acquiesced readily in the suggestion.

"Nothing I should wish for better, miss," he said civilly. "Nobody dislikes this kind of thing more than I do, but a man has to live. Only, I must remain here till your messenger comes back, and it will be my duty to see that you don't go out of my sight."

Adela murmured her thanks. She had fallen a long, long way since the morning. She had been bitterly annoyed and wounded to find that her servants had deserted her, but she was glad of it now. The fewer the people that witnessed her humiliation the better. She handed the note to Cordy, who took up his hat and vanished. The stranger, after a cautious glance round the room to see that there was only one exit, picked up a paper and walked out into the hall, intimating that he should prefer to sit there.

"That is very nice of you," Adela said. "I hope it won't be for long. I expect a friend who will cash a cheque for me."

The minutes crept on, the hour of lunch arrived, but there was no sign of Denne. The clock struck two, and yet he failed to put in an appearance. Then Adela's courage failed her, and she felt she was alone indeed.

CHAPTER XXXVIII

THE LOWEST DEPTH

There was no bitterness in Adela's heart. There very seldom is, even in the most pessimistic of us, when we have sounded the lowest depths of human misery. Disgrace and humiliation hung over her head, but she was past all sense of dismay, and felt that she would have to follow the bailiff wherever he chose to take her. With a calmness that surprised her, she contemplated the certainty of sleeping in gaol that night. She refused to believe that Denne had turned a deaf ear to her request. Probably her messenger could not find him; or he might have been engaged in some all engrossing business that could not possibly be delayed; or he might have been summoned to the Continent at short notice, as, she understood, was often the lot of capitalists. She had not struck the psychological moment, as one so often does in such circumstances.

Meanwhile the clock hands were moving towards the fatal hour. Never had time appeared to fly so quickly before. Adela could not recollect, even in the old days when she pursued pleasure with all the keenness and zest of youth, that time had slipped away as rapidly as it was passing now. She rose and went to the hall. There was no occasion to wait. Denne was not coming, and the sooner the business was over, the better.

"I fear my friend has been detained," Adela said. "I mustn't keep you any longer, I suppose."

The man declared that an extra half-hour would not make much difference to him, for which relief Adela thanked him, and withdrew to her bedroom, much disposed to end the matter there and then, and depart with the man. Whilst those thoughts occurred to her the front door of the flat opened, and her maid entered. She apologised, more or less incoherently, for her absence.

"It doesn't matter," Adela said wearily. "I shan't require you after this afternoon. I believed you had taken alarm and run away like the others. Why did you come back?"

The maid looked at her reproachfully.

"I daresay it is natural you should think so, miss, but I hope you don't suppose I am quite heartless. I had to go out after breakfast, and only learnt what had happened by accident. I am not going; nothing would induce me to leave you in your distress. Take a rest while I bring you a cup of tea."

The tears filled Adela's eyes with a rush. She was not so hard and cold as she thought she was. In her heart of hearts she was grateful for this kindness on the part of her maid, for whom, after all, she had never had much consideration. Well, it was good to find that some people could think of others besides themselves. Adela dropped weakly into a chair, overcome with a strange feeling of dizziness. She was trembling from head to foot, and wondered whether she was dreaming, or whether it was really Douglas Denne who was bending over her chair, and begging her to tell him what was the matter. It was Denne in the flesh, as Adela saw plainly when her head and sight cleared. There was a look on his face which gave her fresh hope and courage.

"My poor child," he said tenderly. "So it has actually gone as far as this? Why didn't you tell me? Why didn't you send for me before? You might have known that I should come at once. Your messenger has been looking for me everywhere, and only caught me by the merest chance at Charing Cross Station. I should have been on my way to Paris in another ten minutes."

Infinitely soothing was the warm caressing tone of Denne's voice. Adela lay back in her chair with a comfortable sense that the direction of affairs was being taken out of her hands—that she would be saved from an unspeakable humiliation. Now, she realised how acutely she had dreaded the possibility of the journey across London with the man outside. But full as she was of her own misery, she found time to think of Denne and his own personal position.

"I did not know what to do," she said with a faint smile; "I am not used to this sort of thing. I sent for you when I was in trouble, but I thought, perhaps, Mark had begun—"

"Callader has not allowed the grass to grow under his feet, but I have given him a counter-stroke that will give him something to think over before he takes the next step. You need not have any anxiety about me. And now, as to your own affairs; I got what I could out of your queer little messenger. I know something of Max's history. He is a graceless scamp, but is as devoted to your interests as he was to those of Mr. Burton. But, in the first place, let me persuade your visitor to depart. I called into my banker's and got some money as I came along, I hope he hasn't been rude?"

"On the contrary, in his own way, he has been very civil. But what have I done that you should be so kind to me?"

But Denne had vanished, and Adela heard the murmur of voices outside. By and by Douglas returned, and took a seat opposite to her. She beheld him through a mist of tears. Covering her face with her hands, she burst into a fit of passionate sobbing. The breakdown did not last long, but it seemed to ease her wonderfully. The pain had left her head, and the hard, cold feeling at her heart was gone. She dried her eyes, and a faint, unsteady smile flicked around her lips.

"You are very good to me," she said. "But I fear you have only postponed the evil day. It terrifies me to think how many more are in a position to treat me in the same way. I don't know whether you will believe me or not, but it is only during the last few hours that I have realised what a wretch I am. You need not shake your head, for it is quite true. I am just as dishonest as if I had forged a cheque, or picked a pocket. I have known for some time how I was situated, and yet I have gone on dealing with my tradesmen in a most heartless fashion. I will make over to them all I possess, and earn my own living after I have had a few weeks' rest. I am utterly worn out, but if you can think of any suggestion—"

"I have a plan," Denne replied. "You had better run down to your cottage at Maidenhead. I know there is bother there, too, but I will easily put that right, and then I will send my solicitor here to meet the claims against you. You do not care to be beholden to anyone, I know, but necessity is sometimes disagreeable. But what can you do. Somebody must help you, and, as you are aware, in the ultrasmart set to which we belong, it is no novelty for a rich man to assist a friend to whom he is attached. You must recollect scores of instances. Let me quote a few."

"You are laughing at me," Adela protested.

"Indeed, I am doing nothing of the sort. You must leave this in my hands, and, besides, it is only anticipating events. You see, if you were my wife, I should have to pay your debts, and if you were my wife, you would not take the slightest objection. I won't hear another word. What you have to do is to keep quiet, drink your tea, and not worry about anything."

Without further words, Denne walked out of the flat, and closed the door behind him. While Adela was trying vaguely to think matters out, there came a ring, and the Duchess of Southampton bustled in. She appeared to know everything that had happened.

"I don't want any explanation, child. I have had one already. Besides, I met Douglas outside, and he posted me up in the latest details. My dear, I was quite used to this kind of thing when I was a girl. My poor dear father lived in an atmosphere of County Court bailiffs and executions. He never found himself inside a debtor's prison, for the simple reason that he was a Peer, who in those days were mercifully exempt from such indignities. It is lucky for you that you have a friend like Denne to look after you. Why do you blush in that absurd way? The man is in love with you, and you are in love with him, and when Callader is out of the running, as he soon will be, you can marry him without further delay. Meanwhile, I will take you to Maidenhead to-morrow, and stay with you a couple of days. At any rate it will prevent the snobs from talking. That is one of the real advantages of being a duchess."

"You are all too good to me," Adela said. "Have you seen anything of Mark?"

"I met him at lunch to-day. He doesn't look particularly happy, though he knows that he is practically Marquis of Kempston. I forgot to tell you that I have been all through Burton's papers, and they are now in the hands of the Callader solicitors. There is not the slightest doubt that poor Samuel's story was true, but it needs confirmation. In a few days the public will know who is the new Marquis of Kempston, and how you have suddenly blossomed into the Lady Adela Callader. Mark doesn't know quite what to believe as to the stories about your benefactor's fortune. In his suspicious way he fancies he has been hoaxed. He was coming around to see you this afternoon, and have it out, but I told him some diplomatic lie about your being at Maidenhead, because I wanted to see you first. I don't think you will have any trouble with Callader. He will refuse to carry out his promise when he finds you are not an heiress."

"He will not have an opportunity," Adela said. "In no case could I marry Mark, and I am not in the least afraid of him for myself. It is what he is likely to do to Douglas Denne that troubles me. I have tried to work it out in my own mind, but I can't think. Every time I try to think my head gets all confused and muddled, and I shake like an aspen leaf. The feeling is coming over me now. Don't be alarmed. I shall be better in a minute or two. It is so unlike me to be miserable."

There was a look of anxiety on the Duchess's shrewd, kindly face as she glanced at Adela. The girl was lying back in her chair, with a white, set face, and a strange trembling in her limbs. The Duchess rose from her chair, and went into the kitchen where the maid was at tea.

"I want you to fetch Miss Burton's doctor at once. I am afraid she is ill."

Adela was still sitting in the same position when the doctor came in. He shook his head gravely.

"Nervous breakdown," he said. "Take her into the country immediately."

CHAPTER XXXIX

RESURRECTION

Adela sat up in bed, and gazed around her. The room was strange, and yet irritatingly familiar. She knew the bed and the hangings, recognised the wall decorations and the blinds. Surely those were some of her own things, but there was a spaciousness about the room which she had never noticed before. In the old days it had been absurdly crowded with luxurious and costly trifles, and as she took in the details, she felt how much more pleasing and more refined her surroundings were. Beyond doubt, she was in her own room in her cottage at Maidenhead.

How was she there and how long had she been ill? Gradually the memory of the recent past returned. It was all coming back to her now. The last thing she recollected was being seated in the dining-room of her flat, and she had a sort of hazy notion that the Duchess of Southampton had played some part in her sudden collapse. Was that a day or two ago, or was it a month? At any rate, the strange confusion of mind was gone, and she could see clearly and think freshly. A glorious sunshine filtered through the blinds, and the birds were calling in the gardens. But though her mind was collected and calm, and recollection was easy, she was aware of bodily weakness when she tried to rise. Then the movement as of one walking with extreme quietness attracted her, and the Duchess disclosed herself.

"So you are awake at last," the latter exclaimed. "You look all right. The doctor said you would be yourself again when once you recovered consciousness. It is only a matter of a day or two now. I shouldn't wonder if you are allowed to get up to-morrow."

"How long have I been here?" Adela asked.

"Nine or ten days. We brought you here on the afternoon that I came to see you at the flat. You came by car, and have been in a high fever. But, thank goodness! that is over. There is nothing whatever to worry about. All your affairs are settled, and we found a tenant, who took the flat just as it was. Many of the things here have been disposed of, too, but I think you will like the change that has been made. To be perfectly candid, my dear child, your taste was too florid; you had too many things here. We have left the pictures and most of the old furniture, but all the costly falderals and knicknacks have been removed, and one has room to move about, and breathe freely."

When Adela went downstairs next afternoon she was bound to admit that he Duchess was right. Everything looked refined and artistic, and yet severely simple. Nothing could interfere with or spoil the beauty of the garden. It was delightful to lie in an easy chair on the verandah, to breathe the fresh, pure air; and listen to the songs of the birds. There was, too, in Adela's heart an ease and thankfulness to which she had long been a stranger. She lay back in her chair, listening, while the Duchess told her all that had happened. The story was not long in the telling.

"There is little to vex you," the kindly old lady said. "In the first place, Mark Callader has had no difficulty in establishing his claim to the title. It is rough upon poor Guy, but he is young, and his tastes are healthy and simple, and he will get over his disappointment. There are a pile of letters waiting for you to read when you feel up to it, and one of them is in Mark Callader's handwriting. You will probably find that he has released you from your engagement. He wants to see you, but you had better postpone that till you are quite strong."

"And Mr. Denne," Adela asked, "what about him?"

"Douglas has been here repeatedly inquiring after you, and, as I have heard of no startling move on Callader's part, I suppose things are where they were. Denne can take care of himself, and will give Callader his quietus when the time comes. Now, no more questions; I'll fetch you a cup of tea, and if you behave yourself, I may allow you to sit up to dinner."

The next two or three days passed uneventfully, but pleasantly. Adela was gaining strength rapidly, and slept well and peacefully. All the restlessness and discontent had left her, and she was happy, without any longing for the old life, which she was beginning to regard with positive disgust. How false and artificial it all was! How foolish the constant craving for unwholesome excitement. What the future held for her she hardly knew, and for the present scarcely cared. She would probably have to earn her own living, but that she was bent upon doing. She was enjoying the tranquility that had usurped the place of her former vexations and anxieties, and for a few days longer she would drift thus pleasantly upon the tide, and then address herself seriously to the problem of her future.

She was alone now. The duchess had gone home for a day or two, promising to return at the end of the week. She had no one to look after the cottage but her faithful maid, but she was doing many things for herself and actually delighting in the work. She partook of her simple food with a zest and relish which a month ago would have astonished her, and she knew now that her former ideas about the simple life were sheer nonsense. She was living it much more nearly now than ever before. She was realising the advantages of the good health which regular hour's and moderation bring in their train. As she sat in the garden one afternoon wondering what had become of Denne, and when she should see him again, he came swinging through the gate and strode across the lawn to the verandah.

He looked singularly brisk and boyish, and an eager, youthful smile lit up his face. For the time, at any rate, he had discarded the worldly mask which he habitually wore. His eyes sparkled, and he spoke with unusual consideration. He held Adela's hand for a moment or two, and looked into her eyes with a glance that, to her, was most precious.

"I couldn't come before," he said. "I have had so much to do, and besides, I had to give you a chance to get better. I should hardly have known you. You are still pale, and so thin, but that dreadfully tired look has gone, and there is some color in your cheeks. You look far more beautiful in that pretty dress than in any of those confections which you used to get at Paris at such exorbitant prices. I can't describe the change, but it is very attractive, and very fascinating. Will you let me stay to tea and a chat? Shall I ring the bell for you?"

"Oh, dear, no," Adela laughed; "I have given up ringing hells. I am waiting on myself, and I rather like it."

She rose lightly from her seat and tripped into the house, Denne's eyes following her with marked approval. To think that only a short time ago she had appeared to be the most idle and frivolous of them all! The old Adela might have answered to that description, but this fresh, clear-eyed girl, who had gone so willingly to fetch the tea, would have recoiled loathing at the mere reminder of it. Nor was he the one to rebuke her, or point a moral, had he been so disposed. In his own past were things which he did not care to dwell upon. Business, as well as charity covers a multitude of sins and short-comings. He would let their dead past bury itself. These thoughts were duly set aside, and Denne smiled brightly again when Adela came up with the tea. Afterwards he suggested a stroll through the garden feeling pretty sure of his ground, and knowing how to act.

"The future will be more pleasant than the past," he said. "Tell me what you propose to do."

"I haven't made up my mind," Adela replied. "I don't know how I shall get out of your debt. It makes me feel uncomfortable when I think about it."

"Then don't think about it," said Denne.

"Ah! but I must, you know. I must. I thought of going abroad. I remember a very nice girl, who was sensible enough to marry a poor man because she loved him. She put all luxury and enjoyment on one side and went out to Canada to rough it as if she had been the wife of a working man. She wrote to me several times to say how happy she was. I used to read those letters with a shade of doubt. I didn't see how such a thing was possible. But in the light of experience one's point of view changes, and I know better. More than once she has pressed me to go out, and be a sort of companion to her. I know she will be pleased to have me, and I think I shall go."

Denne appeared to be pondering some problem.

"That is very brave of you," he said presently. "I like to hear you talk like that; in fact, I like to hear any man or woman talk like that. It shows the proper spirit. But I will show you an alternative. How would you like to stay in England, and do much the same thing as you'd do in Canada? There would be no occasion to rough it, of course, but suppose one had a charming house with a farm attached to it, with a few horses and cattle, where one could devote oneself to outdoor pursuits? Oh, I don't mean an immense showy establishment. I mean a simple refined home where one has time to think and read, and enjoy the blessings and beauties of life. That is the dream I have always had in my mind. But it has unfortunately lacked the one thing needful—the right woman. So far as I am concerned, the quest of the golden fleece was nothing to it. But I have found her, am tired of making money, and shall be only too glad to get out of finance tomorrow. I could do so in a month's time. Now, what do you think of that, Adela? I don't wish to hurry you, but—"

Denne broke off suddenly. The tender light died out of his eyes, and his look was stern and high as he beheld Mark Callader coming down the path towards them. Callader was wearing his most truculent expression, and there was a hard, pugnacious look in his little eyes. He strode forward, and barred the way with an air that caused Denne to tingle, and clench his fists involuntarily.

"So this is the game, eh?" Callader said.

"I don't know what you mean," said Denne coldly. "But I am glad you are here. This meeting has saved me the trouble of a journey. You have something to say to me, and I have one or two propositions to put before you."

"I hope," Adela said anxiously, "that you—"

Denne laid a hand on her arm.

"Please go back to the house," he said, "there is and will be no cause for alarm. I will return shortly. And now, sir, I am at your service."

CHAPTER XL

BEYOND THE GATE

Adela glanced uneasily from one man to the other. At one time, and that not very long ago, things had almost pointed to a personal encounter between Denne and Callader, but she hoped they did not contemplate a fight to-day. It was not that she was afraid as far as Denne was concerned, yet the expression on Callader's face was calculated to arouse anxiety, and he was something of a 'bruiser' from choice. Yet she could hardly misread Douglas' attitude. He looked at her once with lips compressed, and in his eyes site detected the compressed and assurance of victory. She turned slowly away, and walked across the verandah into the house. If she had expected the men would settle their dispute in whatever fashion in her presence, she was disappointed, for Denne strode to the gate with a curt intimation to Callader to follow.

"Where are you going?" the latter asked.

"Outside, if you please," Denne replied. "There's no need to settle this matter on the high road. If there is to be any trouble, I wish to save Miss Burton both anxiety and discredit. The papers get hold of those kind of things too."

Callader followed readily. Whatever his faults were, he had no lack of physical courage. The irregularities of his life had had no effect upon his nerves, possibly because he was entirely devoid of anything in the way of imagination. Moreover, he was certain to have matters all his own way. He walked for a short distance in silence by Denne's side, and then pulled up at a stile heading across the fields, declining to go further.

"I think this will do," he muttered.

Denne remarked coolly that he was quite of the same opinion, took a cigar from his pocket, and lighted it deliberately. He perched himself on the top of the stile, and remarked on the beauty of the afternoon. Callader was puzzled by this behavior.

"Oh, to the devil with the afternoon!" he broke out impatiently. "What has that got to do with it? We are not here to exchange compliments. You are a very clever man, I know, but for once in your life you have been too smart. You don't want me to tell you why I am here to-day."

"Not it the least," Denne replied. "To be candid, you came to blackmail me."

Callader smiled wickedly at the word.

"Just as you please," he said. "I don't care how bluntly you put it. Some people might prefer the word 'damages'; that is what they would call it in a court of law."

"There are two courses open to you," Denne reminded him.

"I can either bring an action and claim a heavy sum as compensation, or I can prosecute you for criminal conspiracy."

"Pity you can't do both," Denne said.

"Yes, isn't it?" Callader sneered, "But one can't eat one's cake and have it, and so I prefer—"

"I know exactly what you prefer. You have given this matter a good deal of consideration, and it is very hard to deprive yourself of the privilege of seeing me in your mind's eye picking oakum and dining regularly upon an appetizing dish of oatmeal gruel. You would have liked that exceedingly, of course; it would have been most gratifying to a vindictive nature like yours. But, on the other hand, such a proceeding would have prevented you from putting money in your pocket. For you agree with Tennyson that the jingling of the guinea helps the hurt that honor feels. I congratulate you upon your choice. Well, what's the price? How much do you expect to get, and what will you do with it when you've got it?"

The perplexed expression returned to Callader's face. His dull intellect always resented sarcasm or humor, which worried and irritated him, for he did not understand it. He had a feeling that Denne was poking fun at him, though the latter was quite grave and appeared to be thinking more about his cigar than anything else.

"Stop that!" Callader blustered.

"Stop what? I thought we came there to discuss business. I have done you an injury, and you think you ought to be recompensed. What a position for the head of the Calladers! How much? Come, you know what I mean. At what figure do you value your wounded feelings?"

The interview was not developing on the lines that Callader had anticipated. He had an uneasy notion that he was getting the worst of it. But if Denne insisted on taking this line, he would not shirk it.

"A hundred thousand pounds," he said.

"A hundred thousand pounds! That is a handsome fortune. Even for me. It is a mint of money. So, to save myself from a criminal prosecution, I must hand over as much as that. Now, have you any idea why I did this extraordinary thing? Can't you guess why I had to take some risk to prove that you are a thief?"

"Drop it!" Callader threatened.

"By no means, there must be no misunderstanding between us. You said you didn't care how bluntly I spoke, and I mean to call a spade a spade. At a heavy outlay I have acquired evidence that you are a thief. It was a particularly mean kind of theft, this purloining of the family treasures, this taking advantage of a young man who thoroughly trusted you. Of course, events have hit you rather hardly. Had you known all along that you would be the Marquis of Kempston I can't suppose you would have stooped to anything so dishonorable. It wouldn't have been worth while. Now don't interrupt me; it is idle to make any protest, because you know that I can prove what has been going on at Callader for several years. Suppose I defy you, tell you to do your worst, refuse to pay a single penny?"

"You dare not refuse!"

"Really! Well, let us assume, for the sake of argument, that I positively do refuse, what will happen then?"

Callader laughed unpleasantly.

"I should apply for a warrant for your arrest."

"Of course, but you would have to give evidence against me. Man! knowing the facts as you know them, you would be reduced to pulp in the witness-box. In spite of your bull-dog courage and tenacity, you would be a broken man at the end of your examination. You would have to admit everything, to confess in public that you were a despicable thief. No doubt you would be arrested before you left the court. You might score against me; in the dispensation of justice I might be picking oakum in the cell adjoining yours. But I am not at all sure that the end might not be held to have justified the means. Have you given all this your consideration? Because, if you like to go on, I am ready for you. Of one thing you may be absolutely certain, you won't get a brass farthing out of me."

"Sheer bluff!" Callader declared. "You forget, or don't know that Paul Lestrine—"

"I was coming to that," Denne said. "I know what Paul Lestrine has done. He betrayed me, and in turn he has betrayed you. He hasn't left the country, for I have taken steps to prevent it. He has robbed me for years. I have known it all the time, made notes on every occasion it happened, but said nothing because he was useful to me. I saw him on the Monday following his visit to Callader, and spoke straight to him. At the present moment he is being shadowed, and with the resources at my command he cannot escape me. Lestrine has your money, and that's all he cares about. He will admit everything because I will call him as a witness, and he will claim an indemnity, and probably get it, against criminal proceedings. He will show you up as a skunk and a scoundrel, but Lestrine isn't the sort of man to mind that. He doesn't care what people say about him; he despises them as cordially as they detest him. He will tell everything. He will expose the conspiracy which has been going on between you and Marner for years. He has a list of the treasures which have been looted from Callader Castle, and he even knows in whose possession they are at the present moment. All this will come out, and when the trial is over you can judge for yourself what your position will be. You won't find Marner disposed to shield you. Yesterday afternoon the police raided Latour's house in Paris, and all his books and papers were seized. You know what this means, and so does Marner. The great gang is broken up, and Marner has vanished. He will die rather than face exposure. The whole vile business is exploded, and you will be lucky if you are not mixed up in the cause celebre which is likely to occupy the French judges for some time to come. Now, you understand, my friend, why I will give you nothing, why I smile at your puny efforts, and tell you to do just what you please. I know I did a hazardous thing, but I didn't do it with my eyes shut. The reason why I interfered was because I did not mean that you should marry Miss Burton. You are aware that she is not Miss Burton at all. But that is a detail. But for her we should not be here holding this extremely pleasant conversation."

Denne stopped as if the subject had no further interest for him, as if he had spoken his last word. Callader stood opposite to him, dogged, sullen, suspicious, and glancing at Denne's face as if he expected to read something there. His mind worked slowly, but he began to see that Denne was master of the situation. If all Denne said was correct, and he knew it could not be doubted, or denied, his own position was full of danger. The more he considered the matter the more he perceived that Denne was armed at every point.

"You are too clever for me," he said sulkily, admitting defeat as a boxer does who owns he has met someone better than himself. "You could have had the girl, so far as I am concerned. I am sure I didn't want to marry her."

"Perhaps not, but you wanted her money, which is about the same thing. Now that you find she has no money, you can afford to play the magnanimous, and set her free. Not that it matters whether you do so or not. But are you not wasting time? Hadn't you better go back to London at once, and put the machinery of the law in motion against me? Nothing will give me greater satisfaction. And now, I shall be glad to finish this interview. Henceforth we shall meet as strangers, and I am authorised to say the same on behalf of my future wife, Lady Adela Callader. Good afternoon!"

CHAPTER XLI

THE SIMPLE LIFE

All's well that ends well. The days were passing evenly and pleasantly in the cottage by the river. Adela thought she had never had so much to do that was profitable and good for her, and wondered hourly how she ever endured her former mode of existence. For here she had light and life and movement, here were the thousand and one responsibilities she had hitherto laid on the shoulders of others. She did not, perhaps, realise that her new-formed happiness, her new health, her new strength, mental no less than bodily, had much to do with the present outlook. There was sheer joy in life now; the peace and comfort which came from regular hours and freedom from excitement had brought back the color to her cheeks, and the sparkle to her eyes. Even the country round seemed new country to her; the vivid green of the trees and the blending blue arch of the sky were painted in brighter and fresher colors than before.

It was irksome to feel under so great a debt to Denne, and even the cottage, simple as it was, cost money. It would be necessary to find means to keep it up. How was it to be done? It was absurd to think of turning to her former associates, for not one of them had come near her since the crash. She had not expected them, either. They did not belong to the class that turned a sympathetic ear to misfortune. Not that Adela minded; she had shrewdly suspected how it would be. She had been in London once or twice lately, and it was impossible to visit the West End without meeting some of them. They had looked at her in a surprised kind of way, and moved on with a more or less faint acknowledgment. Nor was there any sting in this treatment of her. Adela was sincerely glad to turn her back upon them all.

She had not seen Douglas Denne since the day he had so effectually disposed of Callader. On that occasion he had returned to the cottage to tell her briefly what had happened, and then he had gone away with all assurance that she should see him in a few days. Nearly a month had elapsed and she had seen no sign of him.

He came at last on one beautiful July afternoon. His car stood panting in the road, and Adela noticed that he had driven himself. He came to the verandah in his quiet masterful fashion. He wished Adela to go for a drive with him. They would have tea together on the road, and he would see that she was back in time for dinner.

Adela hesitated, but there was no resisting Denne when he was bent on a thing. Besides, if she had missed one thing more than another it was the rapid motion and exhilaration of her car. It had afforded, perhaps, the only healthy amusement in which she had indulged. She cast a longing eye at the big motor beyond the gate, and Denne smiled.

"I knew you would come," he said. "I want to go as far as Hindhead to see a house I am interested in. I should like you to look at it, because, if you approve of the place, I shall buy it. I daresay you have wondered why I have not been lately."

"I have missed you," Adela said.

A pleased, eager smile came over Denne's face. The mask had fallen from his features, and he looked like a boy starting on a holiday.

"I like to hear you say that," he remarked, "because I have missed you, too. But, come along, don't let us waste this glorious afternoon."

Denne tucked her up tenderly in the car, and they started on their journey. There was greater freshness and pleasure in the ride than Adela had ever experienced. She lay back in her seat giving herself over entirely to enjoyment, whilst Denne talked of his plans for the future.

"I have done it," he said joyously. "I have done what I told you I should. For the past month I have been closely engaged in the business of getting out of business, and now I am free to do what I like and go where I please. I have made sacrifices, but that does not matter. So far as I am concerned, I am done with the city. I don't want to see another financial paper, or sit on the board of another company. I mean to settle in the country, and lead a healthy, open-air life. People are supposed to envy a capitalist, but they don't realise what a terrible worry and anxiety his life is. Often, for weeks together, I have hardly been able to speak. But let us change the subject. I don't wish to think of anything else but this house which I have taken such a fancy to."

Denne drew up presently before a pair of lodge gates, of hammered iron, fashioned curiously at the top in scrolls and patterns like rough lace. The lodge nestled amongst a group of elms, and swallows were darting in and out under the thatched eaves. Beyond was an avenue bordered on both sides with magnificent rows of beeches, and as the car sped up the drive the house opened out presently. It was pure Elizabethian in style, and up the gables and around the latticed windows creepers grew in profusion.

"Somebody lives here," Adela exclaimed.

"The house is practically unoccupied. It is fully furnished, and some of the servants are here still. The place was bought by an American millionaire as a wedding present for his daughter, who married a man you know very well. She had a great fancy for a real Elizabethian house in the country, and was crazy about it for a time. Her father was sensible enough to place the house in the hands of an artist, with carte blanche as to furnishing it. He made his commission a labor of love, and did his work magnificently."

A sigh of something like envy came from Adela. A few months ago and she might have admired this as an expensive toy. But now the contemplation of it struck a deeper note, and she could realise what a paradise this lovely house would make.

"Some people never know when they are well off," she said. "'Why do they want to sell it?"

Denne smiled in a peculiarly dry way.

"They got tired of it," he said. "They declared that they were bored to death here. You see, they both belong to the smart set, and there is no escape from that. Once you are bound to the wheel it is hard to break away. But we have tasted of the fruits of society and know that it has nothing to offer us. We have had to pay for our experience, perhaps, but we will be wise in time."

They walked across the lawn, and through the rose garden, along the terraces and thence to the model farm. The dairy was so exceptionally clean and bright and cool that Adela exclaimed in delight. The pedigreed Jersey cattle looked like deer as they moved across the pasture. Nothing was forgotten to make the place complete. Adela drew a sigh of pure delight as she looked around.

"Fancy leaving this," she said, "fancy giving it up. And all to lead a life of unhealthy excitement in town, to breathe a poisonous atmosphere in company with people one dislikes and despises."

"It does seem strange, doesn't it?" Denne observed drily.

Adela laughed gaily.

"Ah! you mustn't altogether blame me. Don't forget that I was dragged into it, before I knew what the pleasure of living meant. I always felt that I wanted to get away from it, but didn't know how. But you won't lose this chance, will you?"

"That," Denne said gravely, "depends upon you. But come inside. They are waiting for us, and I think you will find that tea is ready."

There was no break in the chain of enchantment. Everything had been done to preserve harmony, the symmetry of the charming old house. The furniture looked as if it had been there for centuries, and over the beauty of it all there hovered that spirit of tranquility and refinement which reminded Adela of some of Tennyson's poems. Nor was she amazed, somehow, to find herself in a dim old hall pouring out tea and listening to Denne's plans for the future.

"It wants nothing," she said presently. "There is only one word for it, and that is perfect."

"Not quite," Denne whispered. "You may take it for granted that I am going to buy this place; in fact, I don't mind confessing to you that I have already bought it. But it needs one thing, and that is a mistress."

Adela smiled unsteadily.

"That should offer no great difficulty," she murmured.

"I don't think it will," Denne said gravely. "At least, not now, because I think I have found the right woman. Adela, darling, you know what I mean. I didn't ask you to come just to admire my new purchase. I wished you to see the place which I had pictured as your future home. Unless you consent to share it with me my enjoyment will be gone. Now look me in the face and tell me honestly, didn't you know that I was going to ask you this question?"

"But I have nothing," Adela answered. "I have not even the reputation. I am little better than an adventurer. I should have been leading a life of deceit and fraud now had circumstances not proved too strong for me. And you ask me—"

Something rose in Adela's throat, for she could say no more. Denne reached eagerly over, and took her hands in his.

"I know everything," he whispered. "You have always been frank with me—and I—well, I want you, and there is nothing more to be said. I happen to want you and nobody else, and that being so, what does it matter what anybody else says or thinks? We are both anxious to obliterate the past. I tried not to think of you in this way, I tried—but what is the use of talking like this? If you tell me that you do not care for me sufficiently—"

Words failed Adela. She felt she was being borne away on a wave of happiness, as if she were drifting out across the summer sea into the heart of the golden sunset. Then Denne's arms went around her, and she was crying quietly and happily upon his shoulder.

"This is your answer?" he whispered.

"Oh, yes, yes," Adela replied. "I don't know what I have done to deserve such happiness. In my wildest dreams I never longed for anything like this. You have won at all points, Douglas."

Denne desired to hear no more. For the first time in his life he was wholly and entirely satisfied.

FRED M WHITE – A CONCISE BIBLIOGRAPHY

NOVELS (A-Z)

Ambition's Slave (1916)
The Argus Eye (1919)
Blackmail (1902)
The Blue Daffodil (1934)
The Brand Of Silence (1911)
A Broken Memory (1929)
The Bubble Reputation (1908)
By Order Of The League (1886)
The Cardinal Moth aka The Accused Orchid (1903)
The Case For the Crown (1918)
Claxton's Mill (1912)
A Clue In Wax (1930)

The Corner House (1905)
The Councillors of Falconhoe (1922)
Craven Fortune (1904)
A Crime On Canvas (1909)
The Crimson Blind (US title: The Mystery Of The Crimson Blind) (1905)
A Daughter Of Israel (1892)
The Day: Or The Passing Of A Throne (1914)
A Deal In Letters (1923)
The Devil's Advocate (1924)
Dropped From The Fast Express, or A Daughter's Sacrifice (1911)
The Edge Of The Sword (1907)
The Ends Of Justice (1906)
A Fatal Dose (aka Behind the Mask) (1907)
The Fight For The Child (1925)
The Five Knots (1907)
"Found Dead" (1930)
The Four Fingers (US title: The Mystery Of The Four Fingers) (1907)
A Front Of Brass (1910)
The Garden O' Dreams (1909)
A Golden Argosy (1886)
The Golden Bat (1924)
The Golden Rose (1909)
The Green Bungalow (1923)
The Grey Woman (aka Sinister House) (1928)
The Happy Exile (1920)
A Harbour Of Refuge (1918)
Hard Pressed (1910)
The Honour Of His House (1920)
The House Of Mammon (1913)
A House Of Sorrows (1911)
The House Of The Schemers (1906)
The House On The River (1925)
In Trust (1892)
Jim Crowshaw's Mary (1911)
The King Diamond (1927)
Lady Clara (1913)
Lady Edna's Awakening (1920)
The Lady In Blue (1915)
The Law Of The Land (1906)
The Leopard's Spots (1920)
The Lonely Bride (aka The White Bride) (1907)
The Lord Of The Manor (1907)
Love, The Foe (1910)
A Maker of Millions (1909)
The Man Called Gilray (1911)
The Man Who Found Christmas (a novelette) (1915)
The Man Who Knew (1932)
The Man Who Was Two (1921)

The Man With The Vandyk Beard (1925)
The Midnight Guest: A Detective Story (1907)
A Mummer's Throne (1910)
My Lady Bountiful (1905)
The Mystery Of Crocksands (1923)
The Mystery Of The Ravenspurs (aka The Black Valley) (1911)
The Mystery Of Room 75 (1922)
Naboth's Vineyard (1889)
The Nether Millstone (1906)
Netta, The Story Of Sin (1909)
New Century Calendar Clue (1948)
Number Thirteen (1914)
The Old Secretaire: A Christmas Story (novelette) (1887)
On The Night Express (1930)
The Open Door (1907)
Paul Quentin (1908)
Paul, The Sage (1910)
The Phantom Car (1929)
Powers Of Darkness (1912)
The Price Of Silence (1925)
The Psalm Stone (1905)
Queen Of Hearts (1930)
A Queen Of The Stage (1908)
The Riddle Of The Rail (1926)
The Robe Of Lucifer (1896)
A Royal Wrong (1913)
The Salt Of The Earth (1918)
The Scales Of Justice (1908)
Secret Of The River (1934)
The Secret Of The Sands (1911)
A Secret Service (1913)
The Seed Of Empire (1916)
The Sentence Of The Court (1913)
A Shadowed Love (1905)
The Shadow Of The Dead Hand (1926)
The Silver Stream (novelette)
The Slave Of Silence (1906)
A Society Jezebel (1917)
The Sundial (1908)
Tregarthen's Wife: A Cornish Story (1901)
The Turn Of The Tide (1923)
The Weight Of The Crown (1904)
The White Battalions (1900)
The White Bride (aka The Lonely Bride) (1910)
The White Glove (1910)
The Wings Of Victory (1919)
The Yellow Face (1906)

THE MASTER CRIMINAL (1897-1898)

A series of 12 short stories featuring Felix Gryde, who describes himself as "a really clever soldier of fortune."

The Head Of The Caesars
At Windsor
The Silverpool Cup
The "Morrison Raid" Indemnity
Cleopatra's Robe
The Rosy Cross
The Death Of The President
The Cradlestone Oil Mills
Redburn Castle
"Crysoline Limited"
The Loss Of The "Eastern Empress"
General Marcos

THE LAST OF THE BORGIAS (1898)

A series of stories featuring Professor Victor Colonna, a vigilante physician who murders undesirable people with undetectable poisons.

The Scrip of Death
The Crimson Streak
The Holy Rose
The Saving Of Serena
The Varteg Necklace
The Three Carnations

DRENTON DENN - SPECIAL COMMISSIONER

Drenton Denn is a tough newspaper reporter on the payroll of The New York Post. His hallmarks are a straw hat, a Norfolk jacket, a perennial cigar, and a terrier by the name of "Prince."

The Yellow Moth
The Red Speck
Dust
The Fire Bugs
The Great White Moth

THE ROMANCE OF THE SECRET SERVICE FUND (1900)

This series features Newton Moore, the top agent at The Secret Service Fund.

By Woman's Wit
The Mazaroff Rifle
In The Express
The Almedi Concession
The Other Side Of The Chess Board
Three Of Them

THE DOOM OF LONDON

This sci-fi series of six stories describes a variety of catastrophes which ravage London.

The Four White Days
The Four Days' Night
The Dust Of Death
A Bubble Burst
The Invisible Force
The River Of Death

THE SAGE OF TYBURN (1905-1906)

Each of these stories was preceded by the header The Sage Of Tyburn.

No. 1 - The Chronicle Of The Yellow Girl
No. 2 - The Chronicle Of The Blue-Eyed Syndicate
No. 3 - The Chronicle Of The Inconsequent Princess
No. 4 - The Chronicle Of The Elderly Adonis
No. 5 - The Chronicle Of The Libelled Velasquez

THE DRAGON-FLY (1909)

Six stories about an impecunious but brilliant amateur criminologist, entomologist and ornithologist by the name of Horace Daimler. Each of the stories was preceded by the header The Dragon-Fly.

No. 1 - How Horace Daimler Got His Name
No. 2 - The Three Red Rats
No. 3 - [title unknown]
No. 4 - [title unknown]
No. 5 - A [illegible] Crime
No. 6 - The Mirror Over The Fireplace

REAL DRAMA (1909)

A series of stories published under the subtitle "Being Some Leaves From The Notebook Of A Late Theatrical Agent."

His Second Self
An Extra Turn
"Not In The Bill"
The Plagiarist
The Man In Possession
A Pair Of Handcuffs

THE TELEPHONE STAR (1912)

A series of stories about Keith Marrit, a star journalist working for a fictitious newspaper called The Telephone.

No. 1 - The Case Of El Hamid, The Seer
No. 2 - The Case Of The Genuine Counterfeit
No. 3 - The Case Of The Yellow Car
No. 4 - The Case Of Lord Wintercotte
No. 5 - The Case Of The Rusty Nail
No. 6 - The Case Of The One-Eyed Chauffeur

GIPSY TALES (1903-1916)

A series of stories describing the adventures of a wily British navvy with Romany roots, who is known only as "Gipsy." In his fantasies Gipsy portrays himself as a playwright, and tries to stage-manage the dramatis personae and the situations that feature in the stories.

A Matter Of Kindness
A Liberal Education
A Stranger In Bohemia
Drops Of Water
The Unpremeditated Curtain
Mere Details
Out Of Season

THE DIARY OF A LONELY SOUL (1915)

The Diary Of A Lonely Soul - Story 1 [title unknown]
The Diary Of A Lonely Soul - Story 2 [title unknown]
The Diary Of A Lonely Soul - Story 3 [title unknown]
The Diary Of A Lonely Soul - Story 4 [title unknown]

The Diary Of A Lonely Soul - Story 5 [title unknown]

A Call On The Phone
A Captious Critic
The Case For The Prisoner
The Charlatan
A Christmas Bride
A Christmas Deputy
Christmas Cards
The Christmas Carol
A Christmas in Peril
A Christmas Star
The Clock Struck Twelve
The Colonel's Christmas Pudding
Compounding A Felony
The Convict
Coralie And The Pearls
A Corner In Elephants
The Courage Of Despair
Crossed Swords
The Dancing Shadow
The Daughters Of The Moon
A Daughter Of Nature
The Dawnstar
A Deal In Diamonds
Henny
A Derelict In Clover
The Desert Ship
A Dog's Life
The Doll's House
The Dormer Window
A Dose Of Quinine
The Doubting D, or, A Cranky Cryptogram
A Draught Of Life
Early Closing Day
An Eastern Princess
The Eavesdropper
The Ebbing Tide
The Egg Of The Little Auk
The Emsdam Dispatches
The Empty House
An Error Of Judgment
The Evidence For The Prisoner
Excess Profits
An Eye For An Eye
The Eye Of The Camera
The First Stone
The Foil
Forget-Me-Not
For Love's Sake

The Left Hand
The Lesson The Ants Taught
The Livery Of Death
The Lonely Furrow
The Long Arm Of Bronze
Love In Aether
The Luck Of The Game
Made In England
The Man Himself
The Man Who Got Through
The Man Who Rang The Bell
The Man With The Eyeglass
A Masked Battery
The Master's Voice
A Matter Of Habit
'Merica
A Message from the Flood
The Midnight Call
The Missing Blade
The Missing Note
The Mistletoe Bough
Moray The Traitor
More Than Coronets
The Morning Glory
Music Hath Charms
A Musical Treat
The Mystery Of Room Five
Natural Selection
Nerves
The Night Express: The Story Of A Bank Robbery
The Northern Light
Not On The Records
An Object Lesson
The Odds On Zero
One Day With A Working Ant
One Foggy Night
One Of The Old Guard
On Peace Night
The Onus Of The Charge
The Orpheusia
Ostentation
The Other Man's Story
The Pardon
A Parrot Cry
The Path Of Progress
The Pawn And The Rook
Pearls Of Price
Photo By Lesterre

Pictures In The Snow (a Christmas story)
A Place In The Sun
The Platinum Chain
A Popular Novelist
Poste Restante
A Prize Crop
Proof Positive
The Purple Terror
A Queen In Hiding
A Question Of Money
Rachel's Seventh Year
Rawhide Science
The Real Dramatic Touch
A Record Round
Red Petals
Rob Peter—Pay Paul
A Rope Of Snow
Rose Of The Desert
A Royal Bag
The Royal Train
The Salmon Poachers
Santa Anna
A Satisfactory Reference
Saviour From The North
The Second Chapter
Second In The Field
The Shebeeners
A Single Hair
Sir Jeremiah's Big Shoot
Sister Louise
The Sixteenth Chapter
A Sleeping Partner
Sleeping Partner
A Sound In The Night
"Special" To The Telephone
A Stolen Interview
The Straight Game
The Stranger Within The Gate
Sub Rosa
The Substitute
The Superman
The Supreme Test
The Sword Of Justice
A Table Tragedy
The Thirty-Seventh Month
This Little World
A Thrilling Exit
The Throat Of The Wolf